THE GHOST OF THE FISHERSGATE MARINER

By

P.D.Mitchell

First Published in Great Britain by Jacqui Lessels, Somerset.
November 2017

ISBN 978-0-9955382-2-1

www.pdmitchell.co.uk
e-mail: info@pdmitchell.co.uk

www.theGhostofthefishersgatemariner.com

Cover Artists:
Matt & Harry Mawford

A catalogue copy of this book is available from the British Library

Printed and bound in Great Britain by 4 Edge Ltd Essex SS5 4AD

In memory of my late wife, Julie Mitchell

(née, Bateman.) 1968-2013

For my brother Les Mitchell 1956-2005

and my father Peter Mitchell 1926-1991

For my mother, Mrs. Doris Mitchell.

Special thanks to my editing publisher, Jacqui Lessels, for her complete support encouragement and advice during the writing of this story, without which, this book, the Ghost of the Fishersgate Mariner, would never have been published.

HISTORICAL NOTE

Most of the story told in this book is set before the year of 1971. Before that year the United Kingdom used imperial currency units. This comprised of the pound, as it does today, but with coinage values of half-crown, shilling, sixpence, thru-pence, single penny, half-penny and farthing. The pound before 1971 was made up of 240 pennies. Linear measurements before 1971 were set in yards, feet and inches. In context, this book has used the terminology of this old currency and linear measurement.

On the 15th February 1971, the United Kingdom changed from imperial units to metric SI units.

CONTENTS

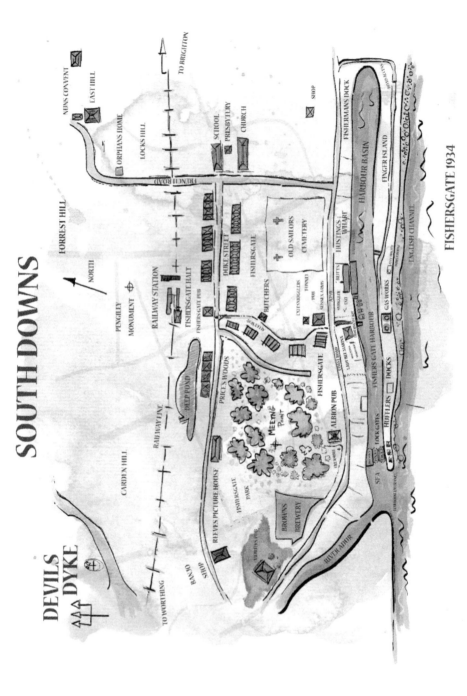

SOUTH DOWNS

DEVILS DYKE

FISHERSGATE 1934

Chapter 1

The ripple on the water - 1934

During the summer of 1934, in a place called Fishersgate, England, an open-air spiritual ceremony was being performed.

"In nomine Patris, et Filii, et Spiritus Sancti," said the high priest to his congregation. The ritual was partly-spoken in an ancient Latin language, fashioned with the hint of a southern English accent.

A golden goblet containing symbolic blood was centrally positioned on the top surface of a religious altar, just in front of the tabernacle. At each end of the altar was a solid-brass candle-stick, each one holding a pure white wax candle. The candles were not burning for there was a breeze in the air. The altar itself was adorned with dahlias and daisies, all creatively placed on a plain white cloth that hid an unsightly piece of furniture beneath its superb clinical exterior. The high priest, only five-foot-three inches tall in stature, was wearing a white cotton robe that flowed in the breeze as he faced the altar - with the congregation seated behind him. He took a circular wafer biscuit from the tabernacle and held it high above his head to show his congregation.

"This represents the body of Christ," he proclaimed in English.

At that point, his assistant, a boy of about nine years old, rang an ornately decorated brass bell - three times.

The high priest broke off a portion of the wafer biscuit and placed it on his tongue, allowing it to melt into a fine paste, before swallowing the mushy substance. He carefully put the remaining part of the wafer biscuit into the tabernacle, before placing both of his hands, palms down with thumbs crossed, just above the golden goblet. The assistant, once again, rang the bell three times. The high priest picked up the goblet and raised it above his head.

"And this represents the blood of Christ," he proclaimed.

The assistant rang the bell three more times as the high priest brought the golden goblet to his lips before taking a sip of its contents.

"Come on, get on with it," shouted one of the congregation. Nathan was his name.

" I have to fillet and prepare these twelve fish that I caught in Fishersgate harbour this morning."

"Okay, okay…" replied the flustered high priest. He wiped the side of his mouth with a white handkerchief to remove the residue of the symbolic 'blood' from his lips.

He then placed the goblet, containing the remaining blood, back onto the central part of the altar before turning to face his congregation.

"Lower the coffin into the ground," he ordered, "while I, as high priest, pray for forgiveness for the late departed."

Two of his helpers proceeded to lower the small coffin into the ready-made hole in the earth, which was situated to the right of the high priest and to the left of the congregation.

The high priest continued his well-rehearsed ritual.

"May God have mercy on thee and, having forgiven thee all thy sins, bring thee to life everlasting, in paradise."

And everyone watching responded by saying, "Amen."

In this single religious act, the high priest had made a direct application to God, for forgiveness on behalf of the deceased.

And having done so, one dead hamster, which had just been buried, was systematically absolved of all his earthly misdemeanours. Forgiven by God, the Great Architect of the Universe, for sins like eating too many nuts on a Friday night and belching his entrails out through to Saturday morning.

Of chewing a hole in the curtains, more than once, and of keeping the occupants of number 56 Duke Street wide-awake at night whilst running several miles on his squeaky hamster wheel. And for antagonising Whiskers the cat, by laying in a sensually provocative manner among the sawdust carpet that decked the bottom of his cage - knowing that Whiskers couldn't get to play with him. You know… the sort of wicked sinful offences that many mortal hamsters often commit… the most serious of which are too numerous for the author to deal with in this short book.

And the ceremony continued. Soil was thrown onto the coffin and soon there was no trace of the hamster's mortal existence, except for a small mound of earth where the hole in the ground had been. Two lolly sticks in the shape of a cross were placed at one end of the clump of soil with the name 'Henry' indelibly marked in blackberry ink, to show the head of the grave. The ceremony was complete. Henry had been buried in a fur-lined shoebox tied with golden string.

The hamster had a long life. Well… as long a life as any hamster could get in the precarious household of the Burton family. Not that the Burton family were intentionally cruel to their pets - just careless. This one, Henry the Hamster number two, got caught by the larder door. It happened one lazy, crazy, Wednesday afternoon. Someone had let Henry out of his cage. The cat, Whiskers, caught sight of Henry and began chasing him. Poor old Henry dived for cover into the larder - just as Mum Burton closed the door. It was there, in that exact spot, that Henry met an untimely hamster end - the poor unfortunate beast had been squashed between the heavy, wooden, green-painted, larder door and the doorframe. And that was that - one squashed hamster with flaking green paint embedded into his fur. Henry was gone. He was on his way to meet his maker somewhere in paradise. But for those left on Earth, the hamster was no more… it had expired and was very dead.

"Probably died quick," said Grandad Burton.

The congregation of some ten young teenagers all heard Grandad, but no-one bothered to reply. He often mumbled to himself.

"Right then, Billy," said Mum. "Put my brass candlesticks back on the mantelpiece; my bread bin… sorry, Billy ... the tabernacle, as you call it - put that back in the kitchen; and give Grandad back his old golden Army goblet, I don't want it going missing. And put that raspberry lemonade, that you call blood, away; before you do anything else."

While Mum was barking her orders, blond haired Billy Royston Burton, the fourteen-year-old five-foot three-inch-tall part-time high priest had fallen over. He had tried to walk while still attired in Mum's summer cotton dressing gown, which he often used as a priest's cassock. He rolled around the patchy green and brown grass burnt by the long summer sun, trapped inside the fabric enclosure. The other laughing youngsters - the disbanding congregation - did not rush to help him escape, they just mocked him.

"It's nice to give them a good send-off," said a dejected Grandad Burton, who was sitting on a garden seat in the corner of the compact but neatly finished garden.

"What?" asked Mum.

"All of our dead hamsters are buried at the end of the garden," replied Grandad. "But I shall probably miss Henry the most."

Mum looked at him candidly. She wasn't quite sure if Grandad was being serious. He broke into a smile and Mum stuck her tongue out at him in a mocking way.

She sat down on the garden chair next to Grandad.

"Would you like a piece of this cake?" she asked.

"No thanks," replied Grandad.

"Go on... I'm going to have a piece," said Gloria.

"Maybe just the one piece," he said, as he reached towards the cake stand.

Grandad chose a small section of the cake and put it onto a plate, which he placed onto the garden table. There was a moment of silence between them as Grandad watched Nathan, galvanized bucket to hand, filleting his twelve fish at the end of the garden. What a magnanimous gesture, thought Grandad, that Nathan had decided to donate the twelve fish he had caught earlier that day to the parish priest at the local church and his guests for their supper that evening.

"I had a letter from John this morning," said Mum.

"Did you Gloria? How is he?" asked Grandad.

"Oh, he's ok… He is settling into the job very well. He likes it. He likes it a lot and says Australia is a wonderful place… He wants us all to join him there."

"All of us?" enquired Grandad.

"Yes, all of us - including you - after all, we can't leave you behind; not you, not my old dad," replied Gloria as she reached out to hold his hand.

"I'm not sure about going to Australia; I'm too long in the tooth for all that travelling," said Grandad. "I mean… it's best that younger people go - not old people like me."

Grandad paused for a moment to allow himself to swallow some cake before speaking further.

"It's a marvellous opportunity for you, John and the children. Go and join your husband in Australia, and have fun; you should get away from this dismal place, this trading port called Fishersgate. I'll be all right on my own Gloria," said Grandad.

"No you won't Dad. I want you to come with us. Anyway, there is plenty of time for you to get used to the idea. It will take at least three months before we can even begin to arrange things," replied Gloria.

"I simply couldn't go," exclaimed Grandad.

His silver-white hair was stirring from side to side in the slight breeze as his eyes welled up with tears behind his black circular spectacles.

"Who would visit your mother if I came with you to Australia?" he asked. "There is no-one else apart from me, you and your sister Mary," he continued.

"I know, Dad," said Gloria, "but sometimes we have to move on. Mum has been dead now for twenty years. Do you remember? It was on my eighteenth birthday, that was the day… that was the day she passed away."

"How can I ever forget that day?" interrupted Grandad.

Gloria continued as she took Grandad's hand, "I remember you coming through the door to tell me. I knew something was wrong, just by the look on your face."

Grandad interrupted again as their clasped hands broke.

"She was a wonderful woman. We grew up together. I was eighteen years old when I first met her. You know… Gloria, when me and your mum were young, when I was young, she took my hand and she led me on this journey of a lifetime. It lasted for over twenty-five years. How I wish that I could hold her hand once more. How I wish that I could hold her close to me, just for a moment. She would comfort the pain that my body has lived through. Luckily, she did not live to see the terrible war of 1914-18. That is one relief. I loved her so much. She was powerful in character and strong worded when she needed to be, yet there was a softness that made her glow. She was magical. Even when there were tears in our house, you know, like when your elder sister Mary was taken gravely ill she guided us through it. She was the strong one in the family."

Grandad began to recite a poem he had once written. Gloria had heard Grandad's poem so many times before, but she sat quietly while he slowly began to recite it once more.

"She held my hand
And led me on a journey...
Lasting many years
She forged this boy
Into a man, with happiness
And sometimes tears
And then one day...
She was gone.

I yearn for her
To hold my hand
I can't describe or understand
This pain that never ends
Within my heart
And as the years go by so
fast
I'll never know..."

Grandad rarely got to recite the whole of his poem and today was no different, for Gloria interrupted, as she usually did. She stopped him because she could see that the more he continued the more he was getting upset by his own rhythmic words.

"Don't upset yourself anymore Dad. We can talk about this later. Anyway, as I have said many times before," she continued in a teasing manner - to try to cheer him up, "your poem does not rhyme properly in all of the right places." Gloria smiled and so did Grandad. And as was usual during their goading ritual about his poetry, he nudged Gloria on the shoulder in a scornful but friendly way before saying, "I have told you Gloria, my dear... many times before," as he sat with a mocking look of shock on his face, "my poem does not have to rhyme in all the right places and anyway, it's my poem and I can do what I like with it. I don't want it to rhyme in all the right places, I want it to rhyme in all the wrong places. Just as the uncertainties of life touch us all, mostly in the wrong places at the wrong times and when we least expect it."

Gloria smiled again, but did not otherwise respond except to say that she believed that Grandad did have some sort of a poetic talent, but wondered how a retired boiler cleaner of Fishersgate Gas Works, a man who once chipped clinker-coke from the inside of an empty gas boiler during routine maintenance procedures, had learned such skills in the gentle art of poetry.

Grandad smiled once more and told Gloria that writing poetry kept his old mind active and that she would be surprised at what retired clinker boiler cleaners knew.

"Don't judge a book by its cover," he argued.

He soon returned to a serious moment as he thought about his late wife once more.

"No... I have made up my mind," said Grandad. "I cannot leave her. Who would put flowers on her grave? Who would make sure the weeds are pulled and the grass trimmed?" Grandad paused for a moment as he observed the flowers at the end of the garden swaying in the breeze.

"You know... How I yearn for her. I wish she was with us," said Grandad.

"I said, don't upset yourself Dad," replied Gloria.

"And what of your sister, Mary?" Grandad continued. "How can we leave her here in Fishersgate, in that institution?"

"Dad, she doesn't even know us anymore," said Gloria. "She gazes out of the window all day long. Her mind has gone. She doesn't know where she is. I know it seems selfish and cruel of me, but John and I need this new life in Australia, for the sake of our two boys, Terry and Billy. There are so many opportunities in Australia. Mary won't miss us she doesn't even know us anymore. She is better off where she is at the institution."

Grandad did not reply. He stared into the distance.

Gloria put out her hand. Their hands momentarily touched again. Gloria stood up, brushed away the cake crumbs from her apron and ran her fingers through her long dark hair down to the back of her neck. She looked towards the end of the garden to where Henry the Hamster had just been buried. Then she turned towards Grandad and took his hand once more.

"As I said Dad, we can talk about it later," said Gloria, "but I really think that we cannot leave you behind."

"Have you told the boys about it?" asked Grandad, "what do Terry and Billy want to do? Do they want to go to Australia?"

"They don't know about our plans yet," said Mum. "All they know is that their dad has gone to work in Australia for a year or so and he will be coming home in a few months. We didn't tell them there was a possibility that it might lead to all the family moving out there..." she sighed, "well, we didn't know, did we? But John and I realise that we can have a better life out there. A better life for all of us - and that includes you, Dad."

"Anyway, shall I make some tea?" she said.

Grandad smiled. "That would be nice."

Mum disappeared into the kitchen to leave Grandad pondering about this potential move to Australia.

"Come on then Billy," a deep voice shouted. It was Billy's older brother, Terry, who was standing by the back door to the house.

"We're off down to the harbour to hire-out one of the rowing boats. Do you want to come along with us?"

By now, Billy had escaped from the dressing gown that had imprisoned him and was carrying his mother's brass candlesticks back into the house.

"Of course, I do," replied Billy, "can you help me put all this stuff away?"

"Not likely brother - you made the mess - you sort it out," replied Terry, "we will take a walk towards the harbour - you can catch us up."

"Oh - all right," said a disgruntled Billy.

Billy disappeared through the back door of the council house that he lived in with his mother, grandad and older brother, Terence Norman Burton, otherwise known as Terry. At six feet two inches tall, with blond hair and a clean-shaven chin, Terry was the athletic type at twenty-one years of age. Extremely good looking and popular with everyone, he was accustomed to winning friends by his charm, when it suited him, and his excellent ability to put on a high-class voice, which he often did for a bit of a laugh. However, there was a sensitive side to Terry; especially when he became passionate about something special involving historical or political matters. Maybe one day he might become an actor or a politician, if indeed post-war council estate kids could ever attain such respectable heights. Terry had a vast interest in the history of the United Kingdom which he had learned at school. In better times, he would have gone on to University, but in the austere days of the nineteen-thirties there were few opportunities for off-springs from the working classes. Times were indeed tough, but they were about to get tougher for the Burton family.

The Burton family lived at number fifty-six Duke Street. To the south of their house, a five-minute walk, was Fishersgate bay. To the east of their house, another five minutes away, was St Mary's school, next to that was Our Lady Star of the Sea church. In-between the school and the church was the presbytery, where the Catholic priest lived. Billy Burton attended both the school and the church. It was a religious affair, not that Billy was particularly religious. The school was managed by the nuns of the Blessed Mary convent and they lived to the north of Fishersgate, at East Hill. Every morning they left their convent to walk down the hill, in formation, two by two, military style; they collected the children from the Locks Hill orphanage on their way; then they continued the one-and-a-half-mile walk to school. Every evening they walked back; up the hill, past the Locks Hill home for orphaned children, where they escorted those children into the building, then onwards and upwards back to the convent. They were the school teachers, managers, gardeners, dinner ladies, cleaners and mentors to the children; all under the watchful eye of the mother superior, Sister Albany. The youngest of the nuns was a fun-loving, twenty-two-year-old Irish born Sister Alisha, a novice nun and junior teacher, who loved the children she looked after. She would play games with the children whenever she could, games like skipping and hopscotch, rather than teach them anything boring or too academic. The older nuns did not always appreciate this playful approach for they were much more serious. This was a time of transformation in the Catholic church and in the wider world. The younger generation of nuns would soon see real change in the world around them. All the older nuns had a very deep solemn commitment to the church and they dressed accordingly. There was nothing sexy about them and rightly so. They were all married to God and each one wore a ring on their wedding finger to prove it. They wore long black habits that covered their entire body and a black flowing headdress. Under the veil was a white coif, a type of cap that fitted over the head and only allowed the front of the face to be seen. It extended upwards from the chin and covered the ears and forehead. This made all nuns have egg-like shaped faces. To children, these scary outfits that the nuns wore were the first line in a strict disciplinarian school. For discipline was a key to their commitment in this mortal world. The nuns lived, prayed, and worked by the rule of discipline and that is exactly what they expected of their pupils at the school. So, if a child was disobedient a quick rap across the knuckles or the backs of the legs, with a wooden measuring ruler or a cane, was often the shortest and sharpest punishment that they administered.

The parish priest, Father Lemmon, a large portly fellow with circular spectacles, lived in the presbytery between the school and the church. He held religious services three times a day for the local congregation. The shift workers at the power station and the gas works in Fishersgate harbour had no excuse for non-attendance at the church, as there was a church service to cover every rest period for every shift worker and at least ninety-five people attended each service. Anyone missing for more than a week would receive a home visit from Father Lemmon, who would not leave until he had administered a scolding and drunk at least one glass of their finest whisky or, if whisky wasn't available, anything else with a hint of alcohol. He was known to have once drunk a whole bottle of home-made dandelion wine before being malleable enough to be ushered, by a slight force, through the front doorway of the house of one of the very tired but polite parishioners. Seen waddling around the streets of Fishersgate on many occasions, holding onto walls and fences for support, most times of the day and night between church services, Father Lemmon was indeed a religious character of distinction.

Father Lemmon had helpers at his church services. These were known as 'altar' boy assistants. They would light candles, ring bells, sometimes swing golden pots from side to side which produced plumes of grey mist that gave off a pleasant smell of incense. All these things were done at notable parts of the ceremony, to give good dramatic effect... and the bell ringing kept a lively pace to the proceedings. The oldest altar boy was eighty-year-old Mr. Duncan and the youngest was fourteen-year-old Billy Burton. Mr. Duncan was a kindly old man - white hair, balding on top; he was so experienced at being an altar boy, his actions and timing during the service were performed to complete perfection. He knew all the Latin words in the repertoire and was often heard whispering prompts to Father Lemmon during the ceremony, especially when a hung-over intoxicated condition was affecting the priest's concentration. But though Mr. Duncan thought he was whispering - whispering he was not! Old Mr. Duncan was as deaf as a post, so when he thought he was speaking in a whisper, he was, in fact, talking very loudly as far as the congregation were concerned. In a sense, Father Lemmon and Mr. Duncan could be described as a pair of elderly doddering thespian actors performing the same play three times a day, almost every day of the year. Billy helped them out a couple of times a week. There was quite a selection of altar boys to choose from in the school. They were a bit like a football team's reserve list of players and the school rotated the programme so that every willing boy took part in a church service at least once a week. This religious outing from school to the church did not unduly disrupt their academic education.

As Billy could get out of some of his lesser preferred school lessons to help in the church services, he was a very keen altar boy indeed. He also learned quite a lot of the Latin language; and the one phrase he liked the most was 'In nomine Patris, et Filii, et Spiritus Sancti.' It really did sound good, had a nice rhythm to it, no-one knew what it meant and it was handy for his regular hamster burial services, which he periodically held in the back garden of number fifty-six Duke Street. This was not the only pastime that occupied the children in the back garden of number 56, but it was the most unpredictable one - for nobody knew when a hamster was likely to die. Hastily arranged hamster funerals were being enacted all over Fishersgate town. Not only that, funeral services were also performed for the local cats, dogs, rabbits, gerbils and other pets belonging to the families in Fishersgate. Billy, by no means, performed all the funerals in Duke Street or indeed Fishersgate - for there

Fishersgate public house, past the butcher's shop, where a portly Mr. Rowland was chopping up his meat; and then he walked through the alley, which wound its way around the back of a row of terrace houses before coming out onto the coastal road by the Sussex Arms pub.

Nearing the end of the alleyway, Billy turned the corner to see Wheeler and Garrett approaching along the coast road from the west. Billy momentarily thought about turning around and heading back up the alleyway, but it was too late. The two bullies had seen him.

"Look, it's the little choir boy," shouted ginger haired Garrett to Wheeler as he rushed towards Billy and pushed him against the wall. "Come here little choir boy, we want a chat with you," shouted Wheeler. Both Wheeler and Garrett were large boys - each a little over six-feet tall and built with muscles like elephants. They both had obese looking faces, though dark-haired Wheeler was the fattest by far. They were a year older than Billy and had attended another school in Fishersgate before leaving nine-months earlier. Garrett and Wheeler had applied to join the merchant navy and were awaiting a response. Unruly behavior and bad manners ran in their family. Garrett and Wheeler were cousins and their respective parents were just as unpleasant. 'Why?' one might ask. Well, simply because this was a deprived area and those that shouted loudest, intimidated the most and bullied all others were the ones who would usually do well in life, in the rough and tumble world of Duke Street. Neither Garrett nor Wheeler had much guidance from their respective fathers. They weren't around very often. Garrett Senior was at present locked-up in Lewes jail and Wheeler Senior was on the run from the police. Some said they worked for 'Barlott', a local criminal, thug, pirate and smuggler.

Before long, Billy was being battered around like a cod-fish fillet. Garrett and Wheeler stood five feet apart batting Billy between them with their large hands. They pushed Billy from one to the other; from side-to-side, twisting and turning his body in the process. As they pushed him they taunted him with despicable suggestions of his perceived religious beliefs, which were entirely false. But the two bullies had no brains between them to realise that Billy was not seriously religious. Eventually, Wheeler held Billy's arms behind his back while Garrett slapped him around the face so hard that his cheek immediately flushed a bright red colour.

"Did that hurt… little choir boy?" whispered Garrett in Billy's ear.

"No," said Billy.

It really did hurt, but Billy did not cry and he wasn't going to let on that it hurt. Billy was more concerned with looking to make his escape - somehow.

He caught sight of his friend, fifteen-year-old Clifford, the cleverest child in all of Fishersgate, well, there is always one clever-clogs in every community. Clifford was on the other side of the coast road and had just climbed the long concrete stairway onto the high road from the harbour basin below. Billy shouted out, "Wait for me Clifford." Fortunately, Wheeler became disorientated and let go of Billy at that precise moment. Billy weaved around Garrett and ran towards his friend Clifford.

As Billy got to him, Clifford asked, "You OK Billy?"

"Yes, I'm ok," replied Billy. "Can't stop right now as I am on my way down to the harbour to find my brother."

Billy went to grab the handrails of the staircase leading down to the harbour but stopped when Clifford continued talking.

"I have been walking around the harbour for the last couple of hours," said Clifford, "and now I am off to the church hall for banjo practice."

"Ok," said Billy as he watched the two bullies approaching.

"It's really nice here today," continued Clifford, "I counted six new ships in the harbour this morning - look! Three of them are over there at Hufflers Dock and the other three are to the east, moored at Hustings Wharf. Can you see them? I have recorded their individual names in my record book," said Clifford.

Billy briefly looked at a page in the book that contained the names of a dozen or more ships, each showing the date, time and place that Clifford had spotted them. He then looked over the entire harbour from the vantage height of the coastal road, some ten yards above the harbour, where the pair of them were standing. It was a magnificent sight. It was a huge expanse of waterway containing ships and boats of all sizes spread along its four-mile length. Cranes, tackle and lorries embellished its docks, men and machinery spread out among various quays that extended towards storage buildings. The huge gas works dominated the scene with the smaller newer electrical power station gleaming brightly beside it. And beyond those buildings, due south, was the English Channel.

But Billy was in a hurry. He had no time to chat.

"Yes, yes, Clifford, I see all the ships, thank you for pointing them out to me - Bye Clifford," said Billy, without giving a second thought to what Clifford had said.

As Billy looked down from the top of the long concrete flight of stairs he saw his friend Nathan at the foot of the stairway, walking towards Fishersgate bay. Beside him were Billy's brother, Terry, and Terry's girlfriend, Lilly.

"Wait for me," shouted Billy.

Billy quickly descended the steep concrete steps, beside the sloping grassed banks, which led to Fishersgate bay.

He soon caught up to his brother and friends.

"You're a bit red in the face Billy!" stated Lilly.

"I've been running," replied Billy.

"Are you all right?" asked Terry, sensing something was wrong.

"Yes, I'm fine," replied Billy as he turned around to see Garrett and Wheeler descending the concrete staircase, clearly following him - but keeping a safe distance. They would not bother Billy when Terry was around and Billy was not going to admit a weakness by telling Terry about what these two thugs usually did to him.

They found Albert the boat keeper inside his workshop. This was a workshop that was built into the steep grass bank beside the concrete steps. It was more like a bunker, with only the two large entrance doors visible. He was varnishing one of his boats.

Albert, a short stocky man with a full ginger-coloured hairy beard, which was beginning to go grey at the sides, was always decidedly grumpy. Today was no different.

"Hello Albert," called Terry.

"You kid's back again then?" said Albert, with a grump and a growl.

"Yes, of course we are," replied Terry. "Can we hire one of your boats please?"

"Course you can son… mind you, no messing about like you did last week. And keep away from those ships in the harbour; I don't want my rowing boat damaged."

"We'll be careful," said Terry, winking at Billy.

Albert picked up two timber rowing oars, which he kept in a rack at the back of the workshop. He put them over his shoulder and marched towards his boats in Fishersgate bay. The boats were tethered together at the water's edge.

"Ruddy kids," he muttered under his breath.

"Take the boat *Doris* today," he ordered. "I have refurbished her and she is as bright as a new pin."

Doris looked spectacular, painted in a pale blue colour, edged in white around the entire top rim. The black rear seat backrest was adorned with hand-painted daffodils and in-between was the name **'Doris'** in a bold white handwritten text.

Fishersgate bay was a small untidy pebbled beach which fell away into the waters of the harbour. It was no more than a ten-yard-long strip of shingle. It was generally hidden from view from the rest of the harbour by two concrete quays; one at each end of the beach. Both the quays extended into the waters of the harbour by about eight yards. On the quay to the right was a very small building known as the *Crab House*. It was no more than a little concrete hut with an asbestos corrugated roof. It had a door-less opening on its north side. It also had a window, without glass, that faced south towards the harbour waters, through which the giant gasworks could be seen. The view of the gasworks was as prominent in size as it was overpowering in smell. The Crab House was quite a draughty place on a windy day. The gas workers used this little hut to shelter from natures elements, while waiting for Albert's ferry on a blustery rainy day, to take them to the other side of the harbour. The Crab House was also used by local fisherman resting in-between their tidal excursions.

Little did Billy and his friends know that a mariner was murdered there, in the labyrinth of tunnels and sewers below the Crab House, some two hundred years before.

The other quay, on the left of the shingle beach, was owned by a timber company called Butts. They often sold timber to Albert, which he used to repair his rowing boats. Fishersgate bay was not a delightful scene, yet it became a haven for those who ventured to the area to hire a pleasure boat at weekends.

Albert laid the oars in the boat named *Doris*, untied the knot in the rope and pulled the boat up the shingle beach on the shoreline so that the youngsters could get in. Albert checked around the boat to make sure it was seaworthy and looked in the bottom to see how much water was laying there. Often, he had to bail out water with an old tin can before he could let a boat out for hire. Not seawater, as his boats rarely leaked; but rainwater which might have fallen into the boats overnight.

Seeing that Garrett and Wheeler were waiting to hire another boat, Billy had a change of plan.

"I think I'll walk along the banks of the harbour, towards the lock-gates," said Billy. And with that, he was gone.

Billy wanted to be alone for a while. He needed to think about this bullying that he was experiencing. Garrett and Wheeler had a profound effect on him and he needed to contemplate.

were many other children who wanted to say a few words for their own late-departed pets. However, Billy was the only boy in the street who could perform a ceremony in the mysterious Latin language and bring a certain kind of magic to the solemn performance. Billy was, without doubt, an organiser - not a pushy type but he could encourage others to fulfill their aspirations. He was a very popular boy among many of the children in the town. In summer months - weather permitting - he organised talent contests and jumble sales in his back garden. In autumn or winter months, on cloudless nights, he gathered those interested in the moon and stars into his back garden for some stargazing - using Grandad's old army binoculars. His best friend was Nathan Martin, a boy of African descent who spent a lot of time in the Burton household and who shared Billy's interest in the moon and the stars as well as fishing and boating.

Now that Henry the hamster's funeral was complete and all of mum's stuff had been cleared away, Billy left his front gate for a short walk to the harbour in a southerly direction. His brother and friends had already left the house, so he walked quickly to catch them up. He passed the railway station, Fishersgate Halt, which led in one direction to the lively town of Brighton and in the opposite direction to the more sedate place of Worthing. He passed by the

"What's up with him?" asked Nathan.

"I don't know," replied Terry. "Let him go."

They ignored Billy and clambered into the boat. Nathan wedged a galvanized bucket he had brought with him at the front of the boat. Terry boarded last.

Albert held his hand out. "That'll be sixpence and I want you back here at two o'clock... and don't be late, otherwise I shall charge you some more money."

Terry gave Albert the sixpence.

"Right then," shouted Albert, "all of you to the back of the boat while I push you out."

The three of them moved up to the far end to lessen the weight of the boat on the shingle beach. This was the only way to push a boat from the shoreline. Albert gave the boat a shove and they were away.

The boat glided fully into the water and each one of them found themselves a seat. Terry sat at the centre of the boat. He put the oars into the rowlocks and gently propelled and directed the boat, turning it one hundred and eighty degrees so that the bow faced southwards, towards the deep waters of the harbour.

Albert went back to his workshop to get two more oars, before he hired another boat named *Frances,* to Garrett and Wheeler. Once they were underway upon the waters of the harbour he turned to walk back to his workshop. Suddenly he was struck by an inner thought, which brought his short ginger haired fat body to a complete standstill. He slowly looked upwards toward something in the sky. It looked just like a ship's anchor, bright but then fading and wiggling. Sitting on the anchor was a Golden snub-nosed monkey wearing a diamond necklace. And then it vanished. As an old sailor who had heard the mysterious enchanting stories of the monkey at sea, he knew exactly what it was. It was a magical sign. Albert turned back towards the harbour waters and watched the youngsters laughing and joking aboard the boats named *Doris* and *Frances*. He stood by the shoreline holding up his hand, statue-like, in a trance, as if to wave goodbye. It was a long silent goodbye which lasted a minute or more. He had a deep stare in his eyes as he watched the children in the boats. It was not the sort of goodbye one would expect from the usually grumpy Albert, the boatman - for the children would surely be back within the hour - but today, maybe not he thought. Terry, Lilly, or Nathan did not notice Albert standing by the shoreline. Neither did Garrett or Wheeler, for they were having too much fun.

None of them heard him slowly mutter under his breath, "Goodbye children of Fishersgate, I think that this is the day it will happen. Today, some of you kids - maybe all of you - are going on a proper adventure. It will be a while before I see some of you again, and one of my newly refurbished boats, come to that. The folklore stories say only one boat is lost. I don't know which boatload of kids will be going on the adventure today - is it Doris or Frances I wonder?"

Nathan was at the front of the boat named Doris, leaning over the edge watching the water hit the forward part of the craft as they headed out into the harbour basin. He was looking for fish, especially eels, he was quite oblivious to Terry and Lilly's romantic glances at each other.

All of the children of Fishersgate were experienced at controlling rowing boats; they had been down to the harbour many times over the past few years, but today Nathan had no intention of rowing as he had brought his and Billy's hand-lines, which he kept in the bucket.

Nathan was hoping to do some fishing in the middle of the harbour and would use the bucket to put his catch into. Billy was supposed to help him - that was, of course, the plan before Billy went off on his own for a walk along the banks of the harbour.

Now it was down to Nathan to catch the fish. A couple of nice slippery eels would do for supper and Grandad loved to cook them, but only if they were brought home, alive, in the bucket. Grandad would often say. "Dead ones taste different… so make sure you bring them home alive…"

Old sailor Grandad would often continue in an old English pirate-style scary voice, "I'll cook 'em alive - me heartiest friends - me landlubber friends."

Then, of course, Grandad would begin to tell those regular stories about the Ghost of the Fishersgate harbour, the Fishersgate Mariner, an honest man, who lost his life somewhere in the harbour because of a devilish deed by smugglers.

"Which way shall we go today?" asked Terry. "Shall we go down to the lock-gates or…?" He changed the tone of his voice to that of one of those new posh BBC announcers, who often had deep rich voices… "Or shall we venture along to Hove, where all the posh people live?"

"Let's go westwards, towards the lock-gates," Lilly said with a smile.

"All agreed?" Terry questioned. Nathan muttered words of acknowledgement.

Nathan looked towards the back of the boat and could see in the distance that Garrett and Wheeler had chosen to row in the opposite direction, eastwards, towards the harbour basin in Hove. So, as agreed, Terry gently rowed the boat on that bright summer's day in August 1934, towards the three giant lock-gates in the west and, unknown to them, into dangers of such an enormous magnitude.

Lilly was nineteen years old. She had blue sparkling eyes and long blonde hair. She wore a blue headband to help keep her hair tidy and she never, ever went out of her house without the golden sign of the Christian crucifix dangling from her neck. From the age of four years old, Lilly had trained to become a classical ballerina at the Fishersgate school of dance and had won many competitions across the region. She had also performed in many amateur stage productions throughout Sussex. Destined for great things in concert dance and movement she had also spent some time training at the Royal Ballet in London since the age of 13. That was until she had a bad fall at the age of seventeen and had broken both her ankles in a fall on platform one at London's Victoria railway station. At the time of the accident Lilly was standing beside the platform edge waiting for a train to Brighton. A resident pigeon in the station, flying within the structure of the iron and glass-enclosure, suddenly swept down low - brushing the top of her head. It startled her greatly and she lost her balance and fell four feet onto the railway track below. She was rescued within seconds but both of her ankles were broken badly. Her career was finished before it had even started. These days she worked as a filing clerk at the local Council offices and some evenings helped the local dance studio students under the principal, Mrs. Goatcher. Terry and Lilly had been seeing each other for around six months - he was a newly qualified plumber working in the construction industry. Of course, they would rather be on their own that afternoon but mum Burton had to go out to the telegraph office, several miles away, to send a message to Australia. She told Terry that he must look after Billy for the rest of the day. Nathan, Billy's best mate, who lived at the orphanage at Locks Hill had just tagged along. He was from London, quite streetwise, tall for his age and black. He had been put in the Locks Hill children's home because, sadly, he had become an orphan when he was only five years old. His father was an African-American soldier named Fred who came to England during the First World War. Fred went off to fight the Germans in 1918 and Nathan's mother, Molly Martin, never saw him again. Nathan had never known his father but kept one old faded photograph of him beside his bed. Nathan's Mother, Molly Martin, died in an accident five years later when a runaway carthorse at Locks Hill trampled her to death. Some said she had been murdered. The horse and cart belonged to the local butcher, Mr. Rowland. He had often been the loudest voice in town, preaching in the pulpit every Sunday at church, about the wrongs of inter-racial relationships. He was also a senior member of a secret group known as the 'klue-less-klan'. The klue-less-klan met once a month, at night, in Fishersgate graveyard to discuss their evil objectives. Each member wore a full facemask and flowing white robe so as to protect their individual identities. They did everything they could to stop the integration of different cultures and ethnicities. It is said that Mr.Rowland let the horse go at a crucial moment, just as Molly Martin crossed the road carrying two wicker baskets - each one full of chicken eggs. Her thirty or so chickens were following her at the time. The broken eggs made such a mess on the road and several chickens also met their maker that day. It was never proven that Mr.Rowland was involved.

The little rowing boat containing the three of them passed the power station and the small marina known as Lady-Bee, where part-time sailors with all levels of expertise moored their pleasure boats. Some of them lived on the boats, which were just a short walk from the Albion public house on the main road.

Billy meanwhile, had walked along the top coastal road beside the steep banks of the harbour. These grassed banks between the top road and the harbour shoreline were very steep indeed, more than a 45-degree angle in some places. Scattered among the long grasses were large quantities of pink shrubs known as *Tamarisk*. These beautifully coloured shrubs had long roots that intertwined each other in the earth below and had the benefit of holding the steep bank in position during rainy weather, without fear of landslides. On this hot sunny day, Billy sat down at the top of the bank in the long grass, among the grasshoppers and grass snakes, looking over the gentle waters of the harbour. He was taking in the view and the harbour workers activities and thinking about his life in general. He sat near to a clump of wild buttercups, which he picked away at, throwing each of the fragile yellow petals into the breeze, as he deeply thought about matters concerning those bullies Garrett and Wheeler. 'Why do they pick on me?' Billy thought to himself. 'I am not a choir boy - why do they think I am a choir boy except for the fact that I go to church and I happen to go to a Catholic school. I never chose to go to a Catholic school!' Billy had not even confided in his best friend, Nathan, who attended the same school as Billy, about this bullying. The bullying only happened when Billy was on his own and Garrett and Wheeler were together - never when others were with him or if he saw either of them on their own. It all seemed so senseless and did not achieve anything - except for the personal enjoyment of the bullies themselves. He continued to think about Garrett and Wheeler's movements around the town and how he tried to plan his days so that he could avoid them. And he thought about how he was the one that felt badly about being bullied - when he himself was the victim. It made him feel physically sick at times - especially at night when he was all alone in his bed. And because he felt so badly about his situation, so guilty, and so embarrassed about his lone vulnerability, he could not bring himself to tell anyone about what was going on. Yet Billy knew that all he had to do was to tell his older brother Terry and once Terry knew he would deal with it and the bullying would stop.

Suddenly, Billy saw something in the harbour! A bizarre looking man wearing a strange naval uniform was rowing a boat across the harbour waters and heading towards the lock-gates that separated the harbour from the English Channel. Billy stood up in the long grass to get a better view of the scene and the man in the boat disappeared completely. The boat was there to see, but the man and his oars had gone. He then reappeared for a few moments and then both boat and man disappeared. Suddenly, this image reappeared again and then faded. Billy had heard stories about the Ghost of the harbour and he didn't believe any of them. Maybe he was wrong to dismiss those scary mariner stories that Grandad had told him about. Maybe this really was the Ghost of the Fishersgate Mariner.

Billy rubbed his eyes in disbelief. Was he seeing things? The boat and man appeared again. He watched the man rowing his boat for a short time before raising his oars and stopping. Billy watched for a few more moments. The man then reached near to the surface of the water and pulled a chain. On the end of the chain was a snub-nosed monkey.

"A monkey," exclaimed Billy.

He had never seen a real monkey before and this one had a diamond encrusted collar around its neck. The chain was connected to the collar. He had only seen images of monkeys in books, but had never seen one clad with a diamond collar that sparkled in the sunlight. The monkey ran up and down the boat as the man pulled in the anchor. He started to row the boat again, this time towards the lock-gates and then suddenly, the man, the boat and the monkey vanished as it hit the closed lock-gates to the dry dock. Billy waited for a while, at least ten minutes, but neither the boat or the man reappeared.

Just then, Clifford came walking along the grass, carrying his banjo.

"Did you see that, Clifford," called out Billy.

"See what?" asked Clifford.

"The man in the boat with the monkey," replied Billy.

"No," replied an astounded Clifford, "you don't get monkeys around these parts," he continued knowledgeably. "Monkeys are not native to this country. They are in fact Haplorhine primates and there are many different species around the world, but none in England. So, I would be very surprised to see a monkey here in Fishersgate... but that is not to say that a visiting sailor could not have brought one here from a foreign land."

Billy sighed on hearing all this boring expert knowledge that Clifford was speaking.

"Anyway, aren't you supposed to be at banjo practice?" said Billy.

"It was cancelled," replied Clifford. "Tell me more about this monkey. I've never seen a real monkey."

Just then, as Billy looked the other way towards the east, he caught sight of his brother in his rowing boat, heading in the direction of the lock-gates. He ran down the banks of the harbour, almost running into the water, shouting, "Terry, Terry."

By now Billy was on the shoreline and Terry turned his boat from the middle of the harbour directly towards Billy on the shore.

"What's up Billy?" shouted Terry, "you look like you have seen a ghost."

"I have… I have," screamed Billy.

Billy was out of breath, but he soon explained what he had just seen. Terry positioned the rowing boat as close as he could to the shore and Billy jumped aboard. But not without a stumble with his left foot on the rim of the boat, followed by a fall that grazed his cheek as he simultaneously, yet accidentally, dangled his right foot into the harbour water.

"Come on *story* boy, sit yourself down," smirked Terry, as he handed Billy a handkerchief to wipe the trace of blood from his grazed face. Billy removed his wet shoe and sock.

"It's really true, I saw the Ghost of the harbour and he looked just like Grandad had said," retorted Billy. But no-one believed him. Terry took the boat back into the centre of the harbour and continued rowing westwards.

Before long they could see the lock-gates in the near distance. Terry pulled back the oars and they drifted for a while. They could see that a large ship occupied the incoming lock, fully loaded with timber, waiting for the inner gates to open so that it could access the harbour. Sailors were leaning over the side of the ship. Wafts of cigarette smoke rose above them at regular intervals. There was little for them to do when the ship entered the harbour - except smoke cigarettes and drink beer. It was the harbour master pilot and his team, who were based at Fishersgate, who were in control of this ship within the harbour until it docked. Once in the designated berthing place, the ship would be tied up by the dock workers known as Hufflers. These were a group of ruffians who looked more like pirates. They had the exclusive right, a birth-right, drawn-up in ancient local law to be the only people allowed to tie-up a commercial ship to its berthing place. The Hufflers lived on Finger Island in little tin sheds beside the dock, waiting for a ship to enter the harbour. They never washed or bathed. They fed themselves on eels caught in the harbour and drank dark rum from wooden barrels. You could see them in the winter evenings huddled around cutaway oil drums converted into fire grates, flames burning brightly in the night, the smell of chestnuts and grilled eel wafting across the harbour as they sang shanty songs until the early hours of the morning. They were a rough lot indeed. However, they would always be ready and waiting for the harbour master pilot to bring the next ship to the dock, at whatever time of day or night.

It would take at least twenty of them to catch and then pull the ropes thrown over the side of the vessel by the ship's crew. They would pull and rest, pull and rest, pull and rest, under the direction of their leader, until finally they positioned the ship in the correct location alongside the dock. The final knot would be tied and the ship would remain dockside waiting to be unloaded of its precious goods by another team known as the Stevedores. The leader of the Hufflers team would demand the money in cash - fresh crisp ten-shilling notes, *if you please*, was always his request.

Whenever the children rowed their boats past the Hufflers it was always an awkward moment. The Hufflers would call out from the dockside to anyone in a rowing boat. They would taunt them. They would chant and beckon the children to row their boats to them with threats that they would cook them and eat them for dinner. The children always kept a wide berth at this part of the harbour and they were not frightened to shout back at the Hufflers, obviously safe in the knowledge that the waters of the harbour separated them.

The children would call out to them. 'Catch us if you can, *filthy beasts* or *scruff bags.*' Even the older ones, like Terry and Lilly, would join in with the banter.

42

The Hufflers never bothered to try to catch the children. It was all a game. And whenever this happened the Hufflers laughed and laughed and laughed, their howling laughter echoing around the dock buildings. But there was one Huffler that really scared them all. His name was Jed Lavell. This individual was so scary that when he emerged from the tin shack he lived in, he would frighten the seagulls and the dockside rats away.

Jed looked like a pirate. Perhaps he was a pirate many years before when he sailed the seas of the Mediterranean. Now that he was older, maybe he preferred to stay local, perhaps he was a smuggler who brought his loot into Fishersgate under the cover of darkness. Perhaps he was waiting for something else, something magical or something mysterious. Perhaps he was trapped in a state of limbo in this place called Fishersgate. Whatever the reason, something had kept him in Fishersgate during the past few years since he first mysteriously appeared on the docks. His long black unkempt hair was tied back with a red handkerchief and his bedraggled beard hid most of the front of his filthy shirt. He walked with a swagger and a limp; helped by a carved walking stick, depicting bizarre nautical themes. The stick helped him to maintain his drunken balance. There was something about him. Something that cannot be explained.

Perhaps it was a dark sinister magical power that emanated from his disgruntled character; an evil streak of nastiness no doubt. Perhaps Jed's disposition was nothing more than the disgusting smell about him.

In his shack - the dockside abode that he called home, rumours were rife that he kept the hands and arms of a man, affixed above his fireplace. They were positioned above the mantelpiece, nailed to the wall in the form of a cross. The folklore story told how he had drained the blood from the arms and filled them with dark rum to preserve his morbid trophy. Did Jed Lavell chop this man's arms off during his wicked days as a pirate on the high seas? Nobody knew the answer to that question. No one asked or even dared to look him in the eye, for he was Jed Lavell, the leader of the Hufflers.

After the children had rowed past the Hufflers, who were stationed in their usual position on the dockside, they approached two giant lock gated chambers, both of which led to the open sea. These giant structures each had two pairs of gates fitted - one pair at each end of their respective elongated chamber. Each of the chambers was big enough to contain a large ship. In the first lock - the incoming lock, both gates were closed and the ship they had seen earlier was floating in-between the two sets of gates. The ship was waiting for the seawaters to lower to the level of the harbour water. As the children continued their journey it wasn't long before they passed the gates of the second lock, the outgoing lock which was empty of all vessels. But there was a third lock, which up until now hadn't been very important to any of the children. This third lock was known as the dry dock. It had only one pair of giant gates, unlike the other two locks which each had two pairs of gates. There was only one way in and one way out of the dry dock in a boat and that was through these gates. The dry dock was normally used to repair large ships. It was entirely covered by a huge timber frame and overlaid with corrugated asbestos sheeting which kept out the rain and enabled work inside to be undertaken in all weathers. The Dockers would power the boat into the dry dock building and close the lock-gates. They would then drain the water out from the lock completely, propping the hull of the ship with giant wooden timbers so that the ship remained upright and stable. Once the waters were drained they could work on the ship in safety, especially on the hull. The dry dock hadn't been used for years; not since the First World War. As was usual this lock gate was closed, it always had been.

Suddenly a creaking noise began to emanate from the lock-gates. "Look," shouted Billy. "The dry dock lock-gates are beginning to open. I saw the Ghost row his boat through these gates earlier. Can we go in and have a look… can we?"

Before long the gates had fully opened and the waters of the harbour extended into its enclosure. Terry looked around. No one seemed to be about, apart from the men on the incoming ship and the harbour-master pilot - and he was too preoccupied navigating through the incoming lock. Terry knew there wasn't much to see, it was just an empty area, full of seawater that was entirely covered by this large grey dirty corrugated building. But then again, Terry thought, if they did have a look inside at least they could tell their friends. And if they found the so-called Ghost then this would be a bonus. Terry really did believe that the Ghost was one of the locals playing a joke on the community. It had to be a hoax for Ghosts simply did not exist. But Billy thought differently. He believed in the Ghost. He had seen it for himself, for it had vanished and then it had re-appeared before him - normal human beings cannot do that. And maybe, just maybe, thought Billy, they might find evidence of the Ghost of the Fishersgate Mariner inside the dry dock.

The rest of the crew in the small rowing boat did not believe Billy's story about seeing the so-called Ghost.

Terry had decided. He put the oars in the water and directed the boat through the open lock-gates and into the semi-darkened anchorage. The further they went inside the chamber the darker it became.

"Can we stay for a while?" asked Billy, as he threw his hand line into the water. "Maybe the fish won't see us in this half-darkness!"

"I reckon you are right Billy," said Nathan, "we could catch loads of eels."

Nathan threw his line into the water and immediately got a bite. "I've got a fish," he exclaimed. He pulled in his line. A long wriggling eel was attached. After de-hooking the eel he threw it in the bucket where he watched it swim around and around in circles. 'Well, what else can an eel do in a bucket?' thought Nathan. Nathan threw his line back into the water, but not before Billy had caught an eel of his own. It wasn't long before they had caught five eels for supper. "This place is brilliant for fishing," called out Billy to his friend.

'Funny thing,' thought Nathan, 'all the eels are swimming around and around in the same direction, clockwise.' He pointed out this new-found information to Billy as they watched the eels in the bucket in the semi-darkness.

By now, they had drifted quite a long way into the darkened watery chamber of the dry dock.

"Let's go back outside… it's scary in here," said Lilly.

"In a minute… let the boys catch a few more eels," replied Terry.

"I cannot see your Ghost anywhere Billy," said a smiling Terry.

Billy ignored his brother.

"Let's go," said Lilly in a frightened, but sterner voice. She was getting quite worried. Out of the darkness she looked towards the light, in the general direction from which they had come. At first, she thought that she was imagining things as she looked towards the lock-gates. She stared hard and could not quite believe what she was seeing.

"The gates are closing," she screamed.

Terry looked around. It was true, the giant lock-gates were slowly closing. They would be trapped inside the building.

"Hold tight everyone," he shouted.

They needed to get out…and fast. Terry grabbed the oars and rowed the boat as quickly as he could… hoping, just hoping to get the little rowing boat back into the main harbour before the gates finally closed. Sweat began to pour from his brow after twenty yards of heavy rowing. The gates were still closing and there was another ten yards to go.

"Faster, faster," screamed Billy and Nathan. In the panic, they lost their fishing lines over the side. The lock-gates were closing fast. And then… as expected, they closed completely. They were on the wrong side of the gates and they were trapped in the darkness of the dock. There was no way out.

Lilly began to weep. "What are we going to do now?" she asked.

Terry pulled the oars back into the boat and laid them lengthways on either side. He moved and sat next to her and put his arm around her.

"I don't know exactly… I do not know what we should do… let me think," replied Terry.

"Albert, the boat owner, isn't going to be happy," said Nathan.

"I know… he's going to kill us," exclaimed Billy. "What are we going to do Terry?"

"Shut up you two," cried out Lilly.

Terry didn't respond at all. He was thinking. His eyes wandered around the darkness. He could see little patches of light on the water and on the sides of the dock. Streams of light were beaming through the gaps and cracks in the corrugated asbestos roof of the building high above them. He noticed that a single beam of light shone down only a few yards away from where they were. He could see what he thought was a steel ladder, fixed vertically to the side of the quay. The ladder extended upwards from the water line, some five yards, to the top of the dock. If he could just climb up that ladder and get himself onto the dock he might be able to find a way out of the building and go and get some help. He grabbed the oars and sent the boat in the direction of the beam of light. As he got closer he saw that the object was indeed a vertical ladder. They would soon be safe.

Suddenly, the boat moved from side to side. It began to judder badly and Terry lost grip of the oars, and they fell over the side into the water. Terry tried to grab them but missed. The oars drifted off into the darkness. They had lost their only propellants of the boat and were at the mercy of the waters, which by now were moving incredibly fast. It moved faster, faster, faster; a whirlpool effect on the water was being created, the boat began to spin; the water was falling below the quay, faster and faster.

"Hold tight," shouted a horrified Terry.

Soon the steel vertical ladder did not touch the water anymore. They were dropping further and further below it. They became surrounded by shooting stars, hundreds, millions of them; swirling around their boat as they descended deeper and deeper into a galaxy of flashing unknown space. Downwards and downwards they continued in a spinning motion into a darker, deeper, scary hole from which there was no escape.

They would not be going home on that day and perhaps not on any other day.

Chapter 2

The future

More than forty years had passed since that little rowing boat named Doris was lost. Time had moved on from 1934 - time was now positioned in the late summer of 1974. It would soon be autumn and the leaves from the surrounding trees would, once again, fall onto the waters of Fishersgate harbour, where they would float on the surface for several weeks, swirling in the wind and creating ever-changing withering patterns. Forty years of recurring falling leaves had passed and there was still no sign of those children.

Tom, son of Albert, was a larger than life character who now runs the boat business that his father had founded. Tom was drawing deeply on his old sailor's smoking pipe while pondering about his usual daily tasks and thinking about old Fishersgate folklore stories of many years before. One of those stories was of those youngsters, Terry, Lilly, Billy and Nathan, who went missing in the harbour during the summer of 1934, forty years before. It was the same year that Tom's own father, Albert, had died in the Sussex Arms public house. But time had moved on and Tom was just reminiscing, just as he often did while working alone in his workshop. The entrance to his workshop, known as the Jolly Boatman, was protected by two large wooden doors, which, when Tom was about, were usually held open by steel chains and when he wasn't about - the building was locked like a fortress. Inside the semi-darkened building was a mass of items - anything and everything to do with repairing rowing boats. Pieces of seasoned timber stood in the corner of the workshop and on the racks across the ceiling. Carpenters' tools were neatly displayed in their individual slots along the walls. Slithers of curly wood-shavings were scattered around the floor. On the shelves were paint brushes, tins of varnish, tins of coloured paint and old rags smelling of turpentine, all wedged in a seemingly haphazard way, in-between any available space in the racking. Usually, one of Tom's rowing boats was laid out inside the workshop undergoing repairs, propped-up on a timber, purpose-made jack. Pieces of boat, oars and rowlocks were neatly laid in the boat, along with more specialist tools like peculiar shaped wood chisels, used to form ornate timber carvings. In the corner of the workshop was a bronze statue of a man and a snub-nosed monkey in a rowing boat. Tom never knew where this piece of art came from. His father, Albert, must have bought it many years before. Tom would often be in the workshop constantly tapping away at wooden materials;

his body hidden in the semi-darkness at the far end of the workshop, his smoking pipe constantly wedged in the corner of his mouth. Often, you could smell his burning pipe before you caught sight of his lanky frame.

Tom was a man in his late sixties, quite tall, slightly skinny yet evenly proportioned with grey swept-back hair fastened to his skull by thickly applied Brylcreem. He wore hideously long hairy sideburns. His thin pointed nose seemed too tall for his face and, from a sideways view, it had a bump near to the top. This bump was very handy for keeping his spectacles in the right place on his well-worn crinkled sea-faring face. Tom had been working in his boat repair business for almost forty years.

Tom was also the water ferry-man, just as his father was before him. Those who worked on the other side of the harbour would use his ferry service, costing tuppence each way. Tom's ferry was, by far, the easiest way to get from the Fishersgate mainland to the other side of the harbour. Another way to get to there was to cycle two miles eastward, along the entire length of the harbour, to a place called fisherman's dock. This was where the peninsula known as Finger Island joined the mainland. Then, cycle a quarter of a mile southwards before heading westwards for a further two miles along the length of Finger Island - to where the industrial part of the docks was located. This industrial area on Finger Island was directly opposite Tom's workshop; though it was separated by about fifty yards of water that formed the harbour.

Tom would row the workmen across the waterway to Finger Island; four or six men at a time; fifty or more in an hour. At the end of their working shift he would row them all back again.

Tom never sat down when he rowed one of his boats. He stood upright. Not bolt upright, but in a peculiar statue-like forward posture. His arms gently moved in a circular manner above his motionless torso. His legs, half bent, straddled the middle seat of the boat, one leg in front of the other, gripping the wooden bench seat with his left shin and right calf. It was a finely balanced position which allowed him to feel every movement of the clinker-built wooden boat, as it floated through the calm harbour waters. Not very easy you might think, but Tom had a certain nautical precision and a boating skill that no one else possessed. Whenever he navigated from one side of the harbour to the other he made it look easy. He effortlessly and silently glided his boats through the water and moored them without the slightest bump or collision.

The little area in the harbour, where Tom's half a dozen rowing boats were kept, was known as Fishersgate bay. The bay was situated at the foot of a concrete stairway that led to the coastal road high above. This little area next to his workshop was Tom's domain. At weekends, Fishersgate bay became crowded with members of the public. They would flock to the harbour waterway in their hundreds. Tom would hire-out his rowing boats to them, usually for an hour at a time, just as his father, Albert, had done many years before. From dawn to dusk the little rowing boats came and went from the Fishersgate shoreline, mostly in the hands of amateur boat people keen to enjoy the waterway and the summer sun. It was during these warmer months of the year that Tom made the most money. The money he earned would support him through the bleak winter months when his only income was that of his ferry service.

It was here, in the harbour, in this very spot, many years before today's year of 1974 and many years before 1934 when those children went missing, that a very wicked thing happened at Fishersgate bay. It happened in 1734 when drunken pirates, smugglers and villains met with each other to exchange their ill-gotten contraband for silver coins. The leader of the smugglers and Chief Paymaster to all concerned was a seemingly respectable businessman known as Barlott, also known as the children-catcher. He was a pied-piper of Fishersgate. Under the cover of darkness, he masterminded an illegal smuggling operation, assisted by his lowly criminal associates. He trained them young, often when they were children, to thieve and smuggle. He and his henchmen tortured and, sometimes, murdered those who stood against them. They would weigh-down the lifeless body of their victim and dump it in the deep waters of the harbour for the slimy-eels, which lived at the bottom of the deep waters, to feed upon. Dozens of villains, vagabonds, and a few foreign pirate sailors disappeared without any trace. No one bothered to look for them for none were reported missing. This was a location where decent law-abiding citizens never dared to venture after sunset.

In 1734 the Sussex Arms public house was a lively place. The landlord and his wife ran this establishment to entertain merchant sailors, dock workers and their women. The sounds of music and laughter emanated from its two drinking bars and the smell of roasted rat, chestnuts, squirrel, pollock, eel or pigeon wafted across the waters of the harbour. Sometimes the cook served a delicious morsel of rabbit or salmon brought to him by the village poacher and crook: known only as Sturrell. Villains and cheats;

smugglers and winos; robbers and aspiring pirates frequented this lively but dangerous place. It was a den of iniquity. The landlord, a man by the name of Ronald Razor and his wife, Elle Nora, kept a neat and impeccably clean house. They let most of their upstairs rooms to passing travellers wanting a bed for the night, but there was another room used for secret meetings. The room, with oak wood panelling adorning all walls, centred on a large coal fireplace; the only furniture was a table and eight chairs. To the right of the fireplace, built into the wooden, ornate panelling, was a secret door. This was opened by pushing the fourth raised panel away from the Bolection moulding that encased it. This doorway led to a labyrinth of tunnels and storerooms where contraband was kept. Barlott and his men controlled this area. The main tunnel, some five feet high, led directly to the harbourside. Hidden in the steep banks of the harbour, by dense gorse bushes, was the stone entrance door. It was so heavy it took a dozen men from inside the tunnel to slide it aside by ropes and pulleys; all so cleverly designed and arranged, that an engineer of some importance must have designed its intricate workings. The tunnel also extended to the Crab House, where a cover in the floor, much like a sewer manhole, was positioned. And it was here that a Fishersgate Mariner was murdered and cut into small pieces, in that very tunnel, just below the Crab House. Barlott did it - along with his henchmen, but before that - he and his men had mercilessly tortured their victim. Screams echoed through the tunnel as the knives sliced into an already scarred and bloodstained body. And those screams wailed down the tunnels to be heard outside, via the open stone doorway in the steep bank as well as in the Crab House; screams that reverberated into the otherwise stillness of the harbour, breaking into the silence of the night. And when the victim's body became lifeless they chopped it up into little pieces and, from the quayside, fed the body bits to the slimy eels that lived in the harbour waters. Barlott had murdered many men but this man was different. This man was a man of the law. A man from the British Admiralty, an officer and a gentleman. The mariner had been working undercover dressed as a lowly sailor. His main occupation was to identify rogue employers who welched on wage payments to ordinary sailors. He was enforcing an act of Parliament of 1730.

So, while Barlott thought he was killing a rival smuggler, who he found in the harbour that night, he had in fact murdered a senior Admiralty man. And unknown to Barlott, for the moment, the wrath of the entire Naval Admiralty was about to descend onto Fishersgate harbour.

But that is a story that must wait, so let us go back to the year of 1974, forty years after those children were lost. No-one went into the run-down Sussex Arms public house anymore because it was said that there was a ghost inside. Maybe it was the Ghost of the Fishersgate Mariner that lived there. The building was derelict, standing shabbily among much cleaner, newer buildings that now surrounded it.

But what of Tom the Jolly Boatman. He had no relatives. His Father Albert had arrived in Fishersgate fifty-five years before, from where, no-one knows, with ancient property deeds, to claim the land at Fishersgate bay. Tom, as Albert's descendant, was now the unofficial guardian of this small area and nothing much happened that Tom did not know about. Smuggling was still going on and Barlott's descendants, also named Barlott, were running the operations. Tom knew a bit more about Barlott's smuggling operations than he let on. He was one of the few people who knew the real identity of the modern-day 1974 Barlott - but their paths rarely crossed. The two of them seemed to have a strange kind of mutual respect towards each other. The secrets of Barlott were known to but a few of his own trusted servants and to one or two people in high places who purchased his illegal wares. Some said that the local Member of Parliament was closely associated with Barlott.

But Tom was more concerned about his own little paradise - that little part of the harbour which he painstakingly looked after - Fishersgate bay. Barlott never encroached upon Tom's little piece of the harbour and Tom never bothered Barlott.

Large families occupied the council houses in nearby Fishersgate town. Four or five children in each household. In the winter months, most families listened to the radio or interacted with each other, playing cards or board games. Sometimes, they would sing along to tunes played on the piano - every house owned a piano. But as soon as the warmer weather arrived the lids on the pianos were closed; the board games put away and Tom's boats were now in high demand.

Each timber boat moored at Fishersgate bay was uniquely identified. A different female name was hand painted in bright colours across the backrest of each boat. His father, Albert, had started naming each individual boat with a female name back in the twenties and Tom knew that he could not name any of his 1974 boats Doris, for Doris was still out on hire - it had been on hire since 1934 when Terry had paid Albert sixpence and taken the boat towards the lock-gates with Billy, Lilly and Nathan.

Some of the boats at Fishersgate bay were blue and white in colour but most were orange and green. In 1974 anyone over twelve years old could hire one of Tom's boats for fifty-pence. Youngsters, who looked twelve years old or more, were his main customers. The children would navigate the enormous harbour, which ran parallel to the English Channel. The 1974 harbour was still protected from tidal forces by giant lock-gates which had been refurbished in the 1950s and extended from the mainland onto Finger Island. These lock-gates kept a decent level of water in the harbour. The harbour waters were twenty yards deep at its greatest depth, a depth that never changed because the tidal forces of the English Channel, outside of the lock-gates, were held back by these giant mechanical devices. Beyond the harbour, out at sea, where the tide regularly ebbed and flowed, twice in every twenty-four hours, large ships heavily laden with coal or timber would appear on the horizon waiting to enter the docks. Coal for the power station and gas works, timber for Butts timber yard. At high tide, the man on the lock-gates would turn a huge handle, which would open the outer lock gate, onto the sea. The ship would navigate into the central area of the lock. After closing the outer gate, the lock-keeper would open the inner gate to allow the ship to proceed into the harbour. The reverse operation was enabled by the lock-keeper whenever a ship left the harbour to find its pre-planned navigational way to its destination, via the open sea. This manoeuvre in the lock-gates often took an hour or more as the water levels were either raised or lowered to suit the exact height of an ever-changing tidal level. The stillness of the waters within the harbour was only disrupted when the big ships navigated their way to their respective berthing places.

Child mariners would wait for the ships. They would race along-side the huge ships in their little hired rowing boats, dodging and weaving through the backwash that the big diesel ships fashioned on the water. Often, sailors would peer down on the children in the rowing boats - waving angrily, telling them to get out of the way. Sometimes, overseas sailors would simply wave and smile, make jokes to each other and shout to the child mariners using unfamiliar foreign words with tones of encouragement and friendliness. Other times, old-fashioned partly-rigged sailing ships would enter the harbour carrying their more specialist cargo, like bananas. Their inspiring presence of sails and rigging would lead to the children to play at being pirates or other such exciting nautical games that their imaginations had created. But as the drab diesel ships became more frequent in the harbour, often, the children would ignore them and simply laze in the sunshine, several boats tied together in the middle of the harbour, drifting, talking, laughing and drinking lemonade; It was so very far away from the overcrowded homes that most lived in and the hard-heartedness that most adults portrayed because of their tough working-class experiences. The brave and more adventurous children would swim in the murky waters of the harbour. Yes, this was 1974 and the nautical games that these children played had not changed in fifty years or more. They were the same nautical games that Billy and Nathan had played in the thirties and many hundreds of other children had played in the years in-between. Some children would run errands for the resident sailors on the big ships that had docked in the harbour, especially the sailors on the Russian ships. These sailors from the communist country of the USSR were not allowed to leave the ship in a democratic country such as England. The penalty for those trying to leave or escape was immediate imprisonment in the hold of the ship followed by death, at the hands of a firing squad, when they returned to their Motherland of Russia. KGB secret agents were aboard those Russian ships, keeping a watchful eye on the sailors who yearned for the freedom of the English way of life. Children ran errands to the local shops to get fresh fruit, or to buy British cigarettes and beer for these sailors, and the rewards were good, often fifty pence or more for a single round trip. Sometimes the young teenagers were invited aboard the ships by the sailors - and they were given beer to drink. Fishersgate harbour was a very dangerous place for young people.

Of course, childhoods don't last very long. These children soon grew-up to become adults. All past adventures were left firmly behind them. Some moved away; some didn't, and some have since died. Every single generation of the Fishersgate harbour children, between 1935 and 1974, could recall being told the astonishing story of the missing youngsters, Terry, Lilly, Billy and Nathan, who vanished during the late summer of 1934.

And they were also told the story of Patricia. She was a mysterious psychic and clairvoyant with flame-coloured waist-length hair. It was old Patricia, who often told her audiences of her mystical premonition. A bit of a nuisance some would say, yet others simply thought she was a foolish misguided old woman. She had revealed her exposé during the late nineteen-thirties and continued to speak of it right up until that wretched moment in 1944 when a Mark 2 German Doodlebug landed flat on top of her while she was tending to her cucumbers on her allotment at Carden Hill. But long before she died, one evening in 1935, when it was her turn to speak to the townsfolk at the local Fishersgate church hall, she climbed onto the stage and she told them for the very first time of her mystical prediction.

"Sometime in the future," she said slowly in a dramatic voice to a hushed audience, "maybe in the year of 1975, a child of Fishersgate, a teenage boy, will return to the harbour. He will arrive at Fishersgate bay in a small rowing boat. The name of that boat will be *Doris*. He will wear a large black hat and long dark trench coat with the collar turned up that hides his facial features from three sides. He has been away from Fishersgate for a very long time - he has been away since 1934.

"And so it shall be, on that early morning - forty years from now - in the year of 1975, on a cold but bright autumn day, the boy will stand by the shore, looking out over Fishersgate bay. That will be the day that he will survey his former playground. Soon, the drugs in his feeble body will wear-off and the shivering excruciating pain caused by his injuries will return. He is dying. He has but a few more hours of life within his mortal body.

"A fine mist will hang just above the peaceful waters of Fishersgate bay. The boy will see rowing boats laying semi-sunken in the calm waters that gently lap onto the shingle beach. The boats are all beyond repair for they have

66

been vandalised. The words on the back-rests of the once colourful boats will be hardly visible but as the boy concentrates his failing vision he can just make out some of the letters which once formed names like Shirley, Rose, Geraldine, Gladys, Mary and Gertrude."

Patricia paused for a few moments, as if to gather her thought. Her eyes were closed as she lifted her head towards the heavens. She slowly raised her hands in unison, before beginning to wail.

"Wakutoo, wakutoo, I am there… I am there… I am there, on the banks of Fishersgate bay - in the future - in 1975," she exclaimed.

"Silly old fool," said Nelly Flanagan, who was sitting in the audience as she drew deeply on her Park Drive cigarette, blowing the smoke in to the air where it mingled with the smoke of fifty other chain-smokers.

"Shush, Nelly," said her friend, "this is getting interesting. Here, give me one of your fags darling, I've run out."

Nelly began rummaging through her handbag looking for her packet of cigarettes.

"Wakutoo, wakutoo," continued Patricia from the stage. "Glancing towards Tom's old workshop, built into the steep grassed bank, I am standing next to the boy. He can see that the doors to the 'Jolly Boatman' workshop are boarded over. A notice that is written on the doors in thick black paint rises at an angle from left to right, in a haphazard way, faded by the past year's stormy weather. It bears the message 'KEEP OUT!' Turning back towards the calm waters of the harbour and to the decaying rowing boats, the old quays, the Crab House and the tranquil view before him, the boy ponders upon these images. It is a reminder of where he and his childhood friends once gathered many years before, in 1934, where they used to hire rowing boats from Albert, the boatman. He feels an air of ghostliness about the place. It is here, and only here, where he believes that his lost memories might appear before him. For the moment, a fragmented vision is all he can see in his mind. Thoughts of a lost friendship held so close to his heart. Yet something is missing. It is something he cannot explain; something so immense but so distant - something so important. He cannot draw this information from his memory. His mind is searching itself, drifting back in time; back to the summer of 1934, he is repeatedly trying to remember what really happened during the time he had been away - right up to the time it ended - here, in Fishersgate bay. As he submerges himself within his own thoughts he does not see a Catholic nun approaching. Yes, it's an elderly Sister Alisha, his former teacher. Somehow, she knows that he has returned to Fishersgate. She knows that the first place he will want to see is the bay. Her Mother Superior, the now late Sister Albany, had told her of this moment, for it was written in the scriptures lodged in the convent archives."

Patricia paused for a moment as she lowered her arms to her side, so as to rest them. A few seconds later she raised them once more before continuing.

"Wakutoo, wakutoo, I am the prophet, Patricia, who often visits the convent to meditate." Once more she paused as she adjusted her posture. She then continued, "Sister Alisha is descending the steep concrete steps that will take her down beside the steep grassed banks, towards the harbour shoreline - I, Patricia, am here, she is hurrying towards the boy. She must tell him something. She must take him somewhere.

"Suddenly, he hears her footsteps on the shingle beach. He turns around and takes a long look at her. He instantly recognises her, even though she is much older than when he last saw her - she has wrinkled facial features."

Patricia paused for a moment before proceeding, in her trance like state, continuing to mimic those who she spoke about.

"The boy gently whispered, 'Is it really you Sister Alisha?'

"Sister Alisha replied, 'Yes, it is, and it is nice to see you again, after all these years. You haven't aged at all my friend - you are still as young a boy as you were the day you left us in 1934.'

"The boy looks puzzled. 'What year is it?' he asks.

"Sister Alisha replies, 'It is 1975.'

"The boy shows no emotion - it is as if he cannot comprehend the situation. He glances around the scene and asks, 'What has happened to Albert, the Jolly Boatman? - Why are the boats damaged and the workshop boarded up?'

" 'Albert died', replies sister Alisha, 'and his son, Tom, took over the business - but Tom has disappeared - he has not been seen for seven months.'

"The boy stares at the wrecked rowing boats in astonishment.

"Sister Alisha continues, 'I somehow knew that you would be here today in 1975, at this precise time. It is written in the convent scripts by the psychic, Patricia.' She pauses before asking, 'where are the others…?'

"The boy falls onto his knees on the shingle beach, holds his head in his hands and begins to cry."

Suddenly, Patricia, the old psychic clairvoyant was interrupted...

"Shut up... you are a sad old woman," shouted a man in the audience. "Get her off the stage."

"Let's have some real entertainment," shouted another. "We don't want to hear stories that are not true. Sadly, all of those children are dead and there is nothing we can do about it. They are dead... do you hear me, dead. Just as those other two boys, who few speak about - Garrett and Wheeler. They are dead too - they went missing on the same day - never to be found, though their boat *Frances* was discovered, floating empty by the lock-gates. We all know the facts. Do not make up stories or give false hope, you wicked, wicked woman."

Patricia was shuffled off the stage by the compere and a violin player immediately took over the spot, playing an Irish jig, and everyone started to dance to the tune.

But the truth of the matter is that years later the old woman Patricia was proven to be right. For time did indeed move on from 1934 and, by 1975, Tom had gone from Fishersgate bay and his workshop was left in ruins. And Sister Alisha did meet a child of Fishersgate on the shore of the bay in 1975. How did he get back to Fishersgate in that little rowing boat named *Doris*? Where had he been for forty years? Why hadn't he physically aged - for he was still a teenager? Why was he ill? And where did he go with Sister Alisha?

This is where the real story about the Ghost of the Fishersgate Mariner will begin.

Chapter 3

The calling of the flute

Suddenly there was a thud. The rowing boat containing Terry, Lilly, Billy and Nathan came to an abrupt halt. Their little boat, *Doris,* had hit the bottom of the dry dock before listing heavily to one side. It was dark and cold. It was so dark they couldn't see their own hands in front of their faces, let alone see each other.

"But this can't be right," Terry thought. "We are a long way down, far deeper than we ought to be - and where has all of the water gone?" He looked upwards and all he could see was darkness. There was no light at all, nor a breeze - just a tranquil, damp, silent darkness.

"Is everyone all right?" he asked.

"I'm ok," whispered Billy.

"So am I," replied Nathan.

"Lilly, are you all right, where are you?"

"I am here," she replied.

He extended his arms outwards until he felt the soft skin of her cheek with his fingertips. He moved across to her side of the boat and they sat together holding hands as he whispered supportive words of comfort to her. Yet he knew they were in grave danger.

"What do we do now Terry?" asked Billy.

"I don't know," replied Terry.

Terry put his hand over the side of the slanting boat and felt the hard-stone floor of the dry dock. The water had drained away completely.

"I think we ought to sit tight for a while, just in case the water returns," said Terry.

They sat for at least a half-hour in the damp darkness, while the eels thrashed about in the bucket. Occasionally their silence was broken by idle chatter which comforted each one of them. But now they were hungry and cold. Nathan resorted to shouting very loudly and they all joined in. But it was to no avail. No one could hear them... for nobody replied. Once more a silence fell upon them all.

More time passed by and they began to drift into sleep. Lilly was the first to be woken by a strange soothing sound. In the distance, she could hear a faint noise. She listened carefully. It sounded like a musical flute. In the air, all around them, a slight breeze wafted past. There was a smell of warmth in the air, like a mid-summers day and freshly baked bread, fish pie and kippers all mixed into one. The sound became louder. It was a flute playing a wonderful sound. It seemed to be a magical calling sound. Maybe a fisherman was playing this tune, or was it a lighthouse keeper; maybe it was a mermaid, or even an angel. The sound of the flute was enticing; it was drawing their minds to this breath-taking unblemished resonance. Then there was light. Not from above, but from the side; not all around, but from what looked like a tunnel that seemed to lead away from the floor of the dry dock.

"Come on," said Terry, "it must be the way out. Let's follow the light. Hold hands so that we don't lose each other."

They formed a line and each one of them stepped out of the boat, in turn, holding hands, edging towards the light in the tunnel, wary that the water could come back at any time. Terry led the way, carefully manoeuvering them towards the distant brightness.

It wasn't long before they reached the light. It was a gas light shimmering brightly in a cave. They could see each other for the first time in hours. They were thankful for that and as they became accustomed to the light Terry noticed something - Nathan had brought the bucket full of eels with him.

"Nathan," he said in a firm voice, "put that bucket of eels down, we are not taking those with us."

"But we can't leave our supper here," replied Nathan. "Grandad will be upset if we return home without his supper."

"Yes, we can," replied Terry angrily. "We are in enough trouble as it is. We can't lug around a galvanized bucket full of eels. I am not even sure we are going home today. I don't know where this tunnel leads to. Leave the bucket right there. If you want to stay with the eels... then stay... I don't care... but we are going through to the end of this tunnel, unhindered by a bucket of eels... it's up to you, Nathan. Are you staying or coming with us?"

"Oh, all right then," said a disappointed Nathan. He wasn't about to stay with the eels - however much he didn't want to leave them behind. Nathan put the bucket down next to the wall of the cave, underneath the gas lamp.

They looked around their surroundings and moved forward about five yards into a chamber. In front of them lay a labyrinth of at least six tunnels, some three yards high, others just two yards, all seemingly going off in different directions. Each one had a sign affixed to the side.

"The signs must show the way, but it's written in some sort of foreign language." said Lilly.

"It's in Latin," exclaimed Billy, "but I don't know what it means."

"A fat lot of good you are," said Nathan. "I thought you knew your Latin language?"

"I do," said a dejected Billy. "but not those particular words."

There was one tunnel which drew their attention - the sound of a flute was echoing through this one small exit. This flute appeared to be a 'calling sound' which drew them towards its entrance. They followed the sound and, as they moved forward yard by yard, as if by magic another gas light illuminated in front of them. Nathan, who was slightly disappointed about leaving the eels, had lagged behind the others by about twenty yards. He was sulking and Terry knew it. He wasn't going to let Nathan influence the others and had told them to ignore him. He knew it was right to leave the eels behind and Nathan would soon come around to his way of thinking. Just then a rat ran across their path. Lilly screamed loudly and the sound reverberated throughout the tunnel. They all stopped in their tracks.

Billy was the first to break the silence once he realised what had made Lilly scream.

"It's only a rat," said Billy. "Only a little bit bigger than the hamsters we keep at home," he continued knowledgeably.

At that moment, they heard the sound of gushing water in the distance. It came from the direction of the dry dock.

"What's that sound?" shouted Nathan to his friends who were further along the tunnel.

Billy listened intently before shouting back to Nathan, "It's water, lots of it... the dry dock must be filling up with water - and it's coming this way. Look, it's beginning to trickle along the floor towards us."

"Come on, come on," screamed Nathan, "we must get back to the boat," and he started to run away from them.

Just then a grinding noise began to vibrate through the tunnel. They looked, once more, towards Nathan's direction. A huge slab of rock was dropping slowly from the roof of the tunnel.

"The tunnel's closing," Nathan screamed. "We'll be trapped, we must get back to the boat."

But the rest of them were too far in front of him to do anything. They would never get back past the stone slab before it closed. They watched as Nathan ran back past the stone doorway and stood on the other side of the giant closing rock. Terry, Lilly and Billy would soon be separated from Nathan and there was nothing they could do.

"Come on... run, let's go back to the rowing boat," an out of breath Nathan screamed, waving his arms at the others; hoping to encourage them to his side of the moving rock. But they knew they couldn't make it - they were too far away from the stone doorway. Seawater began to rise around Nathan's ankles.

"You must come with us," shouted Terry, "you will drown for sure if you stay on that side of the slab - take your chance with us, for you will never make it back to the boat before the tunnel fills with water."

"Come on Nathan," screamed Lilly, "that gushing water sounds more like a torrent now and it will soon engulf you. Maybe the stone door will act like a plug and stop the water hitting us. You must jump onto our side of the tunnel - now."

Just before the giant rock finally blocked the tunnel Nathan made a final decision. At the very last moment he jumped past the closing stone door - back towards the rest of the group and fell to the floor. He was firmly back into that part of the tunnel where the others were standing some twenty-yards away. Billy was the first to shout out with delight. His friend had chosen not to leave them after all.

Nathan lay on the floor of the cave in the position he had fallen. He was thinking about what he had just done. Was it the right thing to do? He resigned himself to the fact that he was now imprisoned in this underground tunnel and awaiting his fate from the rising water, but at least he was trapped with his friend, Billy, and the rest of the gang.

Then he realised - the huge stone had acted like a plug in a sink, the water had been held back by the stone, Lilly was right - they were safe, for the moment.

He picked himself up and brushed himself down and ran along the tunnel to catch up with his friends.

"Well at least the eels are happy now that they are back in harbour waters," said a glum Nathan.

Terry laughed. "Come on Nathan, you'll get over it and when we do get home you can go and catch those eels all over again."

All four of them continued their journey, staying close together, following the sound of the flute.

Suddenly, there was a sound of the wind. It became louder and louder until it became a gale force. It was strong. It was so powerful that it lifted the youngsters off their feet and blew them at a speed of hundreds of miles an hour through the tunnel. It was a magical wind, thrusting them on a magical journey - for they stayed together. Surprisingly, no-one hit the walls of the tunnel.

About an hour later, the high-velocity wind stopped as quickly as it had started, but not before their speed had gradually slowed until they were strolling along at a brisk walking pace. Then it stopped completely and they all came to a halt beside a small quaint shop built into the wall of the cave. It was not what they were expecting. A shop in the middle of a cave would be quite unusual.

The front of the shop had a well-worn dirty timber door with little panes of glass. The door was wedged open and the smell of warm bread and kippers wafted outwards. Through the matching panes of glass in the display window they saw cakes and bread on wooden trays and, in the background, there was a counter with fish and lobster, not embedded amongst chunks of ice as you might think, but simply laid out on a flat stone worktop. The floor was made of wooden boards and dressed in a deep layer of sawdust. The walls were carved out of the rock leaving a ragged yet pleasing sort of reddish coloured finish and a stone butcher's counter stood on the right-hand side displaying joints of beef and pork. On the other side there were tins, jars and bottles neatly arranged on shelves and, hanging above, an array of pots, pans, kettles, telescopes, eyeglasses and all manner of utensils and artefacts that made this the most interesting general store you ever did see. On a low-level shelf outside the shop, there were some books. Billy took one at random.

"Robinson Crusoe by Robinson Crusoe," Billy read.

"Never heard of it," said Nathan.

Billy flicked through the pages of the book but stopped just inside the front cover.

"You must have heard of this book Nathan - it's Robinson Crusoe. He was stranded on a desert island - it says... that this book was published on 25th April 1719."

Lilly called to Billy, "Give me the book you daft thing - I have never seen a book that old. And anyway, Robinson Crusoe was the main character not the author - a man named Daniel Defoe wrote the book."

She took the book from Billy and looked in the same place.

"Well, it's hard to believe," she exclaimed. "It says it was published in 1719... that's really old... this is the original edition and, you are right, the text states that Robinson Crusoe wrote the book called Robinson Crusoe... It must be a mistake."

She put the book back on the shelf.

"Never mind about Robinson Crusoe. We have bigger problems of our own to solve, like getting the four of us back to Fishersgate," whispered Terry "and anyway, Daniel Defoe did write the book, but he was a bit shy so he used the pen-name, Robinson Crusoe."

"Are you sure?" asked Lilly.

"Yes," replied Terry, "I remember my literary history teacher telling the class that when I was at school."

"Hey," exclaimed Nathan. "We are stranded too. Just like Robin Crusoe."

"It's Robinson not Robin," said Billy, "though I have to admit that we are stranded in this tunnel."

"Shut-up you two," retorted Terry. "Lilly's right, we have some big problems of our own to solve and getting back home is the number-one priority."

The shopkeeper stood behind the till. He was dressed in an apron stained with blood and a drab white shirt with a strange eighteenth-century type collar. He put down a musical instrument, a banjo, which he had been holding and began tending to his merchandise without being aware that the children were watching him through the window. They had to look twice at the man for he was remarkably similar, though slightly younger, than Albert, the Fishersgate boatman. But surely it couldn't be him. Yet, he was the same height; same build and with the same facial features as Albert the boatman. He even had the hideous greying ginger beard. It had to be Albert, but why was he wearing funny old-fashioned clothes and how did he get to this place before they did?

In the corner of the shop was another man of Arabic descent sitting cross-legged on the floor playing a flute. He was dressed in brightly coloured robes appearing transfixed by his own music; staring straight ahead looking through the shop doorway into the cave. The smell of freshly baked bread and kippers was all too much for Billy.

"I'm hungry," he called out.

He ran into the shop and the others followed him. The shopkeeper looked up but before he could say anything a large clock fixed on the wall began to chime. The shopkeeper remained static and looked towards a wooden panel at the back of the shop. The man playing the flute stopped and there was a silence, except for the chiming clock. As the clock struck the thirteenth chime the wooden panel in the stone wall opened and three ballet dancers, each dressed in a white tutu, danced their way to the centre of the shop floor. The flute player began a new tune and they danced for a while in unison.

"They dance wonderfully," exclaimed a delighted Lilly, "they dance to perfection - oh, I wish I could dance like that just once more. I so miss not being able to dance at that level of skill."

"Maybe you will one day," whispered Terry as he held her hand.

And while the ballerinas danced a golden goblet appeared from nowhere into the hands of the central dancer. This golden goblet looked remarkably like Grandad Burton's old goblet. She held the goblet above her head, twirled around then lowered it to sip some of the contents before passing it to another dancer. The second dancer carried out the same routine before passing the goblet to the third dancer, whereupon the whole process started again. The children watched all of this with an astonished interest and the shopkeeper remained silent throughout, until the display had been performed three times.

At the end of the third display the dancer handed the goblet to the shopkeeper.

"You must each take a sip of this elixir, it is traveller's brew which must be taken before or after, but certainly within two hours of travel," said the shopkeeper as he passed the goblet to Terry.

"What's he on about," said Billy.

"I am not sure," whispered Nathan.

Terry looked at the contents in the goblet then smelled it. It seemed fine, so he took a small sip of the elixir before passing it to Lilly. Soon, all four of them had sipped some of the contents of the goblet which they all agreed had quite a pleasant taste.

The shopkeeper took back the goblet.

"You are now *free travellers,*" exclaimed the shopkeeper.

"What is a free traveller?" asked Lilly.

"Never mind about that, I haven't got time to explain," said the shopkeeper as he passed the goblet back to one of the dancers.

The dancers then took a low curtsey and as they rose to *'first position'* a huge plume of smoke and a flash of light engulfed the three of them. When the smoke had cleared it became obvious they were not there. They had vanished. As the smoke wafted away Billy blurted out, "That smells just like the incense that Father Lemmon uses at the Star of the Sea."

"Where have the dancers gone?" asked Nathan.

"I don't know," replied Billy.

With that, the shopkeeper called out loudly to them in a broad Sussex accent.

"I am Wentworth, the keeper of mysteries and wares. What can I do for you young sirs and the lady?"

"Where have the dancers gone?" enquired Nathan. He pointed towards where the dancers had been.

"Oh, don't worry about them," replied the shopkeeper, "they are the magicians of time. They will be back when the time strikes once more and calls for the tune of the flute."

Nathan looked puzzled. *"When the time strikes etc. etc. etc."* he mouthed it to Billy, without a sound coming from his mouth.

"What does that mean?" he whispered to Billy.

Billy looked at him and shrugged his shoulders. "I don't know."

There were more important matters to hand than wondering about vanishing dancers. Like *food* for instance, for all four of them were hungry.

Billy looked up at Wentworth the shopkeeper.

"We would like something to eat," he said.

"Well, come over to the counter and I shall see what I can find, you are my second group of customers today," replied the shopkeeper. The four of them approached the counter which was displaying edible goods in abundance. There was cheese, butter, ham and milk. They were so hungry they never looked to see if there was much else to eat. The shopkeeper offered them some cheese.

"That's not cheese," said Lilly, "that's ham."

"Silly me," replied the forgetful shopkeeper, "I am but nearly a thousand years old - the old memory banks lose their function at my age."

Billy took it without further questioning, followed by the others, and they finished off all the ham in the shop before moving on to the cheese and other such foods. They fed themselves until they were quite full. When they were done the shopkeeper handed them the bill.

"That will be one penny," he said.

"Blimey. That's cheap," thought Terry, but nonetheless he put his hand in his pocket and pulled out one shilling and put it on the counter. The shopkeeper picked it up and looked closely at the coin.

"King George the fifth?" the shopkeeper enquired. "Who is that?" He put the coin back down on the counter and folded his arms.

Terry picked up the coin.

"Well, it's the King of England, George the fifth," replied Terry.

"There is no King George the fifth," retorted the shopkeeper. "King George the second rules this forgotten English outpost of the tunnel, well some of the time when he can be bothered, and long may that continue... perhaps."

Wentworth's mood suddenly changed and his eyes glazed over. He appeared to be in a trance for a few seconds. He stood motionless and looked around the store with wide open eyes. Suddenly his body jerked into action and he ran around the store opening and closing every cupboard door in the shop as if he were looking for something, before returning to the counter and whispering, "Can't be too careful what one says around here you know, there are government spies everywhere."

He suddenly stood bolt-upright, his head shuddered and then abruptly, he composed himself.

"Right, it's time to sing a song," said Wentworth before immediately bursting into a musical rendition at the top of his voice. "*Good old Sussex by the sea, Good old Sussex by the sea - you can tell them all that we know...*"

Wentworth suddenly stopped singing. "Funny - I can never remember any more of the lyrics," he exclaimed.

"He's mad," whispered Nathan to Billy.

Billy ignored Nathan for he had a question to ask. "Are we still in Sussex, Mr. Wentworth?" asked Billy.

"Never mind about *where* we are boy," Wentworth continued singing. "*We are, where we are, and where we are, is exactly where we are right at this moment in time and only I know where we are.*"

"And where is that?" asked a puzzled Billy.

"Well… it's here, stupid boy," replied Wentworth.

"What?" said a baffled Nathan.

Wentworth ignored Nathan's comment and once more stated to Terry that only George the second ruled this place.

Terry was puzzled. "George the second? Well that's impossible," replied Terry, "he died years ago?"

"Well, he is very much alive, I can tell you," retorted the shopkeeper. "And unfortunately, so are the King's spies. The King and his unions of Parliament are most definitely our rulers."

The youngsters looked at each other in disbelief. What is this place where magical ballet dancers vanish in a puff of smoke and a shopkeeper dressed in strange clothes thinks George the second *still* rules this Country? Terry wasn't sure exactly when George the second had ruled England, but now the shopkeeper had mentioned his name he knew it was a long time before 1934 because he had read about him at school. He was the last King of England to be born outside of the United Kingdom and was the last King to lead an army into battle as he did at Dettingen in 1743. George the second was also the grandfather of the so-called mad King George the third.

"Can I have another look at that coin?" asked the shopkeeper. Terry handed over the coin once more. The shopkeeper took a magnifying glass from his display and had a second look at the coin. He read out the date on the coin, "Nineteen-thirty... well, that's over two hundred years in the future."

"What do you mean?" asked Lilly.

"Well, young lady," replied the shopkeeper "I don't know where you got this coin or where you come from, but today is the 31st August 1734, and this coin shows the mark that it was made in 1930... so it's a fake - and so are you four young people. I shall call the guards if you don't give me some proper money."

"That is proper money," replied Terry. "I don't know where we are right now, but we come from Fishersgate in Sussex and I would be obliged if you could tell us how to get back."

The shopkeeper stopped in his tracks. He once more stood in a trance-like state, eyes wide open.

"Fishersgate... Fishersgate... I've heard that name before."

He rubbed his chin with all four fingers and a thumb as he delved into his memory.

"Ah, Fishersgate," he exclaimed with a knowing smile.

His face turned to puzzlement once more.

"No, no, it's not that one," he remarked.

"Hmmm, well never mind…it will come to me soon."

His face turned to a thunderous scary look.

"In the meantime, give me my money you, you, scallywags," he screamed with a frustrated anger.

Terry shouted, "We don't have any other money and I don't believe that this is 1734 - we can't have gone back in time two hundred years"

"Well, you have," retorted the impatient but forgetful shopkeeper. "You take my food and you cannot pay with the King's money."

The shopkeeper picked up a large bell with a wooden handle and swung it about. "Guards, Guards," he shouted.

The children looked at each other.

"Guards, Guards." shouted the shopkeeper.

"Run," shouted Terry.

Nathan and Billy went first. Terry grabbed Lilly's hand and they ran past the flute player, who by this time was still in a trance, out of the shop and back into the cave.

They continued their journey in the direction they had been heading before they entered the shop.

"Wait," shouted the shopkeeper, as a spark of memory flashed through his brain. "Where are you from? Did you say you were from Fishersgate?" Did they? He now wasn't sure himself because of the commotion that he had created.

The children were now several yards away from the small shop.

"No, no come back... I know who you are now. I remember. You are the children of Fishersgate. I have read about you in the ancient manuscripts. You can have the food for free," he shouted.

There was no response from the children. They were too far away to hear what the shopkeeper had said.

He began to jump up and down. Annoyed with himself for not realising sooner, he banged his head on the food counter several times, before kicking the flute player in temper. The flute player remained in his trance. Wentworth knew that something was special about these children. He knew that they were the Fishersgate children. It was a missed opportunity for him and now the children had gone.

The youngsters did not stop running until, suddenly, the cave ended and the land opened into a huge expanse of beautiful terrain. A sign stated, 'You are now entering *Namidia.*' In front of them lay a periwinkle-blue sea of almost calm water, with a splash of white surf scattered among its vastness, and squawking seagulls hovered on a warm overhead breeze. In the distance, a fully rigged sailing ship was moored offshore. Nearby, there was a sandy beach where the waters lapped upon the shoreline. A rowing boat containing four men - two guards and two very large chained prisoners - had just left the shore and was heading out to sea towards the ship. 'That's funny,' thought Billy, as he looked towards the men in the rowing boat. 'The outline of the two chained prisoners, against the afternoon sun, look a little like Garrett and Wheeler.' He squinted his eyes for a better view - but he couldn't make out their facial features. 'Surely it couldn't be them,' thought Billy, before turning his attention to other scenes around him

There were palm trees and coconut trees beside the seashore. To their right there was woodland, though this was probably better described as the edge of a jungle, where bananas, mangos and yet more coconuts grew. There was an array of sounds emanating from the jungle. Its sheer size and vastness faded into a hazy distance, where a mountain could be seen. A visible haze of heat rose above the jungle trees which created an artificial perspective of the horizon. Upwards and outwards it drifted, thinning itself into a semi-invisible vapour the higher it ascended and the wider it extended. Much higher in the atmosphere, two silver-white clouds blemished the otherwise clear blue sky.

To the left were a large group of people in a marketplace and beyond that, for as far as one could see, a sandy golden desert with a trail of footprints and not very nice deposits of muck where camels had recently passed by.

Suddenly, two guards dressed in red uniforms came running towards them.

"They went that way," shouted Nathan, pointing towards the men in the rowing boat. The guards ran off towards the sea shouting at the tops of their voices, "Stop thieves."

"Good thinking," said Billy. He smiled at his mate Nathan, "but were they really after us?" he continued.

Terry realised that they were being watched by some of the other people in the marketplace. This was the sort of attention they didn't need.

"Let's get out of here," said Terry. "Quickly now. If we go under those trees for a while I can think about what we shall do next."

"Let's go back and explain to the shopkeeper," said Lilly, "we are not thieves... perhaps we can find a way of paying."

Billy turned towards her. "Are you mad?" he shouted. "We will get arrested for sure and thrown into jail."

Terry angrily interrupted. "Shut up you little squirt". He wasn't going to let his little brother talk to Lilly like that. He gently pushed Billy away. Almost immediately he was apologetic for what he had done.

"I am so sorry Billy," he said.

Terry felt responsible for the situation they were in. He was, after all, the eldest and it was indeed him that had singularly rowed the boat into the dry dock, even though it was Billy who had egged him on. The pressure of responsibility was too much to bear for Terry and lashing out at Billy had released some of that tension within him. But he was also angry with himself. As the oldest, he alone felt responsible for their predicament. Now he was sorry. This brotherly quarrel had done them no good at all. Two Arabic men were now walking towards them from the marketplace. It would be a matter of minutes before they reached them.

With one eye still fixed on the two approaching men Terry turned to Lilly. "I think Billy is right, we can't go back, not yet anyway; the shopkeeper won't believe us and we will be arrested, we really ought to lay low for a while until we can work out exactly where we are and what we should do."

Terry held out his hand to his brother, Billy.

"Come on Bruv… shake hands."

Billy and Terry shook hands as Nathan looked on with an approving nod. Then it was time to go, and all of them ran towards the trees on the edge of the jungle as fast as they could.

Chapter 4

North African lands

It wasn't long before Billy, Nathan, Terry and Lilly were standing beside the tall trees in a strange looking jungle. As they made their way into the thicker wooded areas, Terry glanced behind to see where their pursuers were. He could see that they were not far behind and so he decided that the only way to lose them would be to hide in the bushes, somewhere off the main trail.

They lay low and hid in the undergrowth, amongst the boxwood and scrub wood to allow the two men who were following them to pass by. It worked! A few minutes later the men arrived and continued walking along the path which led deep into the jungle. Terry noticed that they had pistols. They were of Arabic descent - one wore a red fez and the other a beige trilby hat. Both were dressed smartly. The one with the trilby wore a safari suit jacket with breeches and a white linen shirt with a frilly lace edging, while the other wore a cream sleeveless waistcoat, shirt and breeches. They looked like hunters, or maybe they were the government spies that Wentworth had spoken about. After a while Terry was sure that the men had gone and he pulled himself up onto his feet.

"Ok everyone, they've gone - you can come out now," whispered Terry.

The others appeared from the bushes one by one. They brushed each other down to rid their clothes of dirt and twigs and the kind of tiny bugs that are often found in jungles.

"I think we ought to find some shelter," Terry continued. "It will be dark soon."

"But where?" enquired Billy, as he surveyed the area.

The jungle surroundings displayed strange types of vegetation, a mixture of green and beige in colour with the occasional hint of yellow flowers. Tall coconut and mango trees were plentiful and they knew they wouldn't go hungry - provided they all liked fruit of course. Irregular noises, strange to them, emanated from all directions. These were the sounds of the animals, lizards and insects that lived in the jungle. They would soon become familiar with this jungle hullabaloo. High above, towards the dense bush, the branches of trees were moving with a rustling sound, and little green and brown tree frogs were beginning to croak as it became darker. They caught sight of several large, hairy beings, swinging between trees with their young babies precariously attached to their fur. Were these monkeys or gorillas or something else? Were they dangerous? Terry thought to himself - hopefully, there were no leopards in this jungle, but he did not mention this to the others. Only time would tell how dangerous their environment would become.

They began to walk into the thicket. Terry found a sturdy branch, about four feet long, which had fallen from a tree. He snapped the protruding twigs from its stem and used it as a ram to force his way through the thicket and, maybe, it could be used as a weapon if something attacked them. Soon they all had weapons of varying types. Terry didn't know where he was leading the others. All he knew was that they couldn't go back or follow the path where the men were heading as they would be in danger of being captured.

The children were ill-prepared for their new surroundings. Not one of them had a knife or matches or anything that might be useful to survive the potential horrors of jungle life. After all, why would they need a survival kit? They only went boating at Fishersgate harbour a few hours earlier and should have been at home with Mum and Grandad back in Fishersgate in 1934 by now.

Thoughts indeed turned to home. Their mother and Grandad must be missing them by now; it was long after six o'clock in the evening. Lilly's mother would be missing her; she would be very angry and Terry would certainly be in trouble for not taking Lilly home at five o'clock as promised. As for Nathan, he didn't have a mother or father, but the master of the children's home would soon be scouring the streets looking for him.

They pushed their way deep into the jungle, one behind the other, Terry first, Nathan last and the other two in between. Beads of sweat were falling from their brows and their clothes became torn and dirty. They needed something to drink and somewhere to rest but there was nothing in sight in this part of the jungle except for greenery and the odd coconut twenty-feet above them.

Suddenly, Terry heard a muffled sound. He quickly turned around to see that Billy and Nathan had been grabbed from behind and they were struggling to break free from their captors. It was the two men who had been following them and one was holding a gun to the side of Billy's temple.

"Don't move... any of you... otherwise he gets it," said the man.

Terry froze for a moment; arms outstretched with the stick in one hand.

"Drop the stick," the man ordered in broken English with an Arabian accent. Terry let go of the stick he was holding and it fell to the ground.

"Okay, okay," called Terry, "Billy, stay still! Don't fight them."

He was worried that if Billy struggled with the man might cause the gun to go off.

"What do you want?" Terry asked of the men.

"Who are you?" shouted the Arab man.

"I am Terry and these are my friends," he replied.

"Where are you from? - you wear strange clothes," the man said.

"Not as strange as the clothes you wear," murmured Billy.

"I said shut-it Billy," called Terry.

"We are from Fishersgate…" replied Terry to the man.

The man suddenly let go of Billy and stood back. He aimed the gun at Terry who was some three yards away from him.

"Fishersgate," the man gasped.

He spoke in Arabic to the man who was holding Nathan. Suddenly Nathan was released.

"Why is everybody around here so interested in Fishersgate?" exclaimed Billy to his friend Nathan.

"You… are the children of Fishersgate?" the man questioned. He seemed to be mesmerised by the word 'Fishersgate'.

"Yes, we are the children of Fishersgate," retorted Nathan in a sarcastic manner. "But not anymore - because we are here in this place."

"Shut it Nathan," exclaimed Terry. "let's keep it calm, and no-one will get hurt."

Terry wasn't sure what was happening but thought he ought to play along with the men.

"Yes... we are... the children... of Fishersgate," he replied and nodded his head, smiling at the same time. Encouraging the others to copy him, they all nodded their heads, smiling, chanting, "We are the children of Fishersgate."

"Forgive us," the man said in an apologetic gentle voice as he lowered his gun. He stepped forward and held out his hand. Terry held out his hand and the man shook it profusely. Soon the other man was shaking hands and before long both Arab men had shaken the hand of all four of them. Terry was bewildered by events and the children looked at each other in astonishment. They were thankful that this moment of danger had passed.

"You must come with us, and quickly," the man said.

"Where to?" asked Terry.

"Somewhere safe where we can talk," he replied.

Terry looked at the others. Nathan and Billy both shrugged their shoulders as if to accept the invitation.

"Do we have a choice?" Terry asked.

"If you stay here you will soon be in grave danger, there are leopards in the jungle," replied the man.

"Follow me," he ordered.

And they did. Terry picked up his newly acquired stick and they moved deeper and deeper into the thicket until they came to an opening beside a freshwater pond, where ten or more camels were tethered. Several Arab men were tending to the camels.

"Bring me six camels," shouted the man wearing the fez as he raised his hand and waved at one of the keepers of the camels. Soon they were riding the camels and it wasn't long before they arrived at a small white building hidden beside a track deep in the undergrowth.

"This is our castle", said one of the men.

Billy looked at Nathan. "This isn't a castle," whispered Nathan.

The door opened for them and they entered a long exquisite hallway. The house seemed much bigger inside than it looked from the outside.

The man wearing the fez called out, "Abiba, will you come quickly." An elderly Asian lady, about four feet tall, appeared in the doorway. She scuttled into the hallway in her tightly fitting but very colourful bright orange silk dress.

"Abiba, these are our guests. Look after them well and see to their every need. Perhaps you can show them where they shall sleep this evening."

"Yes Master," replied Abiba.

He continued. "I believe that they will also need to bathe… and would you provide clean clothes for them… and would you give them something to drink?"

"Yes Master," said Abiba.

She looked towards the tired bedraggled children and asked them to follow her to the kitchen.

"Before you go, let us introduce ourselves, I am Mr. Josef," said the man who was wearing the trilby, "and this is my brother, Mr. Necho."

Mr. Necho nodded but said nothing.

"Pleased to meet you," replied Terry. "This is Billy my brother and his friend Nathan."

"How can you two men be brothers with different surnames?" blurted out Nathan.

"Be quiet," said Terry who didn't want to antagonise their hosts.

"No… the boy has a fair question which needs to be responded to… Brothers take many shapes and Mr. Necho is my emblematic brother, we are brothers with a single aim."

He almost immediately changed the subject matter.

"And the girl?" asked Mr. Necho, an overweight slimy looking man, who held out his arms as if to embrace Lilly.

Terry grabbed her hand and stood between Mr. Necho and Lilly.

Necho smiled, "She is your woman?"

"Yes," replied Terry, "she is my girlfriend."

"Don't worry, you are all safe in my house," said Necho. "She will not sleep in my room tonight I promise, but neither will she sleep in yours."

He turned to his servant.

"Come... come Abiba," as he clapped his hands once, "take them to their quarters."

"Can I ask something?" enquired Terry. "Where exactly are we?"

Mr. Josef replied. "You are in the tribal land of Namidia which is on the north coast of Africa, by the Mediterranean Sea."

"Why, that's impossible," exclaimed Terry.

"But it's true," replied Mr. Josef with a smile. He continued... "there is much to tell you and I shall do so over dinner this evening."

He looked down to the floor, as if he was struck by a moment of serious thought, then suddenly looked up and clapped his hands together in a single stroke.

"Come… come… please go with Abiba she will look after you and I shall see you at dinner."

"Never mind all that," said Terry. "How do we get back to Fishersgate… We want to go now. We must get back tonight."

Mr. Josef stood upright with his hands clasped behind his back. He took a deep breath. "I am afraid that is not possible for the moment my children."

"But we must get back to Fishersgate, my mother will be waiting for me," exclaimed Lilly.

"You have a mother?" enquired an interested Mr. Necho. "If she is as beautiful as you are, then, I would like to meet her."

"You are not her type," replied Lilly in a sarcastic manner.

Lilly turned her attention to Mr. Josef.

"Mr. Josef, we really must get back to Fishersgate," she said.

"And you will my dear… but all in good time. Now I really must insist that you prepare for dinner," said a kindly Mr. Josef.

Abiba smiled at the children. "Follow me please." She led them into the kitchen where they each drank at least a pint of a truly delicious tropical drink. After that Abiba said she would show them to their quarters. Along the sumptuous corridors, at ten yard intervals, stood an Arabian guard. The guards were all dressed the same in orange and gold Arabian uniforms, all wearing a white headdress, Arabic breeches and each bearing a silver cutlass. They stood within sight of each other, arms folded, and looking straight ahead. Each guard wore an emblem on their headdress consisting of two striking gold and black squares one within the other, crossed by two swords.

"Hello," said Billy as he passed one of the guards. The guard did not respond. He stood motionless, except for his eyes, which followed Billy's every move.

"Do not talk to the guardians of the castle... they cannot talk to you," said Abiba.

"Why not?" asked Billy.

"They cannot talk for they do not have tongues," replied Abiba.

"But why?" asked a surprised Billy.

Terry interrupted. "Leave it, Billy."

"No, I shall tell the boy. He needs to know," Abiba exclaimed.

She continued. "The guardians have seen magical things that happen in this castle and their tongues have been cut out to prevent them telling anyone."

"Castle?" exclaimed Billy. "This isn't a castle, it's a little white house."

"Yeah," retorted Nathan, "his grandad's allotment shed is bigger than this place from the outside."

"Yeah", said Billy in agreement.

"Well, it's a lot bigger on the inside you must agree," replied Abiba. "But it is talk like this... not believing... that leads to..." Abiba poked her tongue from her mouth and brushed her index finger across it... "NO TONGUE," she bellowed; her eyes lit up at that moment and Billy jumped back in fright. He looked at Nathan who took a deep swallow as if to imagine a throat without a tongue.

"OK, that's enough Billy," said Terry.

Abiba showed them the doorway to a room at the end of the corridor. What amazed them was the size of the room. It was huge and paved in white marble. Bronze ornately shaped columns supported the structure and were decorated with patterns of yellow flowers and sheaves of wheat. The ceiling was magnificently painted depicting pictures of ancient gods and cherubs. It was dark outside and a unique skylight fanned the last glimmer of daylight into the building. In the centre of the room was a Roman bath filled with inviting bubbling water. There were several doors leading from the room, each was a bedroom - all with en-suite facilities (a rare thing in those days) and equally ornamented with luxurious fittings more befitting a king than the children of Fishersgate. Four servants awaited them to cater to their every whim and the first thing that Billy asked for was some more of the delicious tropical drink. One servant brought him the refreshment contained in a white goblet placed on a golden tray.

Abiba pointed the boys to their rooms, which were all on one side of the Roman bath. On the opposite side of the bath there were three more doors and Lilly was given one of these rooms.

After they had bathed and put on the fresh clothing provided for them Terry, Billy and Nathan were the first to re-group by the Roman bath. Each wore plain cream slacks and white baggy shirts with boots of Arabic design. They had never seen one another so smartly dressed and this led to the obvious 'mickey' taking. It was the first time that they had really laughed since their ordeal had begun. However, as they waited for Lilly, their laughter turned to the more serious matter of getting themselves back home and Terry made a mental list of questions they would ask Mr. Josef at dinner.

When they had finished composing their list of questions Lilly had still not joined them, so it was left to Terry to knock on the door to her room.

Lilly opened the door and momentarily stood in the entrance.

"Wow," Terry exclaimed.

Lilly was wearing an Arabic style dress with a flowing blue silk wrap which was finished in white lace. Her blonde hair had been dressed upwards by the ladies-in-waiting and her shoes were golden. She wore a dazzling headdress with a lace veil. She was stunning and Terry really was taken aback by her enhanced beauty, which made her look much older than her nineteen years. She removed her veil and Terry lent forward to kiss her crimson lips.

Lilly stepped back unexpectedly.

"Don't ruin my lipstick, Terry," she said with a smile.

"Oh Lilly, you are so beautiful," said Terry as he took her hand in his.

"Thank you, Terry," she purred. "You don't look so bad yourself all dressed up in the finery of an Arabian knight."

They came closer together and then kissed for a lingering moment. The smell of Lilly's perfume mesmerised Terry. It was a fragrance so different from anything he had experienced before. It was almost hypnotic.

"I am so glad that I met you, Lilly," whispered Terry.

"Well, I only live a few doors away from your house in Duke Street... so I suppose it was inevitable... that we would meet," she purred.

Terry smiled.

Suddenly a voice boomed from behind.

"Are you two love-birds finished yet?"

The voice resonated around the hollow interior of the marble structure.

It was Nathan, who had been watching them from the other side of the Roman baths.

"Sickening... isn't it Billy?" said Nathan, turning to his friend standing next to him.

"Yeah," Billy boomed. She isn't that beautiful... she's a girl. "What an idiot Terry is, he used to be all right until he became all lovey-dovey with her."

"He was all right until he got to twenty-one, that's when he changed," said Nathan.

"Shut it brother, and you too Nathan," boomed back Terry at his two young companions. "It's the last time that I offer to babysit for Mum; I don't need *babies* like you *two* hanging around me."

"Yeah, next time we don't want to be anywhere near you either; look at the mess you got us into," replied an agitated Billy.

Billy's temperament changed when suddenly thoughts of Mum and home entered his mind.

"I just want to go home Terry," continued Billy.

"And I am doing my best," exclaimed Terry, not wishing to escalate matters by reminding Billy and Nathan that it was *their* idea that he rowed the boat into the dry dock.

"Look..." Terry continued, "it's time for dinner soon and Mr. Josef has said that he will explain everything. Maybe he knows how we can get back to Fishersgate bay. If we all keep calm, no more arguing, I have a list of questions to ask and we must listen to what he tells us. Maybe, we can find a way to get home"

"He's right you know," added Lilly.

"Terry is right," said Nathan. "He is Billy... and what else are we to do?"

Billy just shrugged his shoulders in agreement.

"Come on then," said Lilly. "Let's go."

One of the male servants who had been silently watching the quarrelling children beckoned them to follow him to the dining room. Billy, Nathan, Terry and Lilly duly obliged and another male servant, along with Lilly's lady-in-waiting followed behind.

They arrived at the dining room where Mr. Josef and his brother, Mr. Necho, were waiting for them. The dining room was as lavish as every other room in the house. In fact, this was no ordinary house; though it looked small from the outside it was enormous inside. It was more like a palace, an Arabian palace disguised as a little white house in the jungle.

The dining table ran the entire length of the room with placemats for at least sixty people. At the far end of the room the entire wall was dressed in displays of battle swords, spears and shields; the sort of armament that foot soldiers used in combat. The wall on the right had two white marble fireplaces - equal distance along its length.

"Who needs a fireplace in a hot jungle?" said Nathan.

"Don't know," replied Billy.

Portraits of important looking Arabian men framed with gold leaf adorned the space in between the fireplaces. The wall to the left was a deep red colour broken only by more paintings and white marble columns, which extended from the floor to the timber ceiling almost twenty feet above. An ornate timber roof, deep brown in colour, stretched over this huge expanse of a room. In between the marble columns stood ivory and ebony busts, separately fitted on purpose-made stands depicting battled-dressed warriors.

More tongue-less guardians of the palace stood along the length of the room, backs to the wall, no more than ten feet apart - protecting the palace and occupants alike. Terry reckoned that he had counted at least fifty or more of these tongue-less guardians since arriving at the palace. The smell of food, a definitive aroma of something jolly delicious, wafted through an open doorway which almost certainly led to the kitchen.

Mr. Josef stood at the far end of the room.

"Come in my friends, be seated," he beckoned in a loud voice.

The servant asked them to follow and they were directed to the central part of the long table. The youngsters, one by one, took their seats. Lilly sat to the right of Terry on one side of the table with Nathan and Billy opposite. Mr. Josef sat at the head of the table and Necho at the far end. Both men were some twenty feet away from them in either direction. It was very odd thought Terry for they would have to shout to speak to their hosts.

Mr. Josef banged the table with a wooden gavel.

"Forgive me for being so far away from you children but it is ancient tradition that I, as Namidian leader, be seated in this ancient chair situated in the East and open the dinner proceedings with the ancient gavel that was handed down through generations of our leaders."

"What's a gavel?" whispered Billy.

"It's that wooden mallet he hits the table with," replied Lilly.

"Shush," intervened Terry.

Mr. Josef continued. "My brother, Mr. Necho, as you can see, is situated in the West, according to ancient law; he is the deputy leader of Namidia. Guests, such as you, are only permitted to be seated at the central part of the table."

"What about the other seats which are empty?" enquired Terry, as he pointed either side.

He was referring to the thirty spaces between him and Mr. Josef and the thirty spaces between Lilly and Necho.

"They are the seats of the Namidia Lords who are spread across the land. We meet three times a year," replied Mr. Josef.

"What do you mean… Lords?" asked an inquisitive Terry.

"I shall tell you about the Lords in good time," replied Mr. Josef.

"Well actually," interrupted Nathan, "we don't have much time - we will be going back to Fishersgate soon, if it's all right with you."

"Yeah," added Billy. "As soon as we find a way out of here we'll be going back to Fishersgate."

Terry looked across the table at the pair of them and gave a look as if to say 'be quiet'. Necho banged the table with his fist and angrily shouted. "You will not be going back."

The two boys openly gasped until Terry interjected.

"How can you say that we will not be going back... we must... How can you say that we will not... are you to keep us prisoners?"

"I shall handle this Necho... if you please," said Mr. Josef. He knew that only the children of Fishersgate could help them and he knew that he had to be honest and kind to them.

"Look my children," he said in a gentle voice, "there might be a way for you to return to Fishersgate... but according to the book of scriptures, it is risky."

The children looked at each other. There was hope. Mr. Josef put both hands on the table in front of him. He looked down at the table for a moment of thought, before looking at Terry.

"First, my children… you must help us. You must help us find the Second Chapter… for that is why you are here."

Billy kicked Terry under the table. "Second Chapter? What's he on about?"

"I don't know," replied Terry in a whisper.

"Sounds like something out of the Bible… I bet it's in Latin," said Billy as he folded his arms.

Mr. Josef, who had not heard Billy, continued.

"The scripture is the ancient writing of our forefathers and written in Latin."

"Told you so," whispered Billy with a smirk on his face.

"Shush," said Terry, "just listen to exactly what he has to say."

"The Latin Second Chapter was written by scribes at a time just after our civilization was nearly wiped out. This was many thousands of years ago. A giant asteroid hit our planet and killed everything - except for a few wise men. Up until that time the people of earth were very advanced with technology. Knowing that they would soon die from exposure to radiation they wrote everything down in the Second Chapter, before planting the seeds of life in an indestructible pod which would create life once more when the radiation had ceased," continued Mr. Josef.

"But how can we help? We know nothing about scriptures or a Second Chapter," said Lilly.

"But you are the children of Fishersgate and you have been sent here to find the missing Second Chapter," boomed Mr. Necho.

"He's crackers," whispered Nathan.

"Be quiet," said Terry. "Okay. Mr. Josef and Mr. Necho," called out Terry. "I can assure you that we know nothing about how to find your missing Second Chapter. We are just lost... Lost in this place where we didn't choose to come to... Where are we again?"

"You are in Namidia," boomed a voice from the other direction, and I am becoming increasingly angry that you make out you know nothing and that you cannot help us," shouted Necho.

"Namidia," repeated Terry firstly looking at Mr. Necho and then towards Mr. Josef. "Of course we want to help you, but we don't know how. Why is it that *you* know why we are supposed to be here, but *we* know nothing about why we are supposed to be here in this place?" asked Terry.

"Let me explain," Mr. Necho continued, "You are from Fishersgate. The prophet Wentworth has written that one-day, young people and children will appear before us in

Namidia; those children being Fishersgate children from the future, and they will find our lost Second Chapter."

"Well, Wentworth is wrong and anyway, who is this Wentworth geezer?" blurted out Nathan.

"Be quiet boy," snarled Necho. "I am speaking to your leader."

Billy began to laugh and Nathan joined him.

"That's no leader... that's my brother Terry," exclaimed Billy.

Lilly leant over the table towards Billy and Nathan.

"I think you two should go along with what's being said by these men. It's no good trying to antagonise them, it will just make matters worse," she said.

"Antagonise?" asked Nathan to Billy... "What's that mean then?"

Billy did not reply because he was not sure.

Terry stood up and cleared his throat with a cough ready to speak with an air of authority as a Shakespearian actor might.

"Ok, Mr. Josef and Mr. Necho," said Terry as he looked towards each man in turn. "At this precise moment in time we know nothing about the Second Chapter that you refer to and nothing about the prophet Wentworth. I mean, the only Wentworth we know is the shopkeeper we ran away from this afternoon. We truly want to help, all of us do." He looked down at Billy and Nathan before looking at Lilly and then directly at Necho. "If you could perhaps tell us a little more about your predicament, we might be able to help. Though I don't know how," he said under his breath.

Mr. Necho called out, "Sit down boy and I shall explain."

Terry sat down and Lilly put her hand in his. They looked attentively towards Mr. Necho.

Mr. Necho continued. "We know that you are from the future - for the prophet Wentworth has written that in his scriptures. We know about the shopkeeper, Wentworth, at the edge of this jungle, we keep our eye on *him*. The prophet told our people about the children of Fishersgate five hundred years ago... Wentworth the shopkeeper is the same man. Perhaps now is the time to call on Wentworth and invite him for dinner this evening?"

Mr. Josef called Abiba and he whispered something into her ear before she scuttled back into the kitchen.

"Anyhow," continued Necho, "back to the matter in hand."

"Many years ago, our learned scribes wrote all of our secrets down in the Second Chapter. The Second Chapter is a book, a hardback volume of information."

"Hang on a minute," shouted Terry, "is this a religious thing?"

"It is not my boy," replied Necho. "Our Muslim religion is quite separate from the writings of our scriptures. Other religions of the world, including Christianity, are also separate. This volume has nothing to do with any kind of religion, for these are the secret *technical scripts.*"

"Technical scripts?" asked Terry.

"Well, it is actually called, *the mysteries and secrets of discovery and invention,*" said Necho.

He continued, "Thousands of years ago Namidia was at the centre of the world. We had a sophisticated lifestyle far exceeding our present-day technology. Then the Scorians came. It is often written that the Scorians were a superior race."

Terry interrupted, "They did have an empire that stretched across Europe… I know that much from my history lessons; which I learned about when I was at school," he said.

"They did have an empire, Terry, but they were not superior in mind or soul, only in their body strength, they were indeed a violent people," replied Mr. Josef. "They extended their violence across Europe. They pillaged and robbed those lands they invaded, but we Namidians were far superior to them."

"I don't get it," asked Terry.

"Let me explain… When the Scorians extended their Empire across the Mediterranean Sea into North Africa they brought nothing except fear and violence. In Namidia we are a peaceful race."

"I've never heard of the Scorians or Namidia," said Billy. "Have you Nathan?"

"Nope," replied Nathan.

"Shush," said Terry who was listening intently.

"Well, let me tell you about them," said Mr. Josef.

"At first, only a few Scorians appeared on our shores. When we realised that their only aim was to rape us of our culture, we fought back. With our weapons, we easily won. We jailed them, then we took pity on them and we fed them and we educated them. We looked after them. We tamed them and we took away from them the only thing they knew… violence. We taught them how to become peaceful and showed, by example, that it was better to live in harmony than to fight. We didn't let them lose their identity… we let them worship their false gods, speak their own language, and grow the food they wanted. It was called *Globalization* by one of our rulers - a man named Blair."

"Gradually more of them came to live in our community. We became a dual-cultural society. This irritated some of the Namidian people, but we were living in a plentiful land that provided a good living for all and, of course, the Scorians would often carry out manual tasks that Namidians had come to dislike. And so we lived, side by side, for a thousand years and, in that time, many more Scorians arrived on our shores to live and work in Namidia."

"The Namidian people had given the Scorians their trust. They thought they had created a society that was perfect in every way; an almost ideal civilization. The Namidians were the dominant race, the clever ones, the masters; and the Scorians were their highly-paid yet equal servants. Or so we thought. Then one day something happened."

Mr. Josef looked sad as he prepared himself for telling this part of his story.

"They rebelled against us. They used our own weapons against us and beat us. They took all our leaders and scholars to a place known as *Ethnos Den* and killed them, one by one by decapitation. The remaining masses of our people were forced to leave these lands and the Scorians remained to rule alone."

"Where are the Scorians now?" asked Lilly.

"They are gone," replied Mr. Josef. "Once they had forced our people out of their own lands they thought it would be easy to rule themselves in a lifestyle of similar proportion. They were wrong. They had no brains among their leaders; none of them were capable of sustaining a pleasurable lifestyle of the type that we enjoy today."

Just then, Abiba appeared in the doorway leading to the kitchen. She looked towards Mr. Josef with an expressionless look, a kind of deadpan look, and announced, "Dinner is ready to be served when you are ready, Master."

"Bring it through now, Abiba, and serve it in the usual manner," he replied.

Abiba disappeared back into the kitchen for a few moments and soon returned, followed by seven servants, each carrying a large identical ornate china bowl on a golden tray. In each bowl was a golden ladle showing its bone handle protruding outwards at an angle from the steaming food.

"Seven dishes!" exclaimed Nathan. "That will do for starters, what you think Billy?"

"It will keep me going. Isn't it great?" replied an excited Billy as he picked up a serviette and blew his nose rather loudly.

"Billy," sighed Terry, "your table manners." He was about to continue when Mr. Josef banged the table with his gavel and said a prayer in Arabic for the food they were about to receive. Well, they thought that he was saying a prayer given the tone of his voice and the way in which he clasped his hands and bowed his head, so each of the visitors copied their host and bowed their head too.

Abiba led the line of servants to Mr. Josef. She stood beside him, lifted the china lid of the bowl and dished a ladle full of a potato-like substance on to Mr. Josef's large dinner plate. In turn, each of the servants approached Abiba and she dished a portion of their wares comprising of meat, vegetables and rice onto Mr. Josef's plate. After they had finished serving Mr. Josef, Abiba led the line of servants along the full length of the table, past Billy and Nathan, to Mr. Necho, whereupon they served his food in a similar manner.

"How long is this going to take?" Billy whispered. "I'm hungry."

"Just be thankful that you are going to get fed," Lilly replied.

It wasn't long before they all had a steaming hot dinner before them and the boys began the urgent task of eagerly filling their bellies. Lilly, on the other hand, took the time to eat her food properly, as all young ladies of distinction, when beautifully dressed, generally do.

Mr. Josef continued with his story throughout the meal.

He told the children that the Scorians had returned to their old ways to display all the unsavoury traits of a barbarous race. After the Namidian enforced absence from their own lands the Scorians fought among themselves until nothing was left standing. The land was barren, the villages destroyed, thousands of Scorians killed and maimed, the people were destitute. Not long after that, the asteroid hit Earth causing an explosion so great and so powerful that it killed millions of people in the region. Those few that remained, those poor severely injured unfortunate people gradually drifted away from Namidia to die a slow painful death caused by an invisible energy force we know little about. Namidia became a sterile place for years.

In time, when it was safe, the descendants of those few Namidian people began to return to the land of their forefathers. They came by sea from the north and by land from the south. They were distraught by what they found. All the things they were told about in the stories passed down through generations had gone. They couldn't rebuild it to a high technical specification because they had no knowledge. That knowledge is contained in the missing Second Chapter. No one, to this day, knows where the Second Chapter is hidden.

"Tell me again about the Second Chapter," said Terry.

"It is the writings of magical design. It is a record of the knowledge that we once had. This information was gathered and written by the hands of the most learned men in the history of our time under the direction of our leader, President Zaffre. It was the map of instructions by which we constructed everything of technical superiority in our land," replied Mr. Josef.

"Once, a long time ago, we had horseless-carriages that were driven by a self-propelled power source, we had smooth pathways to run our machines upon, we could travel hundreds of miles in a few hours. We had sound boxes which transmitted voices and music over long distances, and tiny machines that could calculate and solve the most difficult of mathematical problems. There were flying machines and machines for going deep into the ocean seas. There were automatic machines for washing clothes and other machines for drying them. We had almost eradicated every disease known to humans and life was good for the Namidians."

Terry thought for a moment. Some of the things Mr. Josef had described were items that he had either seen or heard about. Self-propelled carriages, better known as the car or automobile, were invented around 1890 and they were becoming increasingly common in 1934. Sound boxes must be radios; those polished wooden cabinets full of illuminating valves that gave-off a warm red glow when you look through the elongated holes in the back of the box, and which relay sound through the airwaves across many miles. Aeroplanes... these things were luxuries that top-class families used in 1934 - not the likes of the Burton family. The only item that puzzled Terry was Mr. Josef's description of tiny machines that could calculate and solve the most difficult of mathematical problems. Mr. Josef had called those calculators. Terry had not seen or heard of calculators or automated washing machines. Why would anyone need things like automated washing machines when scrubbing boards were perfectly acceptable? Mum had never complained about her scrubbing board, he thought, why would she? Anyway, she would not give-up her scrubbing board because Grandad could play a tune on it and keep the family entertained for hours. Though he did remember a relatively new type of washing machine on the market called a twin-tub, but that wasn't automated. Anyway, electric twin tubs were notoriously inefficient, prone to breakdowns or suddenly bursting into flames and very, very expensive in 1934.

Terry concluded that while he knew of some of the inventions, he had not heard of others. But equally, how could Mr. Josef know about these things in 1734?

All the technology Mr. Josef spoke about hadn't even been thought about or invented in 1734, let alone produced in factories - for there were no factories. Perhaps they had all been fooled. Perhaps it was still 1934?

"Mr. Josef," called out Terry, "what year is it?"

Mr. Josef looked puzzled, "Well, it's 1734, Terry."

"Are you sure?" asked Terry.

"As sure as my 45 years of age, well almost," replied Mr. Josef, "though my mother never kept a record of my exact birth year."

"So, you were born in 1689," piped up Nathan.

"Yes, around that year," replied a still puzzled Mr. Josef.

"You see," said Terry, "we know about these things. We know about cars and aeroplanes and things…"

Mr. Josef interrupted, somewhat surprised. "What do you know?"

Necho interrupted his brother, "No-one knows except our forefathers… it is all written in the Second Chapter."

"But we do," shouted Billy. "We know, we know all about motor cars and things."

"I asked you what you know," replied Mr. Josef. He was becoming increasingly frustrated. "Tell me what do you know."

"What do you want to know?" asked Nathan who realised for the first time since their ordeal began that they might have the upper hand in this conversation.

"Tell me boy, how does a self-propelled carriage work?" Necho boomed.

"Well," said Nathan, with a smirk on his face, as he stood up and looked around at his friends, "a self-propelled carriage is better known as an automobile or a motor car. You lift the lid on the top of the machine and put the petrol in a chamber then switch it on. A thing called um, well it turns and drives the wheels… err."

"It's called a prop shaft and its connected to the wheels," said Terry.

"Thanks Terry," Nathan continued, "the prop shaft turns the wheels on the motor car… I mean the self-propelled carriage… and it moves."

"Haven't you forgotten something Nathan?" asked Terry.

"No, I don't think so," replied Nathan.

"The engine," whispered Terry.

"Oh yes," beamed Nathan, "it's the engine that drives the prop-shaft that drives the wheels and you need someone to steer the car…"

Mr. Necho interrupted. "Enough, I have heard enough."

"Just one question," asked a polite Mr. Josef. "You haven't really told us much at all, Nathan, have you? All you have told us is that this … motor car… a self-propelled carriage merely moves. You haven't told us how it does it; you say it moves… when you switch it on, what is a switch? How does it make it move?"

Nathan thought for a moment before responding. "The switch lets the electricity through from the battery and starts the engine."

"Stop," boomed Mr. Necho.

"What is electricity?" enquired Mr. Josef.

Terry interrupted, "Look Mr. Josef and Mr. Necho, I don't mean to be awkward or rude - but this might be too much for you to understand and I don't think we are getting anywhere." He continued, "I mean, even we four don't fully understand how technical things work but listening to Nathan I do know one thing."

"And what is that?" asked Mr. Josef.

"Well," replied Terry, "you cannot construct a horseless carriage, a motor car, without several important ingredients. Firstly, you need metals like manufactured steel, copper and brass, all refined and produced in distinctive ways. Then you need paint, rubber and glass, and all sorts of other materials that make ingenious devices. Then, when it's all put together you need a power source."

"Hold on," said Necho. "I have never heard of some of those things… like 'rubber'. What is rubber?"

"Exactly," replied Terry. "Do you see what I mean?... even if we found the missing Second Chapter - what could you do with it? You would not have the manufactured materials to be able to make a self-propelled horseless carriage, a motor car."

"And that is because you've got no rubber for a start," said Nathan with a grin.

There was a silence. Mr. Necho and Mr. Josef were thinking these matters through and that gave Terry the opportunity to continue.

"I shall tell you something," continued Terry. "If you had the Second Chapter in your hands right now you could do nothing with it; except wait until various items like steel and copper elements are turned into suitable commercial products and of course rubber, an elastic type substance, has been discovered and refined. You would have to wait until these discoveries are refined or cultivated but most of all you need electricity to power things and until you have that, you cannot have anything... I mean... while I think of it, you cannot have flying machines or self-propelled carriages until you have an alternative power source... like a liquid fuel. Refined petrol or kerosene that's it - that's what they call it. Someone must find a way of refining petrol from crude oil, to drive the self-propelled carriages... There is high-pressure steam-engine power I suppose, but I think that's a long way off too in historical terms of invention."

Terry was quite proud of himself. He had not really thought about these things before in such detail, yet he was able to recite technical matters and material content which he had learned at school. Lilly was proud too. She could see that Terry had put his case to good effect. She put her hand in his as they sat together waiting for a response from the two men. Perhaps they would understand and let them go home, back to Fishersgate.

Mr. Josef left his seat at the table and walked to the far end where he and Mr. Necho spoke quietly for a few moments. The two men were standing that far away that all the children could hear were mumbling voices and they knew that their immediate futures were being discussed.

Suddenly there were three distinct knocks on the giant doors to the dining room and both doors were opened in unison by the guards. Abiba appeared through the entrance and announced that the shopkeeper Wentworth was here.

"Bring him in," ordered Necho.

Billy gasped and whispered to Nathan that this was it. They would be punished for eating the shop food and not paying for it.

"Shush," whispered Lilly to the pair of them.

The shopkeeper, Wentworth, was brought into the room accompanied by two of the biggest tongue-less guards they had seen so far. It was clear that a dirty and bedraggled Wentworth had not come freely for his hands were bound behind his back, his feet clad in chains and a gag covered his mouth. The guards let go of his arms and Wentworth fell onto his knees in front of the dining table where Necho and Mr. Josef were standing. One of the guards untied his gag and almost immediately Wentworth took a huge breath and flung a series of insults at the two men.

"Calm down Wentworth," said Mr. Josef.

"It's a disgrace. Taking a man from his bath in the middle of the evening, while I was playing ships in the water with my woman, and then dragging me through the jungle," screamed Wentworth.

"You look like you need another bath, Wentworth," said Necho with a wry smile.

Mr. Josef smiled at his brother's remark before adopting a more serious stance. He continued, "Wentworth, I have had you brought here because I know that you are the prophet, Wentworth… Do not deny this."

"Dragged here more like," snarled an angry Wentworth.

Mr. Josef raised his arm and gave a signal to the guard. The guards immediately put a noose over Wentworth's head and pulled it tight. Wentworth struggled and wheezed for the few seconds the noose was applied. The guard released his grip on the noose and Wentworth spluttered and coughed before screaming more abuse. Mr. Josef warned him to be quiet and answer the questions.

Mr. Josef continued. "I shall repeat myself only one more time… What is your full name?"

Wentworth whispered, "Albert Wentworth."

Lilly gasped. "It is him… It's Albert the boatman. I told you so Terry."

"It's impossible," said Terry.

Mr. Josef turned towards them and was about to ask Terry a question but then appeared to change his mind. He turned back towards Wentworth.

"I have had you brought here Wentworth because you know about the missing Second Chapter."

There was a silence. Wentworth looked Mr. Josef up and down and then spat on his shiny shoes. Once again, the guard pulled the noose tight for a few seconds and then released it as Wentworth coughed and spluttered.

"Listen to me Wentworth," continued Mr. Josef, "these children are from Fishersgate. They are here to help me find something. Do you know what I am looking for?"

"They are just vagabonds and thieves. They ate my food and ran away without paying. They owe me my money," snarled Wentworth.

Wentworth's mood changed and with a wry smile he said, "and then I let them off once I knew who they were, but by that time they had run away. It's my memory you know - not so good when one gets to a thousand years old."

"Answer the question Wentworth," snarled Necho, "do you know what I am looking for?"

"I know what you seek," replied Wentworth. "You seek the Second Chapter, but it isn't around here."

"Well, where is it?" asked an excited Mr. Josef.

"Unchain me and I shall tell you," replied Wentworth.

Necho suddenly stood between Mr. Josef and Wentworth.

"Why don't we beat it out of him?" he asked.

"No. I don't think so... I think he will tell us in good time," replied Mr. Josef.

Mr. Josef stepped to one side where he had a clear view of Wentworth.

"So, what is it to be Wentworth? Are you to tell me or will my brother have his way? Shall I let him beat it out of you?"

"There's no need for violence," replied Wentworth. "Especially when it concerns my fragile old body," he continued.

"So where is the Second Chapter?" asked Mr. Josef.

"It's in Italy," replied Wentworth.

"Where in Italy?"

"I don't know for sure," replied Wentworth. "It's somewhere in Taranto; buried in an unmarked place. It be a secret that is shared by only a few. The few that took it from this land. But legend has it that it is buried beneath the flag-stones of the Cathedral."

"Well, who took it from our lands?" asked Mr. Necho.

"They be the pirates. They took it along with the silver treasures from the ancient temple of Namidia," said Wentworth.

"You will take us to this place," Necho ordered.

"Hold on a moment," Wentworth replied, "it's a long way from here… and a month's sailing. I cannot help you any further… I need to get back to my bath and my woman, tonight."

"You lie, Wentworth, you know more than you say," shouted Necho.

Wentworth detected a personal dangerous situation and then suddenly changed his mind.

"I have told you all I know… but for one or two things," continued Wentworth. "Only the special child of Fishersgate can unlock the secret of the missing Chapter… that be the secret word given by the Ghost of the Fishersgate Mariner, even I know that, but I can help them if you let me go to Italy with them. The Second Chapter is in the *Cattedrale di San Cataldo,* which is a Roman Catholic cathedral in Taranto, Apulia, Italy. The cathedral is dedicated to Saint Catald. He was an Irish Monk and his original monastery was in Lismore, County Waterford in Southern Ireland. His apparent desire for a life of solitude saw him venture off to Jerusalem on a pilgrimage where he stayed in solitude for seven years."

Wentworth paused and began coughing profusely. "Water, water," he pleaded.

"Guards, give him some water," said Mr. Josef. The guards duly complied and Wentworth took a few sips from a ladle put before his mouth.

"Tell us more," demanded Necho.

Wentworth continued, "On his return home, the Monk's ship was wrecked off the Italian coast, near the city of Taranto. He was rescued and he survived. He was taken in by the populace of Taranto who tended to his injuries. Over the following years he helped them in many ways, mainly as a debt of his gratitude. The people of Taranto asked the Monk to become their Bishop which he gladly did and he later rose to become their Archbishop. Some of the miracles claimed in Catald's name include protecting the city against the plague, growing foods in abundance, making delicious wines and creating engineering designs that persistently protected the city against floods. His mastery of the elements led to him being immortalised and treated as a king. In neighbouring areas, these terrible things did occur - like floods, drought, and famine, but Taranto was saved by the Monk's good-deeds. Seven years after his death,

Canonisation was declared and he became Saint Catald. Some said it was the Second Chapter that gave him the practical knowledge he needed, which gave him the guidance to avoid these natural catastrophes. Some said that there were no miracles only this book of guidance."

"So where did this Monk get the Second Chapter?" demanded Necho.

"I don't know," replied Wentworth, "some say that he was given it by an old sailor during the ship's voyage from Palestine back to Ireland. It was that ship that sank off the coast of Taranto in a storm. The old sailor was saved along with the Monk. He became his confidant and protectorate for the next twenty years until the Monk's death. And the Second Chapter is buried in his coffin."

"In the Bishop's coffin?" enquired Necho.

"No, no, in the old sailor's coffin," retorted Wentworth. "And that's the problem... for the Bishop's grave has been raided several times. Everyone knows where the Bishop's grave is located. People think the book is in his grave, but the Second Chapter is not there. It is in the grave of the old sailor."

Necho pondered on this information.

"And where is the old sailor's grave?" asked Necho.

"It is in the same area of the cathedral, under one of the flagstones of the church near to the archbishop's grave."

"Are you sure?" demanded Necho.

"I am sure… very sure," replied Wentworth, "but take me with you, I will show you."

"How old did you say you were Wentworth?" asked Necho.

"I be one thousand years old next week," replied Wentworth.

"Abiba, Abiba where are you," called Necho.

"Yes Master," she said as she appeared from behind a doorway.

"Abiba, send word to the ship's captain of the *Star of the Sea*. Tell him to prepare to sail tomorrow morning. We sail for Taranto, Italy. All of us except for the girl Lilly," ordered Necho.

"No. No. I am not leaving Lilly behind," shouted Terry, as he ran toward Necho.

"You shall do as you are told," boomed Necho.

"What about me?" enquired Wentworth, "aren't I going too?" Necho did not answer him.

Fearing a physical assault by Terry, Necho stood back and ordered the guards to seize him. Two guards took hold of Terry's arms and held him back.

"Remove him," ordered Necho, "and put him in the high-security jail room."

Terry was dragged out of the room by the guards. He called out to Lilly several times. She hurried towards him, but the lady-in-waiting followed her and held her back before she could get close to him.

Terry's calls for Lilly faded into the distance as she watched him through the open doors as he was dragged away down the long corridor.

"Take these two boys, Billy and Nathan, back to their rooms; do not let them escape," Mr. Josef ordered. The guards took hold of the boys and carried them away in the same direction as they had taken Terry.

Billy and Nathan were taken to a room on the other side of the house and the door was locked. They were now prisoners, separated from Lilly, as was Terry.

Necho squeezed Lilly's cheek, as he looked her over, before staring into her eyes and whispering, "Yes, you are a pretty little thing and you shall be mine." Lilly slapped Necho around the face and called him a wicked pig, but this just made Necho smile.

"Save your energy for when I get back pretty girl," he drawled. "I shall have you put into my harem." And that is what Necho did as Mr. Josef shook his head in disbelief. Soon, Lilly was with the other ladies in Necho's harem.

Mr. Josef went up close to Necho and whispered in his ear. "I do wonder about you my brother Necho. We are a peaceful people but you tend to have more aggression than most, and I also wonder about your motive, with regards to this innocent young girl."

"Brother Josef," replied Necho, "I do what is best for our people, for us also, so leave me be."

Necho's attention returned to the matter in hand.

"As for you Wentworth," bellowed Necho, "you will not reach a thousand years old. Guards... Kill him." And shortly after that command, Wentworth was strangled by the neck with a short piece of rope and he dropped down dead on the spot.

And in a parallel time, in 1934, Albert, the Jolly boatman suddenly dropped dead too. He choked as he was drinking a pint of Kemp-town brewed old speckled chicken beer in the Sussex Arms public house. The beer-glass mysteriously stuck to his lower lip, while his hand tipped the beer-glass profusely upright and forced his head to tilt backwards. The whole pint of beer went down in one go. Some said the old sailor drowned like a sea-dog would on a sinking ship, but most agreed that he choked to death on the Kemp-town special speckled chicken brew.

Mr. Josef looked on in despair before turning towards his brother and asking, "Was that really necessary?"

"He deserved it, and now my brother Josef," said Necho, turning to face Mr. Josef, "it seems we are getting somewhere; tomorrow, I shall sail the Mediterranean Sea for Taranto, Italy. Wait here for me in Namidia and keep control of our wonderful country. Soon I will bring back the secrets of the Second Chapter."

"Try not to kill too many people," replied Mr. Josef as he looked at Necho with piercing eyes and a knowing look.

"You are too soft my brother," said Necho. "And now it is time for bed, I have a busy day tomorrow." And with that, he was gone.

The next day Billy and Nathan were taken to the dockyard where they were put onto the ship. Both had been blindfolded so they had not seen their exact whereabouts. Deep into the hold of the ship, where little daylight shone, was where they were entombed.

"Better get used to it," said Necho as the guard and an accomplice undid their shackled hands, removed their blindfolds, and threw them both into a windowless wooden room, secured with an iron gate. Necho bid them goodbye and said he would next see them in Italy.

"Where's Terry?" shouted Billy.

"Oh, I left him languishing in the dungeon back at my castle… but don't worry my friends, he will survive provided you do as you are told. One wrong move and I will send a message by pigeon carrier and he will be executed. Do we have a deal young sir?"

"I guess we have no choice," answered Nathan.

The door was slammed shut, the lock fastened and they were left alone in their prison cell below the decks of the Star of the Sea sailing ship. They could feel the ship gently moving, rising and falling in a static position; the hull rubbing against the dockside timbers where it was tethered. They could hear the thrashing of the waves in the distance but guessed that they must be in a harbour protected from those thunderous seas that lay beyond. A small dim light shone from an old oil lamp fixed to the wall of their chamber and they could make out each other's facial features. At least there was straw on the floor to bed themselves down. It smelled so bad, in fact… it stunk down there below decks, where they occupied a space in the cargo bay with sheep and cattle that were penned in various adjoining areas. Through the gates they could see the guards sitting on cut-down

146

wooden barrels playing some sort of card game and drinking brew.

"I wonder where Terry and Lilly are?" asked Nathan.

"I wish I knew," replied Billy in a tearful moment as he sat down on the floor amongst the straw carpet.

It was at least another six hours before the ship moved. Then there were voices and shouting. They could make out by the tone of these voices that the ship was about to sail.

Then there was a scuffle nearby and some more shouting as other guards pushed two large silhouetted figures through the darkness of the under-deck, towards the prison occupied by Billy and Nathan.

The door opened and the two bulky figures were thrown into the cell causing dirt and straw to scatter about the room. One of the falling prisoners landed on his back with his head finally resting in Billy's lap. Two eyes stared up at Billy through the semi-darkness.

The door was slammed shut and the distinctive noise of the key in the lock with its unique hollow 'click' was prevalent once more. As the straw settled, Billy began to focus on his new fellow prisoner, almost at once he realised who he was looking at.

"Garrett," he blurted out loudly.

It was indeed Garrett. Looking over he saw the other prisoner. "Oh no," Billy exclaimed as he looked in the direction of the other figure laying on the floor. "Wheeler as well."

This was Billy's worst nightmare. Locked in a room with his arch-enemies and nasty bullies of repute, for a month at least.

Automatically, and without any thought, Garrett grabbed Billy by the throat and began to throttle him, but Wheeler pulled him off saying that now was not the time to play with Billy.

'Playing', is that what you call it thought Billy, as he smoothed his neck with his hand to alleviate the pain.

The four of them sat on the floor gazing at each other, wondering what was in store for them all as the mighty ship, the Star of the Sea, glided through the waves toward Italy.

Chapter 5

Poor Old Grandad

Three months had passed since those youngsters went missing. The month of December 1934 was already in progress. What puzzled the police the most, was that they found no trace of any parts of the little timber boat or anything belonging to Terry, Lilly, Billy, or Nathan. They and their little rowing boat had vanished, without a trace. There were no clues. The dry dock was, once more, full of the waters of the harbour and the gates were firmly shut. Of course, the police did completely comb the interior of the dry dock, as they did in the outlying areas, but they found nothing. The Army and the Navy were called in to help with the search. The police knew that the little timber boat had not gone through the lock-gates out to sea, as the lock-keeper would have seen it. And the youngsters could never have opened the lock-gates themselves. Only a lock-keeper could do that with his special keys. So, it was concluded by the police that they did not row the little timber boat, called Doris, out to sea.

Another theory was that the small boat and the children were taken by sailors from one of the larger Russian ships that had moored along the docksides. It was suggested that the sailors smuggled the little timber boat onboard their own large ship and sailed away. But this theory was dismissed, for all the ships in the harbour on that day were British. No Russian ships or any other nationality - come to that - were in the harbour on the day that the children disappeared. And of those British ships in port on that day, none had left the port without firstly being thoroughly searched by the police. All sailors in the area had been interviewed by the police and all other harbour masters of the port, and private boat owners had confirmed that they had seen nothing unusual. The chief-superintendent of Police was satisfied that all masters of ships and sailors had told the truth and none had any reason or motive for abducting any of the youngsters or, indeed, for stealing a timber clinker boat of little value.

No. The only valid remaining theory was that the little boat lay upturned at the bottom of the harbour with the children trapped under the boat - presumed drowned.

The mystery of the two other missing youngsters, Garrett and Wheeler, was a bigger challenge for the police. Their boat *Frances* was found in the harbour, floating beside the dry dock lock-gates with the oars neatly placed in the boat. A rope tied the boat to a steel ladder that extended upwards from the waterline to the quay. These two boys could have gone anywhere. Had they climbed the ladder onto the quay they could have made it back to the mainland quite easily. But there was no sign of them. They had vanished. There were two possibilities - they had either drowned in the waters of the harbour or they had reached the mainland and run-away. If they had drowned where were their bodies? Unless of course, they had boarded the boat Doris with the other four children and all six of them were now at the bottom of the harbour.

Even the French Navy had helped to look for the youngsters, but to no avail. The French had the most advanced underwater breathing equipment in the world by 1934. They could dive deep into the waters and swim around without being fixed to ropes or airlines from boats above, they were completely unhindered. Their Le Prieur rescue breathing apparatus used special weights that allowed the user to dive down and swim and search the area with complete freedom. If anyone was to find the children it would be the French Navy. Before the Le Prieur system had been invented, only static lines could be used - which dropped the diver vertically, from a boat above to a specific spot on the harbour bed. From here the diver only had a 10ft radius to view the vicinity of the harbour bed, as the diver could not move very far from his static fixed cable-line. In these waters, which were murky and dark, the fixed line diver would have had few chances to spot the children.

However, with the benefit of the modern technology that the French Navy had, along with British Navy assistance, the French Navy could find nothing, using their Le Prieur equipment, deep down in the murky waters of the harbour or indeed, in the depths of the now, waterfilled, 'dry dock'. Lots of other things were found, like old metal bed-heads, bicycles, various types of sinkable rubbish and rubble that was chucked in the harbour waters by fly-tippers. In fact, the mass of rubbish on the harbour bed, combined with the murky water, gave only a limited vision to the divers. This had made the search much more difficult. But the conclusion was that the children were dead and their bodies trapped in their upturned boat at the bottom of the harbour, within the mangled mass of rubbish and rubble.

The coroner's court, held at Worthing on a cold bleak Monday morning during the last week of November 1934, recorded that, because of the absence of the bodies of the youngsters, an open verdict must be recorded, with the proviso that the court believed that all of them tragically met their maker on that day. And so, the matter was closed and reported as such to the local and national newspapers.

Grandad sat in his chair at home, beside the coal fire that emitted yellow and blue flames which flickered shadows on the dimly lit walls in his living room. He hadn't moved much from his favourite old chair in the last three months, except to go to bed, have a wash in the scullery sink or to go to the toilet at the end of the garden. The loss of his grandchildren and their friends was all too much to bear; it was constantly on his mind. Events had slowly drained all happiness from him. The house was very quiet, almost ghostly, now that the youngsters had gone and his daughter Gloria was in a permanent state of anguish and depression. The torment, the suffering and the pain that both had endured was an ultimate and permanent persecution that no human being should ever have to suffer. Yet suffer they did, since that fateful day when they had been told that Billy and Terry had died in the harbour waters along with their friends. But there was some faint glimmer of hope perhaps. After all, their bodies had not been found and the coroner's verdict could be wrong. Maybe the two of them will come walking through the door of number 56 Duke Street at any moment.

Gloria gazed mostly out of the window throughout the day, hoping to see a glimpse of Billy or Terry. Sometimes she thought that she had seen them in a fleeting moment, but it was not to be. Conversation with Grandad was lost and when they did speak Grandad's voice trembled with a weakness prevalent to a seriously unwell man. Only the sight of their new hamster, George the third, made Grandad smile… but only sometimes. Indeed, Grandad had lost some weight about him and found it difficult to walk. Gone were the trips to visit his late wife at the cemetery and gone were the trips to visit his disabled daughter, Mary, at the institution. The happiness that the family once had together had been shattered.

Gloria's husband, John, had also, unsurprisingly, taken the news of his sons' deaths badly. Gloria held the one and only letter from Australia written by John to her when he found out about the deaths. She kept the letter in her pinafore pocket among the many telegrams he had since sent to her as she waited for the day when he would return home. Indeed, he had left Australia for England a week after the boys had vanished and was still en-route home by ship some ten weeks later. 'Nearly home my darling' was the last telegram Gloria received from John just the day before. He was in the seafaring port of St Helier, in the Channel Islands, and that was the last stop before arriving in Fishersgate harbour in a couple of days' time.

In the semi-darkness of the room, where Grandad sat alone in his old favourite chair, there was - above the open flickering log-fire, on the mantelpiece - the two brass candlestick holders belonging to Mum. In between stood Grandad's old golden goblet that he used during his army days in India. On his lap was the hamster, George the third, silently sleeping. Grandad recalled, in his mind, fond memories of days gone by in India at a place called Madras where, as a young soldier, he was stationed with the Lancashire Fusiliers and, latterly, those fond memories when Billy had used his golden goblet for his 'pretend' church services. Such memories. Such happy times that were no more; for they were gone forever. And the comic actions of Billy that were gone forever, and the seriousness but cleverness of Terry that was gone...forever. For both Terry and Billy, as well as their friends Nathan and Lilly, were missing, presumed dead, buried in a watery grave at the bottom of Fishersgate harbour.

A single tear ran down Grandad's wrinkled cheek as he continued to sit in his chair by the fire. Then, he closed his eyes for the last time. His mortal body soon becoming lifeless, his head slumping forwards, his left arm falling onto his lap, waking George the third, his right arm quickly dropping down the side of the chair for his fingers to just touch the cold linoleum floor. In a single moment of time, less than the blink of an eye, grandad's eternal spirit had left his body to begin an invisible journey that would take his soul to another place. A location far away from this place called Earth, where he would finally be at peace. A place where he would join the company of his wife, in a much happier location, way up in the sky at the far end of the Galaxy. Grandad's inner-self was on its way to a spot that some folk might call heaven, or even paradise. George the hamster looked pitifully upwards at his mortally dead master, wondering, as hamsters often do, where his next nutty meal would be coming from.

A few days later John arrived home from Australia and was, at last, reunited with his inconsolable wife, Gloria. They buried Grandad on a frosty Friday morning at 9:31 am, in the cemetery just up the road from their now ghostly quiet house. His mortal resting place was near to a small timber footbridge, by an old oak tree that crossed the slightly-flowing water of a little stream that ran through the neat cemetery. They interred him into the same grave where Grandad's wife had been laid to rest many years before.

Nothing much more is known about Gloria and John, excepting to say that for many years afterwards the gossips of Fishersgate repeated this tale. A tale that would tell others that by the spring of the following year (1935), Gloria and John had left the area for good. They never returned. There was nothing to keep them in Fishersgate anymore. They never said where they were going. They just went. Gone, one imagines, to live a new life in Australia; away from the recurring horrific memories that Fishersgate bay reminded them of every single day that they remained nearby.

Chapter 6

The rolling waves to Italy

Twenty-four hours had passed since the tall, fully rigged sailing ship had left its Namidian harbour. The doors to the cell on the Orlop deck, the lowest deck of the ship, that contained Billy, Nathan and those ruffians, Wheeler and Garrett, were unlocked and six guards, armed with machetes, grabbed the occupants and escorted them onto the main deck. It took two guards each to hold Garrett and Wheeler because of their individual sizes of great proportions. Both had chains and handcuffs fitted about their person, so as to further restrain them. Billy and Nathan remained unclasped. The boys were ordered to form a line on the upper deck facing the bow of the ship, and wait. Billy smelt the fresh air, a little salty but very pleasurable after having experienced the stench of cattle on the decks below - next to their prison cell.

While they waited, the Master of the ship barked orders to his crew and, in-between, told the boys interesting technical things about the ship.

'Why would they tell us about the ship?' Billy thought.

It was an impressive ship, a Galleon maybe, a type that Billy had only seen in pictures at the Library. Entirely made of timber, the Star of the Sea was 55 yards long with a breadth of 13 yards. She carried four and a half thousand square yards of sail and had a maximum speed of 10 knots. It was armed with 80 cannons; 26 thirty-two pounders on the lower deck, 26 twelve-pounders on the middle deck and the rest on the upper deck. There were also two Carronade cannons on either side of the bow, each capable of firing a massive 100-pound shot. There were three main masts, the middle mast was made from a single fir tree imported from Norway, which was 45 yards tall, with the fore and aft masts being slightly shorter. These three giant masts supported some eighteen miles of rigging that held the sails in place. These gigantic sails were currently full of a brisk breeze capturing the natural wind-power that pushed the ship at a steady rate of knots towards its destination. That destination was Taranto, Italy.

The Star of the Sea had been purchased by the Namidians from the Italians in 1712. It was the Italians who had helped to secure modern Namidia one hundred years before in 1612. They ruled Namidia throughout the ensuing years, right up until 1700. During that period, the Italians had built Namidian's infrastructure, its fine houses, castles and harbour - but then the Namidian's wanted independence. The Italians granted this under a protectorate arrangement in 1701 and the two countries remained mutual friends. That was until the French became involved in Namidian politics in 1715. The French fought the Italians over Namidia with muskets and cannons during the ten-year naval war of the Mediterranean, and by 1726 they had pushed out all Italian influence and formed a partnership arrangement with the two Namidian leaders, Mr. Josef, and Mr. Necho. This allowed many French subjects to re-locate from France and reside in the country. But the Namidian's reliance on France was about to come to an end when France's Cardinal Fleury began to rule with King Louis XV, and France, for various reasons, subsequently abandoned Namidia. The French also found the Namidian's politically troublesome and after that, the Italians could not be bothered to return as a protectorate. That's how important Namidia was to two great states of European power - not much importance at all. So, the British took control for about two years before deciding that there was not much to plunder from the country and so they left. Namidia fell into a slow decline, and all because the Namidians were too much trouble to be ruled or protected by the Superpowers. And the Second Chapter book? Well, perhaps the Italians took the book when they left Namidia and that was how it became lost to the nation of Namidia. Mr. Josef had no idea that the book was in Italy until Wentworth told him.

Because of the sour relations with the Italians, the Namidian ship's Captain had already decided that he did not want to provoke the Italian people when the Star of the Sea reached Italy. Enough had already been done. It was probably best to moor one-hundred yards off the shore of Taranto and take smaller rowing boats into the harbour under the cover of darkness, where a selected group of men could scatter, become part of the local population and search for the book.

Aboard the ship were four-hundred sailors in total, including three officers. Below them were men of all stations below the rank of officers - down to general deck-hands, landsmen and cabin boys.

'But what were they waiting for?' thought Billy, as he waited on deck with the other boys.

Everything was soon to be revealed.

A nod from the Lieutenant officer on the poop-deck caused the Master of the ship to shout at the top of his voice, "make way for the captain."

The men on the main-deck below stood to a sort of rabbled attention as the Captain appeared from a small doorway on the main-deck, before making his way up the steps to the poop-deck.

Captain Alfonso Pickering, dressed in the finery of his upper-class personal naval uniform, was ready to address his men. High above the deck, having a bird's-eye view of the proceedings, were two cabin-boy look-outs, aged about twelve years old and not quite yet promoted to young sailors. Cabin boys, Jack and Austin, were in the crows-nest. They had been up at this great height of about 40 yards above deck for just over two hours. It was their job to look out to sea for enemies and danger. Being so high up on the ship was an advantage - they could see for miles on a clear day and could readily warn the Captain of any unfriendly foe approaching the ship.

"Gather round men," shouted the first officer, who was standing to attention on the poop-deck, immediately to the right of Captain Pickering. Like a crisp clear echo, the words of his command were repeated several times, as it boomed and bounced around the decks, emitted by deep voices of the various undefined ranks in varying regional accents, the next voice immediately following the last. Once the ranks had repeated the orders there was a moment of silence before the final instruction came from the Master… "gather round… gather round, stand easy men." This was relayed again, parrot fashion, by the sharp echoes produced by the lower undefined ranks as they repeated the Master's words, "gather round... gather round."

There was a shuffle of sailors and a wave of movement of the men, both heard and seen by the young lookouts in the crow's nest. The men began moving around the decks to gain a good view of the forthcoming proceedings while securing an advantageous listening point to hear what the Captain was about to say.

The men looked a shabby lot. In 1734 ordinary sailors did not wear standard naval uniforms. Neither did the Captain, his lieutenant or the Master come to that. These three officers were the only official ranks aboard the vessel and were appointed by the ship's owners. They wore their own style of uniform, made of upper-class clothing affixed with insignias of their own choosing, with of course the upper-class hair-piece wigs to denote their social standing. Captain Pickering wore a pure white wig with the first officer and the Master wearing black and brown wigs respectively. And these three Officer ranks were clearly defined. The captain was in total command of the ship, followed by the Lieutenant and lastly the Master. Below the rank of the Master were the men, all 400 of them; all supposedly equal in rank. Well almost. These were the landsmen, cabin boys and the skilled sailors. Landsmen were a kind of adult trainee sailor. Other than the separation of name and seamanship ability between a landsman and a fully-fledged sailor there were no official naval ranks for the men. There was just an unofficial pecking-order. Power was seized upon by those sailors and landsmen with strong character and intimidating natures. This led to about a dozen men of leadership. These were the men who really did control the masses of the sailors, both below and above decks. It was a very frightening world for some ordinary men and boys. Not a place where the shy and the meek could exist for very long. Well, not without the help of a strong character beside them. Strong men to lead them and men to protect them. Men to punish them, to keep discipline among the lowest of the ranks. One such man of leadership was Jed Boot - the beast of below deck. He was the master of misinformation, discipline, corruption, wickedness and murder. He was the unofficial fourth in command of this ship. Below his unofficial rank were a dozen of his trusted bullies who kept control of the masses of men in every quarter of the ship and those bullies reported to him, and him alone, in matters of discipline. He called them his twelve-disciples, for there were twelve men of despicable character, each true to Jed Boot.

Jed looked like a pirate. He was indeed, a man with an undisclosed history of piracy and violence. He seemed quite content to leave the running of the ship to the captain and his officers, but he knew – that any time he wanted – he could seize command of the vessel, for he had the backing of the men onboard. His long black unkempt hair was tied back with a red handkerchief and his bedraggled beard hid most of the front of his filthy shirt. He walked with a swagger and a limp; helped by a carved walking stick, depicting nautical themes, such as a human skull with two fully rigged sailing ships floating inside the head - seen through the open eye sockets. Ship's cannons firing dead rats, instead of cannon balls, and pirate flags fixed to spears that were thrust into the bodies of dead men. The stick helped Jed Boot to maintain his drunken balance. Beside him, as always, was his trusted dog who he called *Shell*. This was a dog devoted to his master, a black dog with pointed ears and almost as evil looking as Jed Boot himself. A dog that would kill a ship's rat in three seconds and so vicious that on his master's command, could kill a man in under one minute. The dog's primary role was to protect Jed himself against anyone brave enough to try to knife him in the back in the dead of night when things were quiet on board and his disciples, who usually protected him, were asleep. There was something about Jed Boot and his dog. Something that cannot be explained fully. Perhaps it was a dark sinister magical power that emanated from Jed's disgruntled character - an evil streak of nastiness no doubt. Perhaps it was nothing more than the disgusting smell about him. No-one even dared to look Jed in the eye or argue with him, for he was the leader of all the sailors below the rank of Master. And Jed reported directly to the Master of the Ship himself. They had a nice cosy relationship. Jed kept the men under control for the Master who, in turn, made sure that Jed received as much rum as he could drink and resided in a comfortable cabin below decks - for him to hold court. Oh, and of course there was the torture-rack which was located down in the hold, where Jed and his ruffians could inflict their punishment on men who broke the rules. These were the rules that Jed himself made. These punishments usually ended in death for the unfortunate man who had crossed Jed or any one of his twelve disciples. Then their dead body would be put in a sack, weighed down with a single cannon-ball, strapped up to make a package and slung over the side of the ship. No prayers were said or even a second glance was made, as the package splashed into the depths of its watery grave.

But the one thing that helped Jed keep order, among the men on the ship, was the promise of Booty. Whenever sailors captured another ship or invaded islands in the south seas they'd share their spoils of war and plunder. It was known as Booty, a prize, a gift, a reward for their time spent robbing and seizing an abundance of valuables. On this ship, the Captain and officers took the largest amount of the Booty, around sixty percent in total. Twenty percent of that sixty percent was used to buy food, rum and supplies for the running of the ship, with the remaining forty percent split between the Captain, first officer, Master and owner of the vessel. They left the rest, the remaining forty percent of the Booty to Jed Boot, who would take his share and divide the remainder among his disciples. He called it Booty after his own surname. It was the disciples of Jed Boot who would apportion the final share to each individual man. Sometimes, if the Booty was in gold or coins, it would be handed straight out for division among the men, but if it was cattle hides or other trading commodities the Captain would sell the produce at the next large port that they set down at and share out the money a few days later. There were no regular wages given to the men of the Star of the Sea. They survived on their Booty spoils alone and, of course, the free food and tots of rum provided by the ship's officers. And as most of the crew was a thief or a former vagabond before joining the ship, petty stealing among the crew was rife. There were plenty of men with kleptomaniacal tendencies aboard this ship, so if something of any value wasn't screwed down or meticulously hidden away it was generally stolen. And when some men discovered their personal losses and accused another of stealing from them, fights inevitably broke out between them. Just the sort of thing Jed Boot wanted, a little bit of sportsmanship about the ship. He even took wagers on who would win those fights; fights that usually ended in death for one of the unlucky crew members.

You may have heard of a Jed before. And indeed, you would be correct. For Jed Boot is the same man as Jed Lavell, who later controlled the Hufflers in 1934, two hundred years later in time. But Jed Boot didn't know that - because he could not foresee the future. What a surprise Billy and Nathan would have when they would eventually see him in the next few hours aboard this ship, the Star of the Sea, in the year of 1734. But for now, Jed was below deck in his cabin - just about waking from a deep drunken sleep.

There was silence among the men as the Captain began to speak.

"All you men aboard this ship – the Star of the Sea - are on a voyage to Italy."

The men cheered.

The captain looked downwards and surveyed his men from the poop-deck, sometimes known as the ship's bridge, while he took his clenched fist to his mouth and coughed.

He continued, "You are all on a special mission to find the Secrets of the Lost Chapter."

A murmur of muffled noises emanated from the men and rose from the main decks up onto the poop-deck.

"Be quiet and listen to the Captain," shouted the First officer who was standing beside him.

There was a hush.

"You men," said the Captain, "are going to Italy to find the lost Second Chapter, but I can see from the looks on your faces that you do not know what it is. Well, let me tell you... It's a Book!"

There was a gasp, followed by muffled voices, followed by a roar of disappointment from the deckhands.

"A book?" one man was heard to say.

Another exclaimed, "We don't want books... we want Booty."

The noise among the men became louder and louder at the Captain's revelation that they were searching for ... a book.

"What good is a book to the hungry belly of a sailor?" one man shouted.

"Books don't buy women when we go ashore," shouted another.

"No, but if you had a book on women you might know what to do with one when you get hold of her," jested another sailor.

A huge roar of laughter erupted among the men.

Just then, from the other end of the ship, a pistol was fired into the air.

The whole ship's crew turned around to see where the shot was fired from. Jed Boot stood at the bow of the ship, on the upper front deck, with a discharged pistol in his hand - which he held up high for all to see. Next to him stood Necho, approvingly looking on, with Shell the dog sat peacefully watching his master.

Jed looked upward, towards the two boys in the crow's nest and shouted, "You boys all right up there?"

The boys shouted back to say that they were fine.

"Missed you with my shot then?" shouted Jed before breaking into a hearty laugh that was interrupted by a wheezy smoker's cough, that seemed to go on for a minute or more. Then he put away his pistol, which slipped nicely between his belt and his hip, before focusing on the matter to hand.

"Listen to me all you men," he shouted. "You men of this ship have done well by the Captain and me over the years. We have fed you, paid you in Booty, given you rum and given you a home on this mighty ship, so I don't want no more moaning and groaning about going to Italy and finding a little old book."

"But Jed there is no money in it," shouted Steve Goose, one of his most trusted disciples.

"Ah, but there is Steve!" retorted Jed.

"Let me introduce you to Mr. Necho, the owner of this magnificent ship. He is willing to pay a Booty to all you men in gold coins. We can convert that gold to hard cash and all we have to do is recover a book called…"

Jed stumbled with his words.

Necho interrupted, "The Second Chapter."

"That's it," shouted Jed, "the Second Chapter… That's what it be… the Second Chapter book."

"But where is the gold?" replied Steve. "Is it in a cut-out inside the book?"

"No, it's not inside the book," shouted Necho, "I have the gold right here." He held up a sheep-skin pouch for all to see. There was a collective gasp from the men as Necho took some gold from the bag to show them. Necho continued, "It's the book itself that I want and the information that it contains. In return, I will pay you men handsomely with this gold that the Captain will share among you all."

Jed, somewhat surprised that Necho had held up a bag of gold, pushed Necho's hand with his before saying in a quiet voice, "put it away Mr. Necho…we don't want it to go missing, do we?"

Necho whispered back, "don't take me for a fool Boot, I know I am among thieves on-board this ship. There is only a fraction of the gold in this bag. The bulk of the gold is hidden in a safe spot on this ship somewhere. Only I know where that gold is hidden. When, and if, I need to pay it to you and your men, then I will seek it out. But only when I get my hands on that book."

"Well, let's hope the ship don't sink then Necho," replied Jed Boot with a wry smile.

Jed turned once more toward the men and banged his walking stick on the wooden deck to gain their attention.

He shouted, "As you will see my men, I have struck a deal on your behalf…"

Jed Boot was prodded by Necho who whispered something in his ear.

Jed banged his walking stick once more on the deck before shouting, "As you will see my men, Captain

Pickering has struck a deal with the owner of this ship, Mr. Necho, and we are to give him safe passage to a place called Taranto in Italy where we will find the book. Once we find it and hand it over to Mr. Necho he will give me…"

Necho prodded Jed Boot before whispering once more into his ear.

Jed turned to the men before shouting, "Mr. Necho will give the Captain the gold Booty who will share it out among you men. I reckon you will each receive about ten shillings in hard cash."

There was a roar of approval among the men, which radiated around all quarters of the ship. The yelling, bellowing, and screaming was indeed music to the ears of Captain Pickering, who had patiently been listening to Jed Boot's address to the crew. As the roar died away the first officer could be heard shouting for 'order' at the other end of the ship, to allow the Captain to speak.

The Captain began his address.

"Good men, I am pleased that I have been able to sort this little matter out and will wish you all a safe voyage under my command."

"Three cheers for the Captain," shouted the Master of the vessel,

"Hip - Hip."

"… Hooray," the men responded.

"Hip- Hip."

"… Hooray," the men responded a second time.

"Hip - Hip."

"… Hooray," the men responded for the final time.

It was clear from the lively chatter among the men that they were happy with this promise of hard cash for their labour. Finding a book should be positively easy, thought some.

But the Captain was not finished yet.

"You men," he boomed from the poop-deck, as they turned towards him.

"You men are to take extra special care of these four prisoners. Mr. Necho and I were going to leave them in their prison cells below the main deck, but we have jointly decided, a few minutes ago, that their welfare is better served above decks. One of them has the secret we truly need to get hold of the contents of that book, though at this stage I do not know which of these four has that magical power." .

The Captain looked the four prisoners up and down, trying to decide which one held the secret.

The captain continued. "They will work amongst you during the voyage to Italy and by the time we reach Taranto

I want them to be in good form and as fit in mind, body and spirit as any boy can be. They are here to help Mr. Necho find the lost book, the Second Chapter, and I want them to do light-duties only aboard this ship. It is far better that they are on deck and in the fresh air rather than in a prison cell - below the main-deck, among the diseased smells and the rats… so look after them well."

"That is all."

Captain Pickering turned around on the poop-deck and looked aft to watch the sea waters trailing the moving ship. This indicated to the men that the meeting was completed and they began drifting back to their various duties about the ship. Jed Boot was making his way down the steps towards the main deck, where he would receive instructions from the first officer regarding the four prisoners. It would be up to Jed to ensure that the four boys were treated properly and given light work duties to keep them fit and well during the four-week voyage to Italy.

Billy whispered to Nathan, "So have you got the secret magic needed to find the lost Chapter? Because I certainly haven't got it."

Nathan responded, "I don't know any more than you do Billy, and I don't reckon them two bullies, Garrett and Wheeler, know anything either, they are too thick to know anything useful, but we must go along with the Captain for now and look for a way of escaping when we get to Taranto."

"Ok," said Billy. He was about to say more but Jed was approaching.

"So, what have we got here?" Jed Boot asked the First Officer, as he viewed the four boys up and down.

"Jed Lavell!" exclaimed Billy, "what are you doing here?"

"I beg your pardon young sir," replied a bemused Jed.

"You're the Jed Lavell who is the leader of the Hufflers in 1934 in England," replied Billy.

"No, I ain't," answered Jed, almost embarrassed by this wild claim of Billy's. Composing himself with several bodily jerks about his being, Jed replied, "You must be mistaken boy, and anyhow, 1934 is two hundred years in the future, AND I have not been to England, not never ever been to England in my entire life. AND there is no such thing as time-travel which, as far as I can see, would be the only way to get there, so you're wrong boy, and my name isn't Jed Lavell, it's Jed Boot!"

"And anyways, I cannot go to England for they know me, they know of the famous Jed Boot, the pirate and torturer. I was known as the Gibraltar Butcher because of the many Englishmen I killed off the coast of Spain when we took their gold. I was just squaring things up. The English took it from the Spanish and I just took it from them. Fair's, fair. They got a bounty on my head, don't you know. So, I stays away from England as I don't want me neck strung-up."

Jed was proud of his past reputation. He swaggered as he boasted of his criminal past. Shell, his trusted dog, followed his every move as he pranced, gesticulated and displayed his gory past to all onlookers.

Billy realised that whoever this man was, even though he looked so much like Jed Lavell, it was not worth arguing with him. No one knew about the reality of time-travelling, except for Billy, Nathan and of course those two thugs Garrett and Wheeler. So why waste time quarrelling.

"I am sorry sir," replied Billy, "I must be mistaken."

"Apology accepted," replied Jed.

The four boys were standing in a line on the main deck as Jed walked around them several times - he was studying their individual features.

"So, what have we here then," enquired Jed, as he invaded the personal space of Nathan.

"A black boy... your name?" he snarled.

"It's... Nathan."

"Who is your master, black boy Nathan?" demanded Jed Boot.

"I don't have a Master," replied an indignant Nathan.

"No Master?" said Jed, "well, in that case, I shall be your..."

"Yes, he has!" blurted Billy. "It's me, my father gave him to me as a present for my fourteenth birthday."

Billy looked at Nathan and tried to tell him, with only facial expressions, to go along with this story. It wasn't right, but Billy had studied the matter of slave labour of the seventeen-hundreds at school. Indeed, the word Slave originates from the medieval Latin word Sclavus which Billy had read about at the Library through his interest in the ancient language.

Luckily, Nathan realised that Billy had made up this story for good reasons and went along with it. They were of course friends, who had known each other for as many years as they could remember, and there was a certain coolness, mixed with honesty and joviality that existed between them. Whenever Nathan called Billy 'Master' from then on - and he did so many times over the coming weeks, in front of the crew members on board the ship - they both knew that this was something that had to be done.

"Well then," exclaimed Jed, as he continued to rotate around the four boys - tapping his walking stick on the decking to enforce his presence.

" You boy, Billy, shall keep your *slave*, but look after him well, and make sure he doesn't make no trouble as black boys often do."

"I will," replied Billy, which was interjected by, "Thank you Master," from a smiling Nathan.

'That was easy', thought Billy as he gave a smile of success to Nathan, who returned the compliment with a similar gesture.

Jed Boot's attention had already turned to Garrett and Wheeler as he studied their facial features as closely as he could.

"Big strapping lads, as tall as I am, why each of you must be 6 feet 3 inches tall?" he bellowed. "We need boys like you two on this ship to swab the decks and raise the anchor." Jed's mood changed to a look of thunder. "I'll keep you fit, you two slobs of an excuse for boys, why... you are both as wide as you are tall." That was indeed an exaggeration, but then Jed usually exaggerated all manner of things and usually followed them with a deep hearty laugh.

Jed paused for a moment more as he looked them up and down.

"Excuse me young sirs, while I once more laugh at your condition." Jed Boot broke out into a raucous laugh. It was an infectious laugh and before long every sailor on the deck was laughing loudly. Even Billy and Nathan were laughing at Wheeler and Garrett's expense.

"I'm going to get you, Billy," snarled Garrett.

"Not with those shackles on you won't," taunted Billy.

But as we all know, Jed Boot's statement was not quite true, for very few people are as wide as they are tall. And although it was a little harsh of Jed to call them slobs, that is exactly what Garrett and Wheeler were, overweight, as well as being bullies to smaller people like Billy.

"Men of this ship behold," called Jed Boot, "before you are two large pieces of tallow, as large as whales, filling the clothing of men with the brains of boys."

The men laughed and laughed.

Jed came ever closer to a furious Garrett, who was still clasped in the irons of his imprisonment. Their faces met - no more than an inch apart. Suddenly Garrett nutted Jed as hard as a ball-pein hammer hitting a conker at ninety miles an hour.

Jed's walking stick was reactively flung across the main deck, as he screamed aloud and danced around in pain with a definitive throbbing bloodied forehead.

He screamed and screamed before shouting. "Right boy, that's you done for. I'll put you to work right now, cleaning the keel underneath the ship."

Holding his bloodied forehead with a handkerchief, to douse the pain and stop the flow of blood, an enraged Jed Boot ordered the sailors standing by to, "prepare for a keel-haul."

"What's a keel-haul?" Nathan asked Billy.

"Keel-hauling is a punishment which often leads to an execution," explained Billy, "It is given to sailors who have seriously broken the rules and is associated with unwritten Pirate Laws. One of Garrett's arms will be tied to a rope that will be looped beneath this vessel from portside to starboard side. His other arm will be tied to a second line. They will then throw him overboard and pull him under the ship from portside to starboard side. He will be dragged through the water right under the boat, across the keel of the ship. The hull of most ships is covered in barnacles. These are sharp - like razors. If Garrett is to be pulled underwater quickly, keelhauling would typically result in serious cuts to his body from these barnacles. He may sustain loss of limbs and even decapitation. But if he is dragged slowly, his weight might lower him sufficiently to miss the barnacles. But this method takes longer and it is likely that this would result in his drowning."

"Blimey," said Nathan "how do you know so much Billy?"

Billy shrugged his shoulders, "I suppose it's because I read a lot of books," he replied.

This was serious. Either way, Garrett would probably not make it out from under the ship, alive. He was going to die in a few minutes time.

Suddenly a voice from the poop-deck boomed out.

"Mr. Boot, you know full well that we cannot keel-haul the prisoner at this precise moment." It was Captain Pickering, who had been listening to Boot.

He continued, "we are under full sail and travelling at 10 knots, it is impossible to keel-haul anyone at this speed, and, in this case, the prisoner you seek to punish might be the only one who can unlock the secrets of the lost Second Chapter, so I really must over-rule you on this occasion. You must save your game of keel-hauling for another day - after we have recovered the lost Chapter."

Jed Boot thought for a moment before replying. "Very good Captain."

Jed Boot knew this deep down and had given the order in temper. He was especially delighted though at the response from Garrett, who by this time had systematically peed himself and was visibly very shaken, his legs trembling all the way into his cotton socks.

In a slow but very determined drawl, Jed Boot came close to Garrett once more and spoke very quietly, "you are a dead man walking, Garrett."

Garrett winced and swallowed deeply before the weight of his own body became too much for his trembling legs and he fell to his knees, wailing at the top of his voice.

"Not so clever now are you, Garrett," shouted Billy. "Now *you* know what it's like to be bullied."

Garrett did not reply. He just looked sorry for himself and very, very, scared.

It was now a much heavier breeze that was pushing the ship briskly along at about 12 knots and the Captain had noted that it was likely that they were heading for bad weather.

It was going to be rough, but there was no way around the storm. They were going to go through it and the Captain ordered appropriate measures, in preparation for what they were about to receive from the forces of nature. The sails were lowered and stowed away.

The Captain spoke, "In light of the matters to hand I think that we should put the two large boys back in their cells, but you two, Billy and Nathan, can assist around this ship as may be necessary, in fact, both of you can attend to my cabin during the storm."

"Batten down the hatches," ordered the first officer and every man on deck ran to their respective posts.

"Billy and Nathan, you are to go with Jed Boot who will assign you tasks. Stay close to him and obey his orders for your own safety, this ship is going to roll in the bad weather, so hold tight.

Chapter 7

The Dungeon and Harem

It had been three weeks since Necho had taken Billy and Nathan to Italy. In all of that time, Terry had been in prison in the depths of the castle. Lilly, on the other hand, was languishing freely inside the harem. The harem was a sacred inviolable place where selected females of the household resided in a protected domestic environment. It was inaccessible to adult males except for Necho, the Master of the harem, and the eunuch guards who protected the area. Necho ran this house of polygamy purely for his own needs and fantasies. The harem housed all his wives, intended wives, girlfriends and female slaves. It was guarded by tongue-less eunuchs who protected the area from unwanted guests. Few of these women - most came from all areas of Africa and the Mediterranean - wanted to belong to Necho or reside in the harem. They were prisoners and although the eunuchs kept unwanted predators out, they also kept the women in. Most of the women in the harem were between twenty-five and forty years old and had access to the most wonderful clothing. They used Adlan oils and kohl, a type of eyeliner, perfumed sticks to gloss their lips and scented aromatics and incense. All of these readily available

185

cosmetics enhanced their natural beauty. They wanted for nothing, except freedom. The whole area was sumptuous. It was a palace area fit for a queen. Its décor was of marble and granite. Bathing areas exuded hot waters from the natural volcanic springs, flowing from solid gold taps. Each lady of the harem had several personal female maids, who were all over forty-five years old. They looked after their every whim, and each lady in the harem had her own private bedroom with adjoining dressing room. Though Necho's first wife, Izabella, lived among the ladies of the harem she was the only legitimate bearer of his children. She was the only one, permitted under Namidian law, to produce Necho's heir to the throne, the future half-ruler of the country. The rest of the women in the harem, all in such enforced relationships with Necho, were known as concubines. Whatever the social status and rights of the concubines within the harem, they were always inferior to those of his wife and typically, neither the concubine or her children had any rights of inheritance. Historically, concubinage was frequently entered into voluntarily, but in the case of Necho, it was enforced. These ladies were as much a prisoner as those men shackled in chains in the dungeons, deep in the castle below.

Lilly had made friends with Teresa, another prisoner in the harem. Teresa was about the same age as Lilly. She was from southern Italy and had been abducted from the shores of Taranto twelve-months earlier. This seemed to be a regular occurrence for Necho and his henchmen. They snatched women from different areas around the Mediterranean, countries such as Spain, Italy, Greece, Egypt, Portugal, Turkey and the Barbary Coast, off the coast of North Africa. Necho's harem was a seriously international affair.

Deep down in the dungeons, Terry lay on straw bedding. He was chained to the wall of his prison cell by one arm. The other arm was left free to allow him to eat the paltry food that was taken into his cell once a day. Also in the cell was a man named Antonio. He was the lover of Teresa. It was a pure coincidence that Terry and Antonio were locked in a cell together while their respective partners, Lilly and Teresa, who were also friends, were locked-up together in the harem. The ladies did not know where their corresponding partners were in the castle, and Terry only knew that Lilly was in the harem because some of the guards had taunted him quite regularly that she was now Necho's newly acquired play-thing.

Antonio had been a prisoner in the cell for about a year. He had followed the entourage that had kidnapped Teresa, led by pirate Jed Boot, all the way across the Mediterranean. Antonio had planned to sneak into the prison, with his troop of soldiers, to get his future bride out - but had been caught by Necho's men, thrown into jail to await trial for burglary of a state castle, war crimes and criminal damage. The charges against Antonio were, of course, preposterous. Teresa had no idea that Antonio had been so brave as to try to save her from the monstrous Necho or that, right now, Antonio was only about 100 yards away from her, below ground.

Antonio was a Captain in the Italian army. At the time Teresa was abducted he had been away on army manoeuvres in Northern Italy with another foreign army - the Austrian army. On his return to Taranto he was told by residents that Teresa had been taken by the Namidians, two days before. They took her for her beauty alone, for Necho had sent Jed Boot and his men to capture the most beautiful ladies in the Mediterranean. Antonio immediately gathered his men, a volunteer group and they sailed for Namidia on the following high-tide. The troops he brought with him, numbering about a hundred and fifty of his trusted men, had been either killed, captured, or imprisoned.

In the days that Terry and Antonio had gotten to know each other they had become firm friends, with one common aim. To escape their hell-hole and rescue their respective ladies. Together, in their prison cell, they hatched the final details of Antonio's long thought-through escape plan.

Antonio's year in the prison cell had not been wasted. Daily he had watched the guards come and go, he had watched the transfer of keys among the guards and, most importantly, he calculated who the weakest and less intelligent guards were. And as a soldier himself, a soldier who had planned to break into the castle to rescue Teresa, he already knew the layout of the building. He had a blueprint of the castle etched into his memory. He knew exactly where the harem was located in the building. He knew the back way out of the castle, the route to where the docks were and where the boats were moored in those docks. It's just a pity he got caught in the first place, one might think. A pity for him of course but not for Terry, because Terry now had a real chance of escape - but only because Antonio was by his side.

The two guards immediately outside their cell on that Monday morning were Berco and Plankto. Of the many guards in the Necho team, and there were at least thirty in number, Antonio had calculated that the ones with the least quantity of brains were Berco, Plankto and another known as Lorenzo.

The men had been waiting for all three guards to be on duty together, for only three guards watched the area around the cells at any one time. Two guards maintained security to the forty or so cells leading off the huge central chamber and the third guard stood outside another locked door at the end of the corridor leading from the central chamber. Beyond that final door lay the path to freedom. This last door led to the ante-room inside the castle where they would be close to the harem itself. This was the office of the chief jailer.

Exactly on time, there was a clunk of the heavy key in the door and the door opened to reveal Plankto. He was carrying dinner which comprised of some meat a few days old and pineapple chunks. He locked the cell door behind himself.

"Dinner time for you men," he called.

Antonio and Terry, who were both shackled to the wall of the cell, each by one arm, sat upright to receive their food.

"What have we today?" enquired a cheerful Antonio.

"Three-day-old meat with a rancid smell," replied Plankto.

Plankto broke into a laugh with Antonio and Terry joining in. It wasn't funny but this was part of the plan

Antonio had hatched with Terry throughout their days in captivity.

"You know," said Antonio to Plankto, "I have really enjoyed my time here with you guards." Antonio kept up his cheerful mood and a pretend laugh as he said those words.

"You have?" said Plankto.

"Yes, I really have and only because of you and your friends, you really are friendly guards," replied Antonio.

"Are we?" replied a puzzled Plankto.

"I see another regular guard, Berco, is in the chamber today, but who is the guard by the entrance gate at this moment," continued Antonio.

"Oh, that's Lorenzo," replied Plankto.

"Oh Lorenzo, yes, he's a nice man too, just like you," replied Antonio.

Looking at Terry, Antonio winked profusely. For Lorenzo was indeed the one they had been waiting for. This was the first time all three brainless guards had been put together during the three weeks Terry had been in the cells.

"Can you unshackle me while I eat my dinner?" enquired Antonio.

"You know the rules," replied Plankto, "you must stay shackled at all times."

"Yes, I know," said Antonio, "but it is difficult to eat my dinner with my left hand when I am right handed."

"Which is your right hand? "asked Plankto.

Terry sniggered at Plankto's stupid question.

Antonio smiled. "Well it's connected to my arm that is shackled to this chain and I really would prefer my left hand shackled instead."

Plankto stood motionless for a while as his brain computed the information it had received.

"Ahhh," he finally called out, as that final piece of information was accepted by his brain cell. "You want me to swap the shackle from that wrist to that wrist," he said as he pointed his finger towards each of Antonio's wrists.

"Well, I can do that," he continued, as he placed the tray of food on the floor, before kneeling in front of Antonio, fumbling to find the correct key from a large bunch attached to the belt around his waistline. He inserted the key and opened the shackle.

"That's great," exclaimed Antonio, as he stood up and stretched his arms.

"Ok," said Plankto, "now give me your right arm, or is it your left?"

"It's my left you need to shackle," replied Antonio, as he smiled and winked at Terry.

"Here it is, come and get it," as he held out his left arm before gathering the chain shackle in his right hand, about 30 inches along its length from the open clasp. And with that, he struck Plankto across the head with some considerable force. The big guard fell from his kneeling position in a slow-motion onto the floor with torrents of blood gushing from his head. Soon a pool of blood mixed with old straw lay congealed before them. It was a horrible sight. And then the blood-flow stopped.

"Have you killed him?" enquired a shocked Terry.

"Who cares," replied Antonio as he quickly reached for Plankto's keys to unshackle Terry.

Now free, Terry stood up and moved towards the door of the cell, keeping one eye on Plankto. Antonio was already at the cell door looking through the window that contained several iron bars. He could see the second guard, Berco, asleep in the chair.

"That's lucky," he whispered to Terry, as he quietly tried to unlock the cell door. It was not to be... for the lock gave off an almighty CLUNK as it opened.

The sound of the lock caused Berco to fidget but he remained asleep.

Antonio went back to the now, clearly dead body of Plankto and took a sabre and a small dagger from his waistband. Handing the sabre to a very shaken Terry he returned to the cell door to look through the window once more. Berco was still asleep.

With the dagger in his left-hand, Antonio gently pulled the cell door open with his right. He crept out of the cell towards the direction of Berco. Looking around all the time, in case there were other guards about, Antonio finally reached the still sleeping bulk of the guard.

Without a moment's notice, he stabbed Berco several times through the neck until he lay dead before him. It was a silent affair except for the gurgling gasps, as a shocked Berco held his neck while he drowned in his own blood.

This killing business was as shocking to Terry as it was normal to Antonio. But Terry did have the presence of mind to notice that Antonio had killed Berco using only his left hand.

"I thought you said you were right-handed," whispered Terry.

"I am actually ambidextrous, my friend," replied Antonio, as he wiped the blood from his dagger on the dead guard's clothing.

"Come on," beckoned Antonio, "no time for chit-chat, we have another guard to deal with."

Antonio grabbed a second bunch of keys from Berco's waist and threw them to Terry.

"You unlock the cells on that side of the chamber and I shall unlock the ones on this side. Tell the prisoners that they are now free but to remain quiet at all times and to follow you back here to the centre of this chamber to receive my instructions."

Terry began to unlock the various prison cells, urging the occupants to follow him and to keep extremely quiet. They followed him to the centre of the chamber where Antonio was waiting with his group of men, that he had just released. Between them, they had amassed a troop of some one-hundred men. Antonio passed details of his plans in a whisper and those details were relayed man to man by further whispers. They had found some seven weapons, but it was not nearly enough for a hundred men. The next part of the plan was a simple one. They would capture the next guard, Lorenzo, and, after that, head in the direction of the Armoury, where all the weapons were kept. They would use Lorenzo to lead them there.

The plan was executed exactly as it had been planned and before long they had captured Lorenzo, who then led them to the Armoury. They were in luck. Lorenzo had the keys. The men took all the available weapons and armed themselves to the teeth before locking Lorenzo, gagged and bound, in the large armoury room. He was lucky too - for he was not to be killed on that day.

Now was a time for greetings. For Antonio had not seen some of his men for many months since they had all been captured. And there were many new men, those who had been captured on earlier escapades, to be introduced to. The men all had one thing in common; all were sailors or soldiers and all were enemies of the regime of Necho of Namidia and his brother, Mr. Josef.

'Some peace-loving tribe', thought Terry ironically, as he recalled in his mind what Namidian leaders, Necho and Josef, had told him about themselves three weeks earlier at dinner. How they had told him they were peace loving. How could they be when they kept so many prisoners in these dungeons in such terrible conditions? How could they be peace-loving when they killed Wentworth in the way in which they did, by strangulation to the neck? He was just a harmless old Soothsayer. A harmless prophet and a bit of a likeable character who, it seemed, strangely did not have the foresight to predict his own death. How sad thought Terry.

But time was short and there was much to do. There was no time for reminiscing recent past events at great length. The greetings between the men were short-lived too.

Antonio sent around a new order to the men, once more in a whisper. The plan was formulated as follows. Four men were to be dispatched to capture Necho's wife, Izabella.

Izabella lived in the harem, which was heavily protected. They would never be able to attack the harem as it was impenetrable to invaders, but Antonio knew Izabella took a daily stroll around the orange gardens. Whenever Izabella went into the gardens only two guards protected her. And this is what followed. Four of Antonio's most trusted men secured themselves in the garden where they hid in the gorse bushes by the pathway leading to the lake in the lower part of the estate. As Izabella passed by with her guards, they attacked and killed her two protectorates dragging their bodies into the gorse. Izabella was now captive and they took her to Antonio.

"Where are your husband and his political partner, Mr. Josef?" Antonio demanded.

"You will not find my husband here you pig," replied Izabella, "for my love, Necho, is aboard the Star of the Sea ship somewhere in the Mediterranean. And before you ask I shall not tell you where Mr. Josef is either."

"Kill her," ordered Antonio.

"No wait," screamed Izabella, "I do not know where Mr. Josef is right now but he will be in the mosque later today."

"Take her away and spare her life," ordered Antonio.

"Would you have really killed her?" asked a shocked Terry.

Antonio smiled at Terry before saying, "you will never know, my friend."

Antonio waited until evening for Mr. Josef to attend the mosque to say his evening prayers. And that evening Mr. Josef was captured too, after Antonio's men had dispatched four more of his guards to their deaths. Now that Izabella and Mr. Josef had been captured, both would be used as hostages, to get the castles remaining guards to surrender all their weapons. Things had gone well. In fact, it all seemed too easy, but Antonio had been planning this escape for months and, so far, every single detail of his preparations had come to a fortuitous conclusion.

Antonio and his men had had a good productive day, with Terry following along. But there was one last hurdle and it was nearly upon them.

Having bound and gagged both Mr. Josef and Izabella, Antonio and his men bundled them along the corridor with daggers held to their throats. Each tongue-less guard that they came across surrendered their weapons on being told that if they did not, Izabella or Josef would die. The one-hundred or so men following Antonio collected the weapons and escorted their newly captured prisoners back to the cells where they were locked up.

It was a plan well executed and soon Terry was in the arms of Lilly, while Antonio was caressing his fiancée, Teresa.

Terry asked Lilly if she had been hurt, but she said she had not. This was the first time that Terry told Lilly that he loved her. Lilly did not reply. She found the whole matter of being rescued overpowering and there were tears in her eyes. There were tears in Terry's eyes as well.

But there was no time for any more lovey-dovey stuff for they had to leave… and leave right now.

"Bring the prisoners with us", Antonio shouted. "Release all of the ladies in the harem and as for you two young beautiful ladies…" He looked at Teresa and Lilly dressed in their flowing robes, "please change into something more suitable for we need to find ourselves a boat, hopefully, my own ship, *the Andreina,* which could still be in the Namidian harbour - the one we arrived on about a year ago. Then we shall sail for Italy. We shall go home to Taranto but before that, I shall find Necho, wherever he is in the Mediterranean Sea and kill him myself."

Terry smiled at Lilly and she let go of his hand to disappear for a short while into the changing room. On her return, and now clad in more practical clothing for the long journey ahead, she hugged Terry once more and whispered that she loved him too. They kissed lovingly and longingly; that was until Antonio nudged Terry on the back of his shoulder which caused them to break their clasp. He then told them to leave each other alone. There would be plenty of time for kissing on the voyage ahead.

And before long they were all on their way to the seaport in search of a ship that would take them to Taranto, Italy.

It was at this point that Terry remembered what Necho had said three weeks earlier. Necho had called the guards to prepare to sail the Star of the Sea ship, shortly before Terry was jailed in the dungeons.

What Terry remembered were the words, "We sail for Taranto, Italy."

'I am sure that is what he said...he said Taranto,' thought Terry to himself.

Terry turned to Antonio, "You know, I really think that Necho and my brother are on their way to Taranto. They may already be there."

"What makes you think that?" asked Antonio.

"I don't know," replied Terry, "but when you said you were returning to Taranto I suddenly realised that this is the same name where Necho said he was going to three weeks ago. They are in search of the lost Second Chapter book."

"The lost Second Chapter," replied Antonio, "I have heard of that - or something like that if, of course, one believes the folklore story which indicates that it could be something to do with Taranto."

"So then... I must be right, they must be in Taranto," replied Terry.

"Very well," said Antonio, "we have real reasons to find them now and save your brother and friends. And my task to kill Necho will be made all the easier, for if you remember correctly Terry, and Necho is indeed in Taranto then our paths of destiny will cross much sooner."

Antonio, Teresa, Terry, and Lilly, followed by the one-hundred or so fighting men headed towards the Namidian harbour. They took with them their prisoners, Mr. Josef and Necho's wife, Izabella.

It was time for a new plan to be made, a plan to capture Jed Boot, Necho and the Namidian flagship, the Star of the Sea, containing its 400 men and to rescue Billy and Nathan. There were only a hundred of them under Antonio's command travelling by foot and, as they neared the harbour of Namidia, Antonio was hoping that a seaworthy vessel, maybe Antonio's own ship - *the Andreina,* would be there, in the harbour, for the taking.

Chapter 8

Taranto

"Come-on, Shell," shouted Jed to his dog. The ugly looking black and white animal with a deformed right front-leg and spiked collar, bounded across the main deck of the Star of the Sea ship towards its master. Shell had been hiding throughout the night underneath an upturned lifeboat, taut ropes clamping the small boat firmly onto the deck of the ship. The ship had been through the centre of a storm that had produced a variety of thunder and lightning bolts coupled with a continuous howling hurricane. Waves, sixty-feet high, had thrown the ship and its occupants forcefully from side to side, ripping timbers, fixtures, fittings, and men from the ship's deck. The storm had ended sometime during the hours of darkness, just before daylight struck and the wind was beginning to calm. There was plenty to do now that daylight had risen above the horizon. Clearing the decks and repairing the timbers that usually held the sails in their respective places was one of many tasks to undertake. At least one-hundred and fifty sailors manned the decks, effecting these urgent but necessary repairs. Another smaller group of sailors tended to the dead and the injured. Later that day Captain Pickering would be busy addressing the men and performing the funeral ceremonies for the unfortunate deceased, who had met their mortal end - being thrashed about below decks or hit by falling debris on the main decks during the ravaging storm. But for now, Captain Pickering was busy on the upper deck with his first officer, surveying the damage caused by the storm and determining exactly where they were in this vast expanse of a sea known as the Mediterranean. Before the storm had encircled their ship, he had ordered that the sails were to be lowered and stowed away. He ordered this so they would not be damaged during the gales. It had been a wise decision. Damage to the structure of the timber-ship was slight, but still, it was enough to prevent them from immediately continuing their journey to Taranto. It would be another two and half-days before all repairs had been effected and they could continue their voyage without hindrance. This delay, while repairs were carried out, would prolong their expedition. Luckily, the hull of the ship was completely intact and the real damage done was only prevalent to the fore and aft sail-spreaders. These were the large horizontal timbers that were centre-fixed onto the masts. It was parts of these falling timbers that had killed or injured some of the sailors, who were on deck during the storm - most of whom were washed away, never to be seen again.

Later that day, after it had become dark, Captain Pickering was able to determine exactly where they were in the Mediterranean Sea. Using the stars in the sky, particularly the constellation of Lyra, where the brightest star is Vega, he pinpointed their exact position. The storm had blown them off-course by about fifty miles. It could be worse, thought Captain Pickering to himself.

The weeks went quickly as Billy and Nathan began to learn the skills required to master a sailing ship. They were taught everything from swabbing the decks, stitching the sails, cooking in the galley, to undertaking skills with ropes and tying the most amazing kinds of knots. Captain Pickering even showed them how to navigate using the stars in the sky. From time-to-time, the boys were tasked with taking food to Garrett and Wheeler in their cells. Billy relished this as he could taunt the two bullies through the bars in the cell door. Garrett vowed to get Billy when his chains were removed but Billy reminded him that his keel-hauling punishment had yet to be carried out by Jed Boot.

"I might just remind Jed Boot of your impending punishment… in case he forgets," Billy would say with a smirk to Garrett. This statement always temporarily caused Garrett to stop his barrage of abuse.

These visits to Garrett and Wheeler were also moments of glory for Billy, who saw the two bullies' predicament of being locked-up in the cells below deck, as a form of social justice and chastisement. This was their just-desserts for all the pain they had personally instilled upon Billy during the past year. And yet sometimes, when Billy had quiet moments, mostly before he went to sleep, he felt sorry for them. Sorry for their situation in the cells, sorry for the situation they all found themselves trapped in, two-hundred years away from home and he sometimes, just sometimes, wished they could all be friends. After all, Garrett and Wheeler did come from the same place and time-zone as Billy and Nathan. They should be on the same side, they had to be on the same side, for they all originated from the same place - yet the attitudes of Garrett and Wheeler themselves had made any form of friendship with Billy impossible.

Billy also thought about his mother, father and of course his old grandad, who were all in 1934, two hundred years in the future, though technically none of them had even been born yet, for Billy was living in 1734. Then he thought about his brother, Terry, and his girlfriend, Lilly. Where were they? Sometimes, he just cried himself quietly to sleep, only to awake the following day thinking the same things that he thought of the night before and hoping that one day he could return to England, to be back in 1934 with his brother and friends.

Billy and Nathan also spoke to Jed Boot from time to time during their voyage and sometimes they played with his dog, Shell. Once the boys got to know Jed and Shell they realised that neither were as scary as they looked. And Jed would tell them chilling tales of his life as a pirate many years before. All of Jed's tales were fully animated, to dramatise his story to the greatest extent, as the former pirate waved his arms about, sometimes pretending he had a deadly weapon in his hand when he fought off his most dangerous of imaginary foes. Billy thought that Jed exaggerated most of his stories and if the truth were told he was probably right. Billy even got to like Jed Boot and, in a funny sort of a way, Jed liked Billy too.

The one person they saw the least, but never spoke to, was Necho. He remained in his cabin for most of the sea-voyage. Sometimes they might see him on the poop-deck at the distant end of the ship, but he never acknowledged them. This growling nasty man kept away from almost everyone on board the Star of the Sea ship. He only spoke to either the Captain or to Jed Boot.

Some six weeks after they had left Namidia, land was sighted in the distance by Jack and Austin, the two young cabin boys in the crow's nest. It was confirmed by the navigator of the ship that they were near the coast of Italy, by the village of Taranto. They had almost reached their destination. It was a bright sunny day without a cloud in the sky and very hot. Captain Pickering directed his ship to a spot 100 yards off the coast of the village, where he laid anchor. Garrett and Wheeler were brought from their cells below, up onto the main deck and drenched with bucket upon bucket of seawater to remove the smells about them that six weeks in the prison cell had accumulated. Two sailors, each with a bucket tied to a rope, continually lowered each container into the sea to fill each one full to the brim with the salty water. A dozen sailors or more formed a chain and passed the buckets across the deck to the end-users who threw its contents over their smelly victims. The process was repeated several times.

"Can I have a go?" shouted Nathan as he was handed a bucket of water - which he threw over Wheeler's head from his elevated position on the ladder ropes that stretched up to the top of the main mast.

"Want a go Billy?" shouted Nathan.

Billy scrambled up the rope ladder and threw several buckets of water over the two former bullies.

"I will get you for this Nathan," shouted Wheeler.

"But not just yet," replied Nathan. "Ha, ha, by God you both smell... Poo."

Billy threw a couple more buckets of water over Garrett and Wheeler before suddenly realising that these two ruffians were not the bullies anymore. He and Nathan were now the bullies, but only because they had the might of the fifty or so sailors' patronage behind them. Billy felt quite sorry for Garrett and Wheeler, for he was not a natural bully.

However, Garrett and Wheeler's ordeal was not yet over, soon the responsibility for this game was taken away from Nathan and Billy as one of the sailors took the buckets. The next part of the process of cleaning Garrett and Wheeler and making them *smell* better was about to begin and the two boys were not to be involved. This was man's work.

Some of the largest sailors and landsmen descended upon Garrett and Wheeler, stripped them of their clothes, which they threw overboard, before washing them down with scrubbing brushes and what looked like a black tar soap. Garrett and Wheeler fought them all the way but were constantly overpowered by the sailors. It was a very entertaining spectacle for the rest of the crew, who jeered and taunted the victims during this energetic display. After about twenty minutes, they let go of their prey and allowed them time to dry their red-raw, but sparkling clean bodies in the Mediterranean sun. Then, the pair of them were given a hair-cut, rough and ready sailor style. And soon they were given fresh clothes, clasped back in irons and chained to the main mast of the ship for a good breezy airing in the wind, which was to last for the rest of the day. But it was clear that by the end of their ordeal, primarily because of their six weeks incarceration in the cells, and to some effect their humiliating moments that day, Garrett and Wheeler's confidence was broken. They were indeed submissive to their many masters aboard the ship - the sailors of the Star of the Sea.

Early the next morning Jed Boot woke Billy and Nathan.

"Come-on, look lively you two - get up, get dressed and I shall see you on the main deck in ten minutes. Don't be late."

Billy and Nathan did as they were instructed and, once on deck, were told to climb down the side of the ship on a rope ladder. This led to a small rowing boat tied up alongside the ship. In the boat was Jed Boot and Necho.

"Ever used one of these here boats before?" Jed Boot enquired.

"Of course we have," replied Billy.

"Good," said Jed, "pick up them there oars and start rowing."

Billy and Nathan took an oar each and sat beside each other on the bench seat centrally positioned, before putting their oars into the respective rowlocks. Billy sat port-side on the left looking towards the stern, Nathan, starboard side on the right.

"Good morning," said Necho with a growl, "now turn the boat towards that dock over there and head for the east-end of the harbour, by that Church steeple in the distance."

Necho pointed his cat-o-nine-tails whip in the direction they should head and then flexed his whip, indicating that if they did not comply he would strike them.

Billy and Nathan were both experienced oarsmen simply because of their considerable use of the rowing boats in Fishersgate harbour. Soon they had this boat under their total joint control and were gliding through the waters of the bay of Taranto towards the harbour.

It was after they had turned their boat around towards the harbour they noticed that Garrett and Wheeler were in a second boat, accompanied by two of Necho's guards. It became clear that this second boat was heading for a different part of the harbour - the west end of Taranto harbour.

"No time for breakfast then?" enquired Nathan.

"You'll get your breakfast once we get ashore," replied Necho. "And just remember, any thoughts of running away or talking to anyone else when we get to the harbour will mean that I will send a message by pigeon post to Namidia to tell my guards to kill Billy's brother, Terry."

Necho continued, "I will not be killing the lovely Lilly as she now belongs to me and, on my return, I shall consummate our bond. But your brother - he means nothing to me."

"You really are a disgusting man," bellowed Nathan.

"Be quiet boy," retorted Necho.

"No, you listen to me," shouted Nathan, "if it takes me all my strength I will get you for this somehow, someday."

"Shut-up boy, you will never have the strength or the brains to get one over on me," and with that Necho struck Nathan across the face with his whip. Nathan fell backwards onto the hull of the little rowing boat writhing in pain. The oar he had been using fell into the water and began to drift away.

"Look what you have done now, Necho," said Jed Boot. "How are we going to get to shore with one oar?"

Jed called to his dog, "Shell, go get that oar." The dog sat there in the bottom of the boat without moving an inch. He looked at his master in wide-eyed doggy-style bewilderment. He was not the brightest of dogs.

With that Jed stood-up, removed his boots and exclaimed, "Oh well, I suppose it's time to get wet, I have the only dog in the world that gets his master to do the barking," before almost instantaneously diving into the water to swim a short distance to capture the oar.

Nathan, with a bloodied face, got himself up from the hull of the boat and sat up. He wasn't hurt badly. Holding his face with his hands trying to stem the trickle of blood, he looked at Necho in a disparaging way. He was trying to understand why someone from a peaceful race, such as the Namidians, could be so ruthless and violent. Billy went to help Nathan, but as he did so he also dropped his oar into the water.

"Shell, Shell," shouted Jed. "Go fetch that other oar." This time the dog jumped into the water and began swimming towards his master who was treading water after having caught hold of the first oar.

"No, no, don't come to me Shell, what a daft dog you are, go get that other oar on the other side of the boat."

The dog duly complied and swam around the back end of the rowing boat to the port-side, where he retrieved the oar by clamping it in his huge jaws.

"Good boy," shouted Jed Boot, "now take the oar back to the boat."

The dog swam back towards the boat pushing the oar along with his jaw. Nathan grabbed the oar from the dog at the gripper end before cautiously standing bolt upright, raising the oar above his head and striking Necho as hard as he could. Necho bellowed loudly and tried to stand up but the force of the blow to his head caused him to become dizzy and he fell backwards. Nathan continued to batter Necho with the edge of the paddle until Necho moved no more.

"You won't be sending any pigeon post to Namidia or anywhere else," said Nathan, as he turned to Billy. "Quick, Billy, help me throw him overboard," shouted Nathan.

Billy and Nathan struggled to lift the heavy body of the fat man from the stern of the boat, but they managed it somehow and, before long, Necho was floating face upwards in the water.

"What have you done," screamed Jed Boot. He swam close to the boat and Nathan snatched the recently retrieved oar from Jed's hands.

"You have killed our cash master, the man with the gold booty, you crazy boys."

With that, Billy placed both oars in their respective rowlocks and he and Nathan rowed the boat away from the occupants of the water as fast as they could.

Once they had distanced themselves by some twenty-yards Nathan threw the pirates boots into the water and shouted, "You will need these when you get to the shore, if you make it."

"I'll get you for this you... you... scallywags," retorted a very wet Jed Boot as he and his trusty dog, Shell, paddled their way towards Necho who was laying face-upwards, unknown to the boys, not dead, but unconscious in the water. The last the boys saw was Jed Boot performing a sea-faring rescue as he grabbed Necho from behind his body, held him around his upper chest and began a backward paddling swim towards the Star of the Sea ship. The dog duly followed. Billy and Nathan carried on with their journey and within half-an-hour were scrambling up the vertical ladder onto the dockside of Taranto. They abandoned their boat, as they found there was no rope anywhere nearby to tie it to the ladder and anyway, the last place they would want to go was back to the Star of the Sea ship.

In the distance, they could see the small rowing boat containing Garrett and Wheeler and their guards, heading for the other side of the docks - so they hatched a plan and ran as fast as they could to the west end of the harbour.

It was here that their plan came to fruition.

The boat arrived at the dockside and one of the guards tied a rope in the boat through a loop, fixed to a crudely built assembly of water drenched timbers situated at the foot of some wooden steps. The steps led upwards some seven yards to the head of the dock. The guard who secured the boat was at the bow of the boat, Garrett and Wheeler were in the middle seated on the rower's bench-seat, with the second guard positioned at the stern. Billy and Nathan had found something heavy on the dockside. It was a fortuitous find. It was a small timber barrel full of something - maybe rum. It wasn't a full-sized barrel, more a quarter size. But whatever it was... it was heavy - and exactly what they needed. Together they rolled it near to the dock edge. With one final push and a little bit of luck, they propelled it off the top of the dock for it to fall onto the rowing boat below.

Luck was certainly with them on that day for the barrel fell directly onto the guard at the bow end of the boat. They had knocked him out completely - maybe even killed him. He sprawled forwards, half-hanging over the side of the boat as the barrel bounced off his shoulders and head, continuing its journey on a gravitational downward motion. The barrel then struck the bottom of the boat and the force of the barrels' rim tore into the wooden structure causing a large hole. Immediately, sea water began to fill the boat - it was sinking.

"Get the other guard," shouted Nathan as he looked down onto the sinking vessel.

Garrett and Wheeler simultaneously lunged at the second guard who, on seeing the danger to hand, pulled out a dagger from his belt. What followed, appeared to be a slow-motion stand-off as the guard stood, dagger in hand, pointing it towards Garrett who was the closest. A few seconds later the guard suddenly thrust his dagger forward and, though Garrett was a very large boy, he was able to move out of the way very fast, but not fast enough. His upper arm had been caught and the blade caused a superficial cut. Blood seeped through his shirt as he fell backwards in shock, into the bottom of the water soaked boat. The salt in the seawater acted as a kind of antiseptic solution, for when the wound contacted the water Garrett screamed like a demented elephant. At this moment Wheeler picked up one of the boat's oars and struck the guard between the neck and the shoulder blade with the edge of the paddle. The guard was instantly disabled, he dropped his dagger into the boat and fell overboard into the water. Wheeler scrambled for the dagger and picked it up from the shallow water, which was by now gushing into the bottom of the boat.

"Quick," shouted Wheeler, as he helped his friend stand up. They clambered out of the sinking vessel and onto the dockside steps where they made their way to the top. Billy and Nathan were waiting for them and, as they arrived, both Wheeler and Garrett looked attentively at the two youngsters who had helped them escape. Garrett was whimpering in pain, but Wheeler began to stare into Billy's eyes. This was a stand-off. There was a moment of reflection during this single engagement as Billy recalled all the moments these two despicable characters had physically bullied him back in Fishersgate. What Wheeler was thinking now was anybody's guess. The stand-off seemed to last forever but the reality was it could only have been a fleeting moment. The glares and the silence were broken finally by Wheeler who spoke in a soft voice.

"Thank you, Billy, thank you, Nathan, for saving us."

Garrett nodded in agreement before looking down at his bloodied left arm, which he was holding with his right hand.

A sense of relief hit Billy full-on as Wheeler patted Billy on the back and said, "well-done mate."

"Come on," said Nathan," no time for sentimentality." He pointed to what looked like a dockside storage building with an open door.

"Let's get out of sight and fix Garrett's arm before we decide what to do next."

They made their way towards the storage building across the cobbled dockside of this uncannily quiet area - for no other human souls were about, though in the distance they could hear church bells ringing, so they knew that people were around.

Once inside the building it was clear that this was indeed a storage area for goods. It was a huge expanse of space, some 30 yards long, 20 yards wide and 5 yards high, pitching into a roof eloquently constructed with huge timber beams that were interlocked. It was completely empty and it looked as though nothing had been stored there for many months. In one corner of the building was a smaller room that contained some chairs and a table on a stone floor. They made themselves comfortable and Billy tended to Garrett's bloodied arm. The cut was not as bad as it looked. It was a shallow gash of about two inches, though there was a lot of blood to be cleaned away. Billy went in search of some clean water and something to dress the wound with, while the others stayed in the room.

Back outside, by the docks, it was clear once more that there was no one around. He walked up and down the dock area and still he saw no-one. So, he went down a side street where he saw a little cottage. He looked through the small window of the cottage to see a young girl of about his age sitting in an armchair sewing what looked like a ballerina's bodice. Just as he saw her she looked up towards the window to see him looking in. She jumped up from her seat, put down her sewing task and ran to the door at the front of the cottage before charging out into the street screaming something at him in Italian. It sounded quite nasty, but Billy couldn't understand what she was saying. Then she slapped him around the face.

He grabbed her wrists, one with each of his hands, to try to restrain her and calm her down but this just made her more determined to make as much noise as she possibly could.

Just then a group of very well-dressed people, of all ages, including a Catholic priest, turned the corner into the small cobbled street. Billy found out later that they had come from the church. It was Sunday. That was why the area had been so quiet. The whole village, except for the girl - who was a Muslim - had been at a Catholic church service.

Seeing the scene before them, two of the men from the group ran towards Billy as he restrained the girl. They grabbed him and he let go of the girl's wrists, whereupon she slapped him across the face once more and shouted something derogatory to him. Everyone in the group was talking in an excited manner though Billy could not understand a word of it. From the back of the group came a man wearing a huge walrus-style moustache. He seemed to be in charge. He said something to the girl and she replied. Billy could not comprehend.

He then approached Billy and asked him "Che cosa stai facendo qui boy?"

"I cannot speak your language," replied Billy.

The man looked puzzled and then repeated himself. "Che cosa stai facendo qui?" [What are you doing here?]

Just then an elderly woman came forward, ably assisted by her walking stick to help her keep her balance, and said something to the man in her native Italian.

"Credo che egli è in lingua inglese?" she said.

"Inglese," said the man.

221

"Sì, Inglese," she replied.

She turned to Billy who was still being restrained by the two men, and in a kindly but firm voice and with an enquiring smile asked, "Are you from England?"

"Yes, I am," replied a relieved Billy, who knew that now someone could understand him he might be better able to explain his situation.

The woman turned to the man with the walrus moustache and said, "Egli è l'inglese. Permettetemi di chiedere di lui alcuni le domande." [He is English, let me ask him some questions.]

"Molto bene," the man replied.

She then returned her attention to Billy.

"My name is Priscilla and I am pleased to meet you. An English boy, it is a real honour for me to meet you for we do not get very many English people in this village. What is your name?"

Billy responded sheepishly, "It's Billy."

"Well… Billy, we would like to know what you are doing here in our village?"

She seemed like a very kindly old lady and Billy warmed to her immediately. They spoke for a short while in English and, by the time introductions were over, Billy had learned that she had been a teacher of English to Italian students in her younger days. She had lived in Spain, as well as having lived in England for over five years after she married a Spanish Captain of the Merchant Navy, who regularly called at Taranto harbour. They moved to England at the beginning of the long war against France, under a Naval exchange programme. After he died, in about 1695, two years before the end of the war, she moved back to her beloved village of Taranto in Italy. It was a bitter-sweet return, for Italy was still under the domination of the Spanish. Since then Spanish power had waned and the Austrian nation had seized power. How sad she looked when she spoke of this part of Italy being in an impoverished state under the Austrians. This was Billy's lucky day for it transpired that she really did like the English. And when Billy said that he was from Fishersgate the old woman's eyes lit up with delight.

'Here we go again,' thought Billy to himself, 'every time I mention Fishersgate... people get excitable.'

But no-one else got excited at the name Fishersgate - only the old woman.

The crowd of people of Taranto gathered closely around to hear what Billy had to say and every now and again the old woman broke into Italian to give them an update of exactly what Billy had said. By this time the two men restraining Billy had released their grip and everyone around was smiling at their newly found English friend. And Billy told them the whole story, about his mother and father, about his grandad who lived in the year 1934. He told them about the day he travelled back in time with his brother and friends to the year of 1734 and of all their adventures since then, right up until that present moment in time. During the conversation, and as soon as the old woman found out about others hiding in the warehouse, she summoned a group of Italian men to go and fetch them. By the end of Billy's story, Garrett had been medically patched-up with a suitable bandage on his arm and he, Nathan and Wheeler were smiling at their enthusiastic supporters who had brought them out into the sunshine.

The old woman was interested in the fact that the boys had recently travelled from Namidia. "Did you see my son while you were there?" she enquired, "He is Captain Antonio Sorrento of the Italian army and he went to Namidia to look for his fiancée, Teresa, who was abducted."

"I am sorry," said Billy "I have not heard that name before and I did not hear of him while I was there. I hope you find them both someday."

"There are few days left for me," said the old woman, "for I am 102 years old."

Billy changed the subject. "And I wish my brother Terry was with me right now. He always knows what to do in difficult situations."

The old woman looked sad as she pondered briefly on memories of her son Antonio. "He has been missing for many months and I fear for his life. The Namidians will tell you they are a peaceful nation but they are not. There is a particularly nasty person called Necho among them, a so-called leader. The Namidians come here sometimes to rape and pillage. So do the Scorians and when both tribes are here at the same time they fight each other. We are only safe from the Namidians and the Scorians when the Austrian armies are here, but they rarely bother to come down to this region anymore."

"We know about him, we know Necho," said Billy. "We left him half-dead, maybe dead and that pirate Jed Boot was swimming around him in the water about seventy yards off-shore. In fact, I am very surprised we have not seen Jed Boot yet, he must have swum back to the ship. Unless he did swim to shore... who knows?"

"Good," said the old woman, "I have heard of Jed Boot as well, I hope they are both dead."

The old woman said something to one of the men in Italian and he dispatched several men along the dock-side at intervals of fifty yards to stand guard.

As the crowd began to disband the woman said that they were going to the City Hall with another man. She would go with them to translate until they saw the mayor, who could also speak English.

Over a late lunch that afternoon, consisting of boiled goat's head, onions, cabbage, sprouts and some red grapes, polished off with a glass of red wine, all very finely presented at the village hall, the boys told their various stories to the old woman and the mayor. She passed on the details, in Italian, to all those in attendance - those prominent, important and pompous people that every city has.

Of course, their story of time-travel sounded a little far-fetched and most of the audience listening to the boy's stories did not believe them. They continually questioned this matter of time-travel - for them, it was an impossible concept.

But not for the old woman. She knew about such things. She told the boys that she was a benefactor of secrets. She knew they had come from the year 1934. She had heard of the child of Fishersgate who could unlock the secrets of the Second Chapter.

One of the things the old woman, Priscilla, spoke about was that sometime in the future, maybe in the year of 1975, over two hundred years in the future, a former child of 1934 Fishersgate would return to the harbour. He would arrive at Fishersgate bay in a rowing boat. The name of that boat was *Doris*. He would wear a long dark trench coat, with the collar turned up, and a large black trilby hat that hid his facial features from three sides. He had been away from Fishersgate for a long time. He had been away since 1934. He wanted to see Fishersgate bay as soon as he possibly could.

"And so, it shall be, on an early morning on a cold but bright autumn day he will stand by the shore, looking out over Fishersgate bay. This is the day that he will survey his former playground. And he must go there, though I do not know the reason - but it has something to do with the Second Chapter which must emit its magical power from and into the First Chapter," she said.

"How do you know about the Second Chapter?" blurted Nathan.

"It is written in folklore," replied the old woman, "I do not know where the Chapter is located. But let me tell you what I do know. These skills came from my late husband who told the story of magnificent technical achievements that swept right across Italy, Spain and North Africa many years ago. Our nations had horseless-carriages that were driven by a self-propelled power source, we had smooth pathways to run our machines upon, we could travel hundreds of miles in a few hours. We flew men into space, to the moon and back. We had sound boxes which transmitted voices and music over long distances, and tiny machines that could calculate and solve the most difficult of mathematical problems. There were flying machines and machines for going deep into the ocean seas. There were automatic machines for washing clothes and other machines for drying them. We had almost eradicated every known disease known to humans and life was good for all of us."

"Yes," interrupted Billy," we have heard a story like this before."

The old woman continued, "Then it happened. A natural phenomenon damaged this planet. It was a large asteroid. Millions of people died and just a few hundred survived. Before long we had poverty, disease, and famine. We had lost all of our abilities to build fantastic machines, grow food efficiently, build infrastructures and cure all known diseases."

"But people don't just forget how to do things overnight," said Nathan.

"No boy," replied the old woman, "it took nearly a hundred years to forget those technical secrets. The whole area, from Northern Italy to the Sahara Desert, from England to Egypt, the most civilized areas of the world were blown apart by the asteroid. There were no raw materials to make anything with - everything had been wiped out."

"But we were told that it was a race called the Scorians that ended technology," said Billy.

"No," said the old woman, "it was not them. However, they did make matters worse after the asteroid struck, they are a warrior race - we see them around here from time to time looking for the Second Chapter, but it was not them that finally ended civilization, it was the giant asteroid."

Billy and Nathan were confused but had too many questions to ask of the old woman.

"But when did the asteroid hit our planet?" asked Nathan, "there are plenty of people about these days, more than just a few hundred, why... we must have seen thousands of people since we have been in 1734."

Billy nodded in agreement.

The old woman responded, "it was thirteen thousand years ago that the asteroid hit our planet."

Billy and Nathan both gasped before Nathan added, "So this technology has been lost for thousands of years?"

"Yes," replied the old woman. "The secrets that could be remembered were written down by those few survivors after the asteroid struck, for they knew that one day the raw materials would again be readily available once man had learned to mine them and they wanted future generations to know their secrets of technology. But only to worthy people, not the warring tribes like the Scorians or anyone else like them. That is why they set a date and a time when the books could be opened and named the people who would open them."

"And who would they be?" enquired Billy.

"A child of Fishersgate," came the reply from the old woman.

Billy and Nathan both looked at each other in amazement.

"But how would they know about Fishersgate all those years ago," asked Billy.

"Only God knows the answer to your question," said the old woman.

"But what about this monk named Catald?" said Billy, "he was the man that was shipwrecked off the Italian coast, near to this city of Taranto. He was rescued and he survived.

I have been told that he found the Second Chapter and used its contents to protect the city against the plague, growing plentiful foods in abundance, making delicious wines and creating engineering designs that persistently protected the city against floods. His mastery of the elements led to him being immortalised and treated as a king. Was this city not saved by this Monk who later became the Archbishop and later Saint Catald. Some said it was the Second Chapter that gave him the practical knowledge he needed which gave him the guidance to avoid these natural calamities."

"Yes", interrupted the woman, "Catald did save this city but he did not do it with the Second Chapter. That is a myth that could never be true for Catald never found the Second Chapter. Catald saved this city by performing miracles created by God himself. I believe that fact to be true."

Billy asked, "So what about this early morning in 1975, that you told us about. What did you say? When a child of Fishersgate will stand by the shore of Fishersgate bay. Why must he go there?"

"I do not yet know the answer to your question," replied the old woman, "but let me tell you this - it has been said that only a child of Fishersgate can unlock the secrets of the Second Chapter, so this visit to the future has to be coming soon. Surely, you as the children of Fishersgate will make that happen."

"But why the Second Chapter," asked Garrett. "Where is the First Chapter?"

Billy and Nathan looked over towards Garrett in amazement.

"That's quite an intelligent question coming from you Garrett," said Nathan

Wheeler laughed as a puzzled Garrett looked at him in bemusement.

"A very good question," said the old woman, in a very matter of fact response that any school teacher would give. "We already have the First Chapter here in our village."

"You have it!" exclaimed Wheeler.

"Yes, we do," said the old woman, "but do not get excited for it does not tell us any secrets about mastering technology because we cannot open it. It is bound by a clasp, a magical clasp that cannot be opened. Believe you me, many men have tried to open this book using all sorts of implements and sometimes just with their bare hands... all have failed. And anyone attempting to open the book forcibly more than twice is burnt alive in a ball of flames. There is no trace of them after the flame of death has extinguished itself. They vanish."

"Wow," replied Billy.

"Can I see this book?" asked Wheeler.

"Me too," said Garrett.

"I think that we would all like to see the book," said Nathan. Billy nodded in agreement.

"No-one can see the book at this moment for the mayor has ordered it to be locked away from public view. Only the master of the keys can open the safe it is contained within," said the old woman.

"But we know where the Second Chapter is located."

The mayor gasped, "You do?"

"It's right here in Taranto. Wentworth the old soothsayer told us," said Nathan.

The old woman spoke in Italian to the mayor of the town. The conversation became energetic and animated as question after question was asked by the mayor with the old woman responding. The conversation ended when the old woman asked the boys if they were sure that the Second Chapter was in Taranto. The boys said it was and the old woman once more engaged in an Italian conversation with the mayor.

"Very well," said the old woman, "the mayor has agreed that you can see the First Chapter provided you think you will find enough information to be able to take him and his officials to find the Second Chapter immediately afterwards."

The boys agreed to this and were then told that they would be sleeping in the City Hall that night and that the First Chapter would be brought to them in the morning, once the 'master of the keys' who was out of town that day, returned to begin his weekly official tasks. It would be the next day, a Monday, that the safe containing the book would be opened.

That evening, around seven o'clock, the boys were taken to a ground floor hall where they were given supper and supplied with sufficient bedding for the night. After they were left alone Billy reflected on the day with Nathan and his newly found friends Garrett and Wheeler. They all made each other laugh as they mimicked Jed Boot, Necho and some of the pompous Italian officials who had been their hosts earlier in the day.

Suddenly there was a distinct knock on the door.

"Who is that?" asked Garrett.

"How should I know," replied Billy.

All four boys laughed. Wheeler went to the door and opened it. The old woman was standing outside with the girl Billy had first encountered at the cottage.

"Hello boys," said the old woman. "I have brought Catrina to see you, she wants to say sorry to Billy for screaming at him earlier today."

A slightly embarrassed Billy said that she did not need to apologise and it was him that should apologise for looking through the cottage window and frightening her. Billy thought Catrina was a pretty girl and he suddenly became very embarrassed in her presence. Up until then he had not really thought much about girls and they certainly had no effect on him. But Catrina was different. He had previously thought that girls were just an annoying breed who stopped boys from playing all sorts of exciting games with other boys. He had seen this change in his brother Terry, after Terry had begun to fall in love with Lilly.

The old woman explained that an apology was not the only reason they were there.

"Catrina makes dresses for ballerinas. She sells them to the clockmaker - the master of time. He employs the services of the ballerinas and a flute player."

"So, what," said Nathan.

"Look out for the clockmaker, for he appears with his flute player and ballerinas whenever a time-portal to the past or future is nearby."

"You mean we can get back to 1934?" asked Garrett.

"It's possible, but dangerous," said the old woman.

"Wait a minute," said Nathan, "do you remember, Billy, when we came across old Wentworth's shop in the tunnel… that had a clock and flute player and ballerinas."

"Yes, I do," said Billy, "and it was near to a portal into time because that is when we first arrived in Namidia after having travelled from Fishersgate through the lock-gate compound. That lock-gate was a time-portal and so was the tunnel by Wentworth's shop. We need to get back to Namidia and find Wentworth's shop."

"No, you don't," said the old woman. "These portals to time are all around the world and can only be used by those who are selected to use them. There is probably one here in Taranto, but you can only use it when you have completed your task."

"And what task is that?" enquired Wheeler.

"To unlock the secrets of the Second Chapter, of course," came the reply.

"Can Catrina take us to the clockmaker?" asked Billy.

"She cannot, for no-one has seen the clockmaker. She makes her ballerina outfits and leaves them in the warehouse near to her cottage. By the next morning, they are gone and payment is left in gold. People have waited and hidden to see the clockmaker but he has never appeared; yet still, the ballerina goods disappear and the gold is left."

The old woman continued, "But remember this; when you find a time-portal you must remember that as the clock strikes the thirteenth chime the wooden panel in the stone wall will open and three ballet dancers, each dressed in a white tutu will dance their way to the centre of the room. The flute player will begin his tune as they dance for a short while in unison. And while they dance a golden goblet will appear, as if from nowhere, into the hands of the central dancer. She will hold the goblet above her head, twirl around then lower it to sip some of the contents before passing it to another dancer. The second dancer carries out the same routine before passing the goblet to the third dancer whereupon the whole process starts again. It is at this point that one of you must take the goblet from one of the dancers and take a sip of its contents yourself. You must then pass it to each of your friends who are travelling in time with you on that day and lastly, after all of you have drunk from the goblet, you must pass it back to the same dancer you had taken it from. Then you must go to the tunnel and select your route. If you choose the wrong tunnel you will not go to the place you desire. But you must be quick. After they have performed their dance routine they will take a low curtsey and as they rise to '*first position*' a huge plume of smoke and a flash of light will engulf the three of them and they will disappear. You will have missed the opportunity and have to wait until the next thirteenth hour."

"Well, that's a lot to remember," said Garrett.

"I know," said Wheeler.

"What happens if the drink in the goblet has gone before the last of us takes a sip?" asked Nathan.

"It will never run dry for it is a perpetual fluid, an elixir of time-travel," replied the old woman.

"Leave it to me," smiled Billy, "I will remember all of those instructions. But how do we find one of these time-portals?"

"Once you have unlocked the secrets of the Second Chapter you will know where they are," said the old woman, "and now it is time for us to go, so I bid you goodnight."

Catrina smiled at Billy and said, "Buonanotte", [Goodnight]. There was an obvious mutual attraction between the two of them as they looked deeply into each other's eyes and Billy felt the butterfly effect in his stomach. This was something he had not experienced before. Soon the four boys were on their own again, so they settled down for the night and fell asleep.

Chapter 9

The battle begins

"You really are a lucky man, Necho," slurred Jed Boot as he loomed over his poorly ungrateful patient, laying before him in the semi-darkened sick bay of the Star of the Sea ship.

"Go away Boot," murmured Necho, as he lay on the side of his body with his eyes closed, facing away from Boot.

"Oh, that's the sort of thanks that I get for saving your life," replied Boot as he took another swig from a half-empty bottle of rum. Boot staggered, then held onto an overhead beam to steady himself.

Necho swung his large frame onto his back as he opened his eyes and looked Jed Boot straight in the eye.

"You only saved me because of my gold and I bet you rifled through my pockets while I was unconscious."

Boot did not reply.

As Necho moved his body about the bed he groaned with pain more than once. Jed Boot smirked and took another gulp from the bottle.

"Drunk, I am and all 'cos of you Necho; drenched through I am with that blasted sea-water, after jumping in the drink to get that oar for the boat."

Necho held his forehead, which was covered in several dirty-white swathes of bandages. These were cloaking the entire top of his head.

"I wish this pain would go," he grumbled before returning to the subject of gold.

"Well, you'll never find the gold that's hidden aboard this ship... and you will not get any of it until I have that Second Chapter book in my possession," said Necho.

Then Necho told Boot that he had summoned his personal assistant to send a message by pigeon back to Namidia ordering them to kill Terry. "The two that escaped are stupid boys," whimpered Necho in a manner suited to his injuries. "I warned those two boys, Billy and Nathan, that if they absconded I would kill the older one. It's their own fault that Terry now must die."

Jed turned on Necho, "They are not the stupid ones Necho, you and I are the stupid ones for letting two boys escape. Why, they are not even men and they beat us. It's disgraceful - and we don't even have the book yet. So, killing one of them back in Namidia isn't going to make the slightest bit of difference."

Jed took yet another swig from the bottle. "Here Shell, you have a drink too." He tipped some rum from the bottle into the cup of his hand and the dog lapped it up.

"Good boy," said Boot. The dog barked in delight, though it was clear that Shell was also a bit unsteady on his feet - as was his master.

While Necho was smarting that Terry would be killed, little did he know that Terry had already escaped the castle in Namidia with Antonio and a band of fighting men. In fact, Terry and Antonio were well on their way towards Taranto with Necho's wife and brother, Mr. Josef, who were their prisoners. The hand of destiny was indeed in the favour of Terry and Antonio.

That was the problem with pigeon post in the eighteenth century; it was only a one-way messaging system. These were 'homing' pigeons, they flew home to the castle from any location they were set free from with tightly wrapped messages affixed to their feet. They could not fly in the opposite direction from the castle to the ship, for they would not know where the ship was positioned in the vast seas of the Mediterranean.

Just then Necho's eyes glazed over as he pointed to something behind Jed Boot.

"And get rid of that monkey," warned Necho, "it's been annoying me all night."

Jed Boot looked around to a wooden shelf on the far side of the sickbay cabin.

"Monkey... what monkey?" enquired Boot.

"That one there," pointed a frightened Necho. "Get him away from me! Get him away... he keeps smiling at me."

"I see no monkey," said a puzzled Boot.

"Yes... there he is... right there," exclaimed an ever agitated Necho as he pointed to the corner of the room before trying to get up off the bed - to no avail. "That monkey," he continued, "it just came walking in through the port-hole in that wall and now he is sitting there flashing his diamond encrusted collar and eating bananas - one after the other."

Jed Boot looked again in the direction Necho was indicating.

"There is no monkey in this cabin, Necho. Good God man, have you been drinking my rum?"

"It's there, it's there," pointed an agitated Necho towards the empty shelf in the corner of the room.

"There is certainly no monkey, let alone one adorned with a diamond collar," retorted Boot. "Do you really think

I would stay sitting here if a monkey wearing diamonds was sitting just over there?"

"Get him away from me," shouted Necho.

"There is no monkey," shouted a frustrated Jed Boot, "for I would surely have strangled the bleeder by now and taken the diamonds. If you don't shut-up Necho I will be strangling you in a minute."

At that moment Necho fell backwards, flat on his back and passed out, snoring profusely. Jed Boot decided that this was, therefore, the end of the conversation, for the time being, so he made his way up the steps onto the main deck. He had drunk enough rum. What was next on his agenda was a restful snooze somewhere. He would look for a quiet area on deck and snooze in the sunshine.

It was a fine breeze that blew through the timber masts of the magnificent structure of the Star of the Sea. The ship was at anchor. The sails had been lowered the night before and wrapped around the main horizontal beams, sometimes called rafts.

Suddenly one of the boy's in the crow's nest shouted down to the crew, "Ship Ahoy."

Captain Pickering, who was on the poop-deck discussing matters with his first officer, casually raised his telescope to view the approaching vessel in the distance.

With a look of horror stretched across his well-worn face, he quickly lowered his telescope before handing it to the first officer. "It's the Scorian Santa Nicholas ship, we must make sail fast. We are a sitting duck anchored here by the shoreline."

"I agree," said the first officer, "it is a Scorian ship, much more powerful than ours in cannon alone, much bigger in length - surely they must have two-hundred more fighting men than we have."

Pickering took the telescope back, looked again through its lenses and issued the order, "all-hands-on-deck." This was repeated, the words reverberating around the structure of the giant ship as men of all ranks steadfastly shouted it. This was a matter of urgency. Next to the ship's wheel on the deck was the ship's bell which was rung in a rapid manner by the navigator. Soon the decks were swarming with a hundred and fifty men or more as the orders to 'man the yardarm', 'raise the anchor' and 'hoist the mizzen sails' were given. This was the beginning of the process that would see the ship in full sail within minutes, depending upon wind conditions and the detail of the Captain's orders.

"The leading wind will take us offshore," said the Captain. "That's where we shall head, we have a full hour before we make contact with the Scorian ship. If we can gain position, we will fight them at sea. We will be ready for them on their arrival."

Sailors scrambled everywhere, on the rigging, up the masts, clearing decks of any obstructions, preparing the cannons on the decks below and preparing to empty the gunpowder store in a detailed pre-planned manner. It was a well-oiled procedure that they had practiced many times before... only this time it was real.

Within half-an-hour, the ship had positioned itself out in the open sea. It was clear that the Scorian ship had identified them as the enemy and was sailing directly towards them. Captain Pickering knew he had maybe two chances to get a good shot at the Scorian vessel as it approached his ship, head-on.

Pickering positioned his ship with the bow facing directly towards the oncoming Scorian vessel, adjusting its position as the approaching ship's course changed. Pickering was waiting for the moment he might fire his carronade cannons, which were positioned at the foc'sle, part of the ship. This area is a small part of the bow deck at the extreme tip of the front of the ship. There were only two carronade cannons positioned at this part of the ship, facing forward. Being able to fire one-hundred pounder cannon balls forward, some 100 yards, these were the most useful cannons onboard. A carronade cannonball could smash through the enemies' hull with devastating effect and just one good shot could end this battle before it was likely to begin. If a proper judgement of distance was made, Pickering's men could do some damage to the Santa Nicholas before the two ships met broadside.

Once broadside, the two vessels would be facing each other, side onwards and the might of the rest of their cannons would be tested. The Santa Nicholas had much more firepower than the Star of the Sea as the number of useable cannons they had at their disposal was far greater. It was likely that the Santa Nicholas would win. Pickering's only realistic plan was the carronade cannons which, if judged correctly, would deny the Santa Nicholas the chance of using its broadside cannons on the Star of the Sea.

As Captain Pickering announced imminent action stations he became aware of the need for sustenance for some of his men. He ordered that the cabin boys and those unfit for battle duty should take food to the action stations. Salted beef, dried peas, biscuits and cheese were duly distributed among the soon-to-be warriors. It would be about a half-hour more before the Scorian ship would be in gunshot range of the Star of the Sea, so they took that precious time to refresh themselves, to tend to their personal comforts and to take that tot of rum, to which each man and boy was entitled.

These sailors knew that this could be their last meal - washed down with a final tot of rum. Each man knew that the approaching Scorian ship was far more powerful than their own ship, the Namidian Star of the Sea, and that only a miracle from God could save them. Some sailors openly prayed to him for help; that they might survive their imminent ordeal and return to their family back home in Namidia in safety and with God's speed. The gold Booty promised to them was a far distant memory, for it did not matter anymore.

Necho had no worries at all. He was out cold. His gold was well hidden, for what it was worth, at this time of battle and likely death. He was oblivious to everything for he remained unconscious in his bunk in the sick-bay... snoring like a demented pig. Jed Boot, on the other hand, took another tot of rum and became resigned to the fact that he would now have to forsake his afternoon nap.

The Scorian ship relentlessly forced its way through the resistance of the Mediterranean surf, the wind filling its sails full to the brim - providing a propulsion so powerful and so natural, as to push the might of the entire ship at a speedy rate of knots towards its battle position, with all who sailed aboard her working the ropes and pulleys.

The two ships became ever closer as the minutes ticked away. Captain Pickering ordered his men to stay calm and fire the cannons only on his orders. Pickering could see the outlines of the faces of his enemy and soon realised that this was a ship captained by his old adversary, Captain Rodrigues, of the Scorian navy. The ship that Rodrigues commanded was the Santa Nicholas. Pickering smiled as he heard the drum roll coming from the other ship. It was a variation of the Scorian drum role of impending battle to the death - the distinctive battle drum roll that only Captain Rufus Emmanuel José Miguel Rodrigues himself used, before engaging with the enemy. This was to become a survive-or-perish situation for both Captains. They had met each other in several battles during the past twenty-years and each time both had survived to fight another day. Would today be any different Pickering wondered, and yet he knew that the odds of them both surviving battle once more had to be very slim.

Various other commands were relayed from Captain Pickering to the men controlling the ship's navigation and several sails were re-positioned to place the ship in an advantageous position, relative to the oncoming enemy and all exactly as Pickering had wanted it. Men were posted high above the deck, among the rigging of the ship armed with muskets, ready to pick-off sailors, especially officers and masters of the ship, on the decks of the opposing vessel as it approached. Grappling hooks, boarding axes and cutlasses were at the ready for when Pickering and his men hoped they would have the Santa Nicholas within reach. If the battle took the ships side-by-side they could board and commence hand-to-hand fighting.

"I hope he knows what he is doing," exclaimed Boot to one of his disciples.

There was no time for a response. The bow of the ship gently rose on the crest of a wave and, momentarily, time stood still. This was the critical moment that Captain Pickering had been waiting for. Time, height, luck and bravado versus the perils of misjudging the distance.

"Fire the right carronade cannon," shouted Pickering. "NOW!" A huge explosion emanated from inside the chamber of the right-hand carronade cannon and a mighty thrust of energy forced the 100-pound cannonball out of its cavity towards the Santa Nicholas. A split second later Pickering heard the carronade cannon of the Santa Nicholas thrust a cannonball towards his ship, the Star of the Sea. Time stood still once more as the two cannon balls ravaged ahead of gun-powdered flames that each ship's cannon had thrust towards their respective targets.

Magical history books have long-since written about this moment in time. This moment when the Namidians met with the Scorians in the Mediterranean Sea in the late autumn months of 1734 and how luck presided for only one of the Captains. The other was to die. This was an historical turning point in the history of the two nations as the Star of the Sea battled with the Santa Nicholas.

Pickering and Rodrigues were from two different backgrounds, Pickering from the gentler nation of Namidia and Rodrigues from the warrior nation of the Scorians. Each however respected the other as they had both spent much time together during their teenage years when both had found themselves on the mainland of Taranto one summer in 1689. It was here that they had become friends, at a time when relationships between Namidia and Scoria were less onerous. It was a summer spent in each other's company and the company of young Italian women. This became a summer of lust and love for both young men. It was a summer of learning about their inner selves during that transitional period when boys became men. Both had honed their personal fighting skills with the sword during that year. Both became accomplished in matters of duty that future military officers of the elite members of their respective nations would need. Both were destined to become potential members of the ruling classes. It was also a time for frolics and fun in the hot summer sun. All of this lasted for only one season, not even three months. And when it was done Pickering went back to Namidia and Rodrigues to Scoria, each man to join his respective Navy to learn the skills of handling magnificent sailing ships on the high-seas. They parted as friends but became enemies due to complicated national identities and federal pride, which would not allow them the simplistic pleasures of a continuing personal friendship. It is to both men's individual credit that in later life they both became Captains of their vessels. And now they were enemies. They had been enemies for many years, each fighting for their own nationalistic causes. Such was the mixture of these two warring nations, as was Necho's birth secret. For Necho, who was currently out cold in the sick-bay of the Star of the Sea, was indeed half Namidian and half Scorian. His father a Scorian and mother a Namidian had also met in Taranto many years before. It was a complete secret to his symbolic brother, Mr. Josef, and to the Namidian people that Necho was half Scorian. No wonder his personal characteristics were sometimes aggressive. Necho had used the Namidian pedigree of his mother, who came from a high-class family, to rise through the ranks of the Namidian political system, finally attaining the rank of joint leader of the country along with his symbolic brother, Mr. Josef. He was, in fact, a spy - for most of his loyalties were with his father's tribe in Scoria, which is where Necho had fed all his information during the past twelve years. It was all in search of the lost Chapter, which the fruition of his efforts - subject to the outcome of this imminent sea battle - were about to become a reality.

And what of Jed Boot, where was he from originally? This former pirate, now semi-retired, was a prodigy of the pirate Captain Teach, otherwise known as Blackbeard. Blackbeard was a frightening man who wore a large beard with long hair straddling from his hat. His appearance was as terrifying as his reputation which often preceded him. Jed Boot had sailed with Blackbeard, the legendary fearsome pirate, around the islands of the Caribbean during the early part of the eighteenth century and was nearby when he died in 1718. Boot made his escape on a sloop named '*Adventure*' from the Caribbean to Europe where he met Necho in Morocco and, before long, had moved to Namidia to be a protectorate and enforcer of Necho's power.

And here they all were, men with different upbringings and backgrounds. Pickering, Necho and Boot on the ship of the Star of the Sea and Rodrigues aboard the Santa Nicholas, in a moment in time that was, later, to become magical history.

And then, that moment in time became past time and history had been made. The shot that Captain Pickering's men had fired hit the bow of the Santa Nicholas above its water-line, just as the ship rolled the crest of a shallow wave. It was a perfect shot. The ship was soon taking in water at an alarming rate. This single shot from the carronade cannon on the Star of the Sea had crippled the Scorian boat. Luck was on Pickering's side for the cannonball fired from the Santa Nicholas missed its target.

But danger was not yet passed for Captain Pickering and his crew. The momentum of the two ships was on-going. They continued to travel towards each other; each propelled by the forces of nature. But for every yard that the Santa Nicholas travelled water gushed into the newly formed hole in its bow. Soon they would be meeting each other head-on and that would be followed by broadside action. It was less than a minute away.

Pickering knew that the Santa Nicholas outgunned his ship and once both ships became broadside the Star of the Sea could receive a serious battering from enemy cannons. Pickering wanted to avoid this at all costs, so he ordered that his ship be turned hard starboard. This was a risky operation for it meant that the sharp action on the rudder could force it to break under the pressures of the sea's strong current. If that happened, then they would be rudderless - unable to steer the ship and befall themselves to the mercy of the tidal forces and undercurrents. But it was the only way to put some distance between the two ships quickly. It had to be done.

After the order had been implemented the ship diverted heavily to one side. It seemed to work, though a few enemy cannon shots did hit the mast and top deck of the Star of the Sea. It was light damage and easily repairable, once the battle had ended. A few minutes later they were out of range and the firepower of the Santa Nicholas could no longer reach them. A huge cheer went up from the men on the decks as they watched the Santa Nicholas slowly sink beneath the waves as it succumbed to the ravaging sea waters which filled its hold below decks. Hundreds of men abandoned their ship and at least four rowing boats made their way from the devastating scene. Pickering raised his telescope and watched his old friend, Captain Rufus Emmanuel José Miguel Rodrigues, standing firmly on the deck, alone, holding the ship's wheel in a determined and authoritative manner. As the ship sank deeper into the sea and the waters were rushing about his waistline, Captain Rodrigues performed one last act. He saluted in a way that only a Naval captain of stature could. And he held that salute as he disappeared to his grave beneath the surf. It was a poignant moment for Captain Pickering.

Pickering had already decided that he would not try to rescue any of the enemy sailors for they would surely overwhelm his ship. Food and other resources would be used much quicker if he took prisoners, so he left them to die a sailors' death in the warm ravaging shark-infested waters of the Mediterranean seas.

Pickering's thoughts about his ships future were clear. The ship would return to its mooring point off the coast of Taranto and he would dispatch a small crew, including Jed Boot, to find those young escapees, Billy Burton and his friends.

Chapter 10

Ghostly encounter

There was a thud on the door to the council chamber. The door opened and in walked a man of small stature. He was the Master of the Keys and was attired with two large bunches of keys attached to his belt. Following him was the Mayor of Taranto. To Billy's delight, Catrina followed them into the room and he immediately went over to her and smiled. She returned the compliment and they gazed into each other's eyes for one brief moment. Suddenly, something awoke in Billy. It was something that he had not experienced before… something that started in his belly and caused him to pleasantly tingle.

Billy and the boys had been awake for some time. Everyone had slept well the previous night and now they were excited because they would soon be in possession of the First Chapter and, later that day, would hope to find the Second Chapter. This was one step nearer to getting back to Fishersgate. Shortly after breakfast, which comprised of some bread, cheese and red grapes, they made their way into the rooms situated below ground level - directly beneath the city hall.

In the semi-darkness, they watched as the Master of the Keys opened a safe buried into the stone wall. He pulled out a book about foolscap folio size and about half-an-inch thick. They all gathered around this important artefact, though the giant frames of Garrett and Wheeler dominated the scene. The book cover was deep red in colour but it could have been brown, given the dim lighting. On one side of the volume was a hasp and lock that kept the expensively bound impenetrable thick covers firmly closed. Impatient, Wheeler took the book from the Master of the Keys and tried to release the clasp - but it remained firm. Garrett tried too, but the book remained secure. Neither could unlock the secrets of the book.

Catrina, who had been holding an oil filled lantern, brought the flame closer to the cover of the book. Given the additional lighting, it was clear that the book was indeed deep red in colour and from the sparkling golden reflection enhanced by the lantern in the dimmed-light, it was clear that a gold inscription was imbedded in the front cover.

"What does it say?" asked Garrett.

"Don't know," replied Wheeler, "it's in Latin."

"Let me have a look," said Billy, as he gently pushed his way past Garrett and Wheeler. The two giant boys obliged and they made way for Billy and Nathan to get nearer to the hardback book.

"It says, Palma imprimere percipo," said Billy.

"What does that mean Billy?" enquired Nathan.

Billy did not answer for he was looking at the second line of the inscription. *Filiorum autem Fishersgate.*

The word *Fishersgate* had caught his eye.

Nathan had seen it too. "Look, Billy," he exclaimed, "Fishersgate."

"I see it," replied Billy, as he focused on the inscription's meaning.

Underneath the text was an engraved outline of a human hand. Not a man's hand or a baby's hand - it was in-between the two sizes. It was a boy's hand. A hand about Billy's size.

Billy looked at the inscription once more and at the outline of the hand-print.

The whole thing translates, *"Handprint secured; Children of Fishersgate,"* said Billy.

"I wonder what would happen if I placed my hand onto the engraving," Nathan asked.

"Don't know," replied Billy, "try it!"

Nathan placed his hand onto the cover of the book directly over the engraved hand. His hand engulfed the engraving and sight of it was momentarily lost. Nathan tried the hasp - it was firmly closed.

"Let me try," said Billy.

Billy put his hand onto the book's outlined hand. His own hand fitted perfectly inside the engraved outline. It was almost as if someone had drawn a pencil line around his fingers and thumb. The handprint was indeed, unique to Billy.

Suddenly the sound of a flute emitted from inside the book, followed by the faint sound of several twinkling bells playing in unison.

There was a click and the lock and hasp holding the book together released on its own.

A gasp of amazement from the Master of the Keys to the Mayor of Taranto filled the chamber and, as the sounds echoed away, Catrina said something nice to Billy. He did not have a clue what she said but the tone of her voice suggested one of support, congratulations, and excitement.

The mayor pushed himself forward to be nearer the book. "This is absolutely fantastic," he said. "Our people have waited many years for this moment… What is inside?" he asked, as Billy opened the book.

"Let's have a look," said Billy, as he viewed the first page. "It looks like the plan of a building."

Bored with this image, Billy opened the second page. It was completely blank. So was the third, fourth and fifth. In fact, all the pages were blank - except for the last page, which had about five-hundred randomly printed Latin words, each with a Roman numerical marking beside it.

Billy was puzzled. The words did not make any sense for none of them made a cohesive sentence. These were fragmented individual words.

"I don't understand," said Billy.

"Go back to the first page for a moment," said the mayor.

Billy duly obliged and the mayor studied the layout plan.

"You know, I think I know what this is," said the mayor.

"Tell us," said Nathan.

"Well," began the mayor, as he pointed his finger to a part of the drawing. "This is the South wall of the Cathedral of Taranto."

The mayor traced his finger over other lines on the drawing as he continued. "And this is the West wall, where the entrance to the building is located and this is the North wall."

"And look," said an excited Billy "these oblong shapes within the West and South walls must be the graves of the deceased - each is numbered."

"Yes, I think you are right," said the mayor, "they are graves beneath the stone flagstones that form the floor of the Cathedral."

The mayor stood upright for a moment in puzzlement as he rubbed his chin with the palm of his hand.

"Ahhh," he exclaimed. He once more pointed his finger to the drawing.

"This is the East wall but it is not there today - it seems that it was removed when the church was extended. A new wall was built some twenty yards further east of the original wall and that new area now contains the altar, tabernacle, choir seating and two small side chapels. This is most definitely a map of the old church, long before the building was extended to become a Cathedral."

"But look," said Nathan, "there is a cross marked on the drawing, it's in the east - beyond the old perimeter wall of the building."

He continued. "And do you see that arrow pointing to the cross? It leads to an outline picture of a book with the letters 'II' marked upon its front cover."

"Wait a minute… wait a minute… wait a minute," replied an excited mayor, "I have a theory."

There was a silence as they waited for the mayor to speak.

"The markings on the book 'II' indicate the number '2'. This is where the Second Chapter is buried… but I truly hope that it is still there."

"What do you mean, why shouldn't it still be there?" asked Garrett.

"The cathedral building has been extended since the book was buried and now the book has to be underneath the flagstone flooring of the extended church. I do believe that it now lies below the Chapel of Relics."

The mayor sighed. "Of course, there is a possibility that the book has already been found. They might have found it when they dug the foundations for the Chapel extension to the cathedral many years ago."

"But your people would have heard… surely?" asked Billy.

"Maybe," replied the mayor, "maybe not."

"Maybe they did not know what it was - so they destroyed it or cast it aside and never spoke of it to anyone."

"What's this?" enquired Nathan, as he pointed to another part of the page.

The mayor looked at the page and replied. "It's the ancient unit of measurement which is a Pes. It's a linear measurement about one foot in length."

"Well there you are then," said an excited Nathan, "we have the location of the book. We have a treasure map and the scaled measurements from the edge of the cathedral building. We know where it's buried. We can pace the distance out and find the Second Chapter. All we need now is a shovel. Let's go and dig it up... what are we waiting for?"

"I wish I could share your optimism," said the mayor with a brave smile. "As I have told you all, the book could have been excavated when they extended the building - but I suppose we have nothing to lose, so I will organise some men and equipment and we will go to the cathedral."

The boys cheered and they made their way up the steps to the bright daylight of Taranto and into a waiting crowd of local citizens, who were most interested in the outcome of the events that had just occurred below the council chambers. Catrina stood beside Billy in the bright sunlight as the mayor positioned himself on the steps of City Hall ready to address the people of Taranto. Billy held Catrina's hand. On being told by the mayor what had been found - there was a huge excitement in the air as the whole village, the butchers, the bakers, the candlestick makers and many other tradespeople, housewives, grannies and grandads as well as all their children made their way to the cathedral, armed with shovels, picks and buckets.

They entered the magnificent Roman Catholic Cathedral on the 5th October 1734. The mayor had brought the First Chapter book with him. The cathedral's structure and décor were truly magnificent and worthy of its status. Just inside the main doorway to the cathedral was the Chapel of Peccadillo. This area contained a baptism font and a lectern for placing religious books upon for the bishop to read the scriptures. The Roman Catholic purpose of baptism was to remove the 'original sin' that all human beings are supposedly born with. If the baptism font was near to the entrance of the church the 'original sin' could be removed by the religious priest in the single act of baptism before taking the child into the main sacred part of the church, without sin. This Cathedral was built in the shape of a cross. The main entrance was at the west end, situated at the bottom of the cross. A long central aisle, called the nave, and two side aisles ran from west to east. Huge towers and domes adorned the building and around the walls were pictures depicting religious events such as the Stations of the Cross, scenes from the bible and the lives of Saints.

The altar, where the priests and bishop performed religious ceremonies, was situated near to the choir benches at the eastern end of the building. This was a truly beautiful church that was built in the Renaissance period of European history. Near to the altar was a small side room known as the Chapel of Relics. It had an open doorway, about two yards wide, from the main part of the church into its superb interior. On the wall beside the entrance to the Chapel of Relics were four stone cylindrical turn-pieces located beside each other. Each had a series of numbers around their circumference from nought to nine and each moved if pushed with a small force. To the left of these digits was a larger cog that depicted the month. They depicted a month, a year-date and today they were set to display October 1734.

The people of Taranto gathered around inside the main body of the cathedral. Among them was a man who stood out distinctively. He was different from the others who all had that Mediterranean golden olive skin. This man was pale white and he wore an outfit appertaining to a man of authority. At a little over 6 feet 3 inches in height, he stood tall among the crowd though they did not seem to notice him. Was that a naval uniform he was wearing, immaculate in design and presentation, the jacket blue in colour with gold buttons and braided with golden rope and gold-fringed epaulettes? Medals of bravery adorned his breast and a red sash crossed from his left shoulder to his right hip where a leather belt held his pure white breeches in place. The breeches extended downwards and cut just below his knees where they met with the tops of his black socks. His feet were fitted with meticulously clean, shiny black shoes, each having a silver buckle.

He had beside him a snub-nosed monkey with a diamond collar that must have been worth a million pounds. The monkey was busily breaking into a banana before consuming its content. It was Nathan that noticed him first. He nudged Billy.

"Billy, Billy."

"What?" enquired Billy, as he continued to focus on the mayoral activities.

"Billy, look at that man in the crowd over there, with a monkey."

He nudged Billy once more and pointed towards the man - Billy looked in the direction of this finely dressed man who was standing about five yards away.

"My God," Billy exclaimed on seeing him. "That is the Ghost of the Fishersgate Mariner. It was that man who I saw rowing the boat at Fishersgate harbour, you know the one we followed into the lock-gates," said Billy.

"Never," replied Nathan.

"It's true, I tell you," said Billy.

A bemused Catrina could not understand what was being said.

As Billy spoke those words the Ghost smiled and waved at them. The monkey carried on eating his banana, oblivious to events around him.

"He's seen us," exclaimed Nathan, "look the other way." And they both did. They looked towards the centre of the operations - the Mayor of Taranto and his men.

The mayor of the town coughed loudly as he began to direct all of the proposed excavational operations in fine detail. From the information provided in the First Chapter treasure map, he paced out the exact position of where digging should commence in the Chapel of Relics. Once a position had been plotted he gave the instructions to the men standing by with shovels and picks.

Billy looked back, towards the direction of the Ghost, but he had vanished.

But there were now more important things to watch and consider now that the exact spot of the treasure had been identified. The men lifted the heavy flagstones that formed a smooth floor in the chapel of relics and began digging deep into the Italian soil.

"Come on Billy, let's go look for the Ghost while they are digging," said Nathan.

"I don't think so," replied a worried Billy.

Nonetheless, Nathan had his way - so they left Garrett, Wheeler and Catrina watching events in the chapel while they went into the crowd to look for the Ghost of the Fishersgate Mariner. He was nowhere to be seen. So, they moved further into the crowd in the central part of the cathedral and came out the other side near to the internal South wall.

"He's gone," said Billy.

A very well spoken English-speaking voice suddenly responded, "Oh no I haven't."

Both boys jumped with fright.

"Who was that?" asked Nathan as he looked around at the blank whitewashed wall.

"It's me," said the voice, "The Ghost of the Fishersgate Mariner."

"Is this some sort of joke?" exclaimed Billy, who by now began to remember those happier times when his older brother used to play games on him at the family home. Terry used to dress as a stereotypical ghost, hidden under a white sheet making strange ghostly noises. Billy was scared back then in the early days when he was only seven years old, but in time got used to these brotherly pranks that Terry used to pull. So this was no surprise.

"Come on, whoever you are - come out from where you are hiding!" shouted Billy.

"You mean you cannot see me?" said the voice.

"No, we cannot," uttered Nathan.

"Oh, sorry," said the voice, "I haven't pressed the correct button on my belt. Hang on a minute."

There was a pause, followed by several gasps from Billy and Nathan as the Ghost of the Fishersgate Mariner slowly began to appear before them both. The monkey appeared too - still eating the eternal banana - for as he seemed to finish one banana, another appeared.

"You're real," exclaimed Nathan.

"Not quite," said the Ghost.

Billy went to prod him but his hand went right through the ghostly image.

"You see," said the Ghost with that knowing look on his face.

The two boys looked at each other before looking around at the backs of the people of Taranto who were busily watching the digging before them.

"Don't worry about them," said the Ghost, "only the children of Fishersgate can see me. If those people turn around they will think you are talking to a blank wall."

"Thanks," said Billy, "for making us look silly in front of the crowd of people."

"You're welcome," said the Ghost.

Nathan was already thinking. He had many questions to ask of the Ghost and time was running short. The book would hopefully be found and they would soon have to rush away.

"What are we doing here?" enquired Nathan.

"You are here to complete a mission that only a child of Fishersgate can achieve," replied the Ghost.

"But what?" asked Billy.

"To find the Second Chapter book and take it, along with the First Chapter, to a time and place where they can do no harm," said the Ghost.

"But why and where?" asked Billy.

"The knowledge contained in the book is too dangerous for primitive peoples so it must be taken to a place and time in the future where technology has almost equalled the contents of the book. And you must take the First Chapter reference book too. For that contains codes linked to numerical numbers that complements and helps reveal the Second Chapter secrets."

"Why not just burn the Second Chapter?" asked Nathan, "that is if we find it."

"It is indestructible," said the Ghost.

"But, if it's like the First Chapter, no-one can open it - so how can it do any harm?"

"You can open the book, Billy," said the Ghost.

"Yeah, but..." said a puzzled Billy, "if I wasn't here - in this time zone - then surely the contents of the book would be safe."

"You are right Billy," said the Ghost before continuing his explanation.

"The problem is that the learned scribes, who wrote the Second Chapter's contents, set a date way, way, way, in their future when the books lock and hasp would automatically unlock and reveal its secrets to a future generation."

"Why?" said Nathan.

"Because, my boy, that is when they deemed that the so-called secrets of the books would be useful to an advanced civilisation," said the Ghost.

"I get it," said Billy, "they wanted to make sure that their secrets of invention were given only to people who could use them rationally and responsibly."

"You got it, boy," said the Ghost.

"So where is the problem then?" countered Nathan.

"The scribes got their date wrong. The book is due to auto-unlock next week and it is all too much for the peoples of the Eighteenth century to handle," said the Ghost.

"But why can't you take the Chapters somewhere into the future... why us? And anyway, once next week's date is passed the book will open anyway, so wherever we take it in the future it will be unlocked," said Billy.

"You make good arguments my boy, you are a very clever boy indeed," said the Ghost. "I can time travel but I cannot take anything into the future or into the past except all of the things that were personally attached to me at the exact time of my death. My clothes, my boots and hat were all on me when I died. They come with me everywhere. Why do you think that damn monkey keeps hanging around me? I don't know where he came from but I do know he walked across my chest at the precise moment that I died. I am lumbered with the beastly animal for all eternity."

Nathan smiled at the Ghost's predicament and, as he looked at the monkey, he thought he saw him smiling too.

Billy thought for a moment before speaking, "but if you were undercover when you died and dressed as a lowly sailor, how come you wear a very fine naval uniform today?"

'Well Billy," said the Ghost, "those sailor rags did come with me but the Boss relented and let me have my old dress uniform to wear."

"Surely he can rid you of the monkey then?" said Nathan.

"You would think so," replied the Ghost, "I keep asking but the Boss just smiles and says everything comes to those who wait. Anyway, to more important issues - your second point about the book auto unlocking if we travel through time past the unlocking day that the scribes have set is not valid. For by travelling through time we will by-pass that unlocking date. The books will remain firmly locked when they arrive in the future."

"Ok," said Nathan, "I get that."

A more serious Billy was thinking about the death of the Ghost and he asked,

"Who killed you then?"

"It was that monster smuggler Barlott. I was on his case in January 1734 at Fishersgate harbour, trying to do my bit for England and rid the land that I love of his type of criminal fraternity and murderers. But he got me. I never stood a chance. I was working alone monitoring his activities in Fishersgate harbour."

"That's sad," replied Billy.

"I think so too," said the Ghost, "and of course my death had ramifications for the future as well."

"What ramifications?" asked Nathan.

"Parallel death fields," replied the Ghost. "When someone connected to the story of finding the books of the First and Second Chapters, in the eighteenth century, dies a murderous death, then a parallel person in the future dies too. It doesn't always happen that way but often it does."

"You mean when you were murdered in 1734, someone else died in the future?"

"Spot on my boy," replied the Ghost.

"But who?" asked Billy.

"Oh, you won't know him, his name was Tom, the Jolly Boatman - it's a bit complicated but he died a terrible death in 1974," said the Ghost, with a sadness about him.

"We know of Albert the boatman of Fishersgate, but not Tom," said Billy.

"Tom was Albert's son and heir," replied the Ghost. "He was having battles too in 1974 with the smugglers after he and their leader, Barlott, clashed. But let me tell you what happened to Tom…"

Just then the Ghost was interrupted and he held his index finger to his ear. "What's that you say?" he said, as he gazed into the distance. It was as if someone was speaking directly into his ear. There was a faint intermittent buzzing sound, like a bee flying close to one's ear - then moving further away. The buzzing sound being emitted could be weakly heard by Billy and Nathan.

"Ah yes," replied the Ghost to this invisible person talking in his ear, "I will be there in a moment."

"Got to go," said the Ghost to the boys, "It's the boss… he wants me to deal with an urgent matter."

"But wait a minute," said Nathan, "there is lots more we need to ask you."

"No… I really must go," replied the Ghost. "And anyway, if you look over there behind the crowd of people, you will see that they are just about to find the bones of an old sailor and then… the Second Chapter in a wooden chest. Must dash bye-zee-bye… catch you later, love to you all."

"No don't go," shouted Nathan. But it was too late the Ghost had completely vanished.

The boys made their way back through the crowd, and Billy found Catrina. The bones of the old sailor had already been removed from the ground and were neatly stacked to the side of his former resting place. Billy grasped Catrina's hand just as one of the shovels hit something solid in the soil. The men dug around the article below ground to find it was a curved wooden substance. Another half-hour went by as the men excitedly dug around the full extent of the object. This revealed the lid of a wooden chest and they dug some more soil away before being able to release the item from its tightly fitting earthly surroundings. Once loosened from the ground they lifted the chest by its two handles, which were positioned at either end of its oblong wooden frame. They lifted it onto the adjacent flagstones. As they did so a plume of smoke rose from the hole in the ground and the sound of a flute played magical music. The music was coming from the hole in the ground and the clock on the wall chimed. It was twelve o'clock and Billy looked up to see that the clock had thirteen hours marked instead of the usual twelve - but he did not take much notice. The mayor was too busy to take much notice of the smoke or the clock for he was more interested in the contents of the wooden chest. He broke the feeble mechanical lock away from its hasp. The Mayor of Taranto looked at the chest with some trepidation. This was his glorious moment, as he grabbed the hasp and pulled it apart before lifting the hinged lid to reveal its single content.

It was the book they were looking for. It was bound in a similar manner as the First Chapter book. He placed the First Chapter beside the Second Chapter. The books matched in colour and size.

Nathan whispered to Billy. "This seems too easy Billy, I'm sure Long John Silver and Jim Hawkins took a lot longer than we did to find their treasure."

"Don't be silly," replied Billy, "Treasure Island is a fictional story... the author had to make the narrative interesting and that lasted long enough to fill a whole book... and he had a parrot character in his story for tropical effect... but this is real life Nathan and we have found what we were looking for - the treasure - never mind how we got there or how easy you think it is."

"Yeah, but Billy... just think about it, we have a monkey in our story and a Ghost. That's got to be a better story than a parrot and Long John Silver." Nathan made ghostly noises followed by impressions of monkeys. Billy just laughed as they strode forward.

The mayor called Billy. Both he and Nathan made their way towards the mayor, who was by now holding the Second Chapter book in his hands. It was identical to the First Chapter book except for some of the Latin text, which stated on the first line, *Capitulum suarum adinventionum.*

Below that it read *Palma imprimer securitas liber...* (The Second Chapter of their inventions - a palm print security book).

The mayor held the book high at arm's reach to show the people of Taranto.

"This is a marvellous day for celebration," said the mayor, "let us all go back to City Hall, where we can eat, drink and be merry while we study the contents of this book and begin our new adventures with the benefit of the proven technology that the two books will reveal. The contents of this book, the Second Chapter, and the numerical content of the First Chapter will change all of our lives."

The people of Taranto cheered in delight.

"Not so fast," boomed the voice of Necho. His voice echoed around the internal structure of the cathedral walls as he stood in the west entrance leading into the house of worship.

During their excitement, the people of Taranto had not noticed that the cathedral had slowly, but quietly, been surrounded by over a hundred of Necho's men. The people of Taranto, who had attended the cathedral to search for the missing Second Chapter, were now prisoners of the Namidian regime and the half-blooded, most hated half-Scorian himself... Necho. He was now in command, and his henchman, Jed Boot, walked beside him. Boot's trusty dog, Shell, scampered behind them both, as they made their way from the doorway, up the nave and into the main body of the cathedral.

Chapter 11

Re-united

"I will take that book," shouted Necho, "and the other book. Bring them both to me boy."

Nathan took the Second Chapter book from the mayor and placed it on top of the First Chapter laying on the floor.

"No, not you - black boy," barked Necho, "you boy, the one they call Billy, bring the books to me."

Billy lifted both books from the floor and walked with them to where Necho was standing. They were heavy, at least 8 kilograms each, but Billy managed to carry them. He placed the books at Necho's feet. Necho looked down and studied the text written on the cover of the Second Chapter.

"What does this mean boy?" barked Necho.

"It's written in Latin," said Jed Boot.

"I know that," howled Necho, "but what does it mean?"

Billy responded to Necho's question, and read out aloud the lines of the text, *"Capitulum suarum adinventionum*, translated into English it roughly states... *The Second Chapter of their inventions* - and underneath it reads *Palma imprimer securitas liber* and that means that it is *a palm print security book."*

"You shouldn't have told him that," boomed Wheeler.

"Yes, that was a silly thing to do," said Garrett.

"Why not?" said Billy, "he would have found out anyway. I have only given them a translation of the Latin language and these two, Mr. Necho and Jed Boot, do not have the power themselves to open the book."

Garrett, who had been standing next to Wheeler caught the eye of Jed Boot.

"You boy, Garrett," called Jed Boot, "we have some unfinished business I do believe… just you and I and the rest of the crew of the Star of the Sea. You are to be punished."

Boot roared with a haughty laugh followed by a cough and a wheeze.

Garrett tried to melt into the crowd but, due to his huge size, this was not possible.

"Seize them both, him and the other fat boy," ordered Jed Boot to his guards. "Do not kill them just yet, we have a keel-hauling to perform back on board the Star of the Sea."

Ten of Necho's men charged into the cathedral directly towards Garrett and Wheeler. The crowd scattered and the two huge boys were suddenly all alone and unarmed. Necho's men were fully armed with pistols and cutlasses and, after a minor struggle, both Wheeler and Garrett were detained. Shackled in chains and restrained by the guards, they passed Jed Boot. Wheeler spat in his face and called him a monster lunatic.

"Take them back to the ship," ordered Boot as he wiped the spittle from his cheek with the corner of his cuff. "We shall have a double keel-hauling when I return. Garrett and Wheeler are dead men walking."

Garrett and Wheeler were escorted back to the docks of Taranto where they were taken by a small boat to the Star of the Sea ship.

"Mr. Mayor," called Necho. "You spoke of this First Chapter book a few moments ago which I now have in my possession. What is that about?"

"I shall not tell you that," replied the mayor.

Necho turned to his guards and order them to seize five citizens of Taranto and kill them where they stood.

"Wait a minute," shouted the mayor. "Call off your men and I shall tell you all that you want to know."

"You are a wise man," snapped Necho. "Guards - stand down."

The mayor continued, "the two books work in unison, the Second Chapter has all the information with some blank words, while the First Chapter fills in the missing words when cross-checking with corresponding numerical figures. It is likened to a security system."

Necho picked up the Second Chapter book in his hands and studied the text on the front cover. It was a glorious moment for he had waited years to hold this book in his hands. He kissed its cover and tried to open the hasp but it remained firmly closed.

Necho moved into the central body of the church where he found a timber lectern on which he placed the Second Chapter.

"Open the book, Billy," he demanded.

"No don't," shouted Nathan as he ran towards the lectern, grabbing a brass candlestick en-route, which now became a weapon.

BANG.

A shot was fired which hit Nathan on his hip. Blood began to emerge through his clothing as he fell onto the hard slabs that covered the floor of the cathedral. The heavy candlestick slid some five yards across the stone floor.

Jed Boot had fired the shot.

"You fool," shouted Necho as Billy ran towards his friend who was, by now, in considerable pain.

Caterina ran towards Nathan, frantically speaking aloud in Italian before beginning to tear at his clothing so that she could quickly get to the wound. Other women from the crowd helped tend to Nathan, some bringing water, others tearing strips of linen that they had taken from the bishop's wardrobe, in the process, destroying one of his cassocks and a chasuble. The men from the city rushed towards Necho and Jed Boot, overpowering them, bringing them both to the ground in a frenzied attack full of anger because of what they had just witnessed - the shooting of an unarmed boy. But some of Necho's men saw what was happening and they called for re-enforcements from those standing outside. The guards and some of Jed Boot's trusted disciples rushed into the cathedral and beat back the men of the city, killing some of them during the struggle. It was not long before Necho was in command once more, soon to be seeking devastating revenge for the cuts and bruises he had all over his body.

Catrina ran into the bishop's room, where a cupboard adjacent to the bishop's wardrobe contained drugs and various medical implements. She knew these drugs were in this room, for one of her jobs involved repairing the bishop's ceremonial costumes. She brought back these items in a small wicker basket, including a bottle of brandy, which she immediately administered to Nathan's wound. Nathan wriggled with pain as the brandy took hold of the broken bloodied flesh. Then he passed out into semi-unconsciousness. One of the older women mixed some of the drugs together and forcibly administered the solution into the mouth of Nathan, whose health was rapidly declining. Death was very near. However, between them, Catrina and the older women of the city managed to stem the blood loss from Nathan's wound, by applying bandages around his body.

"What's that drug you have given Nathan?" asked Billy.

"It's a very religious medicinal drug that should help to stabilise your friend for a few hours and maybe bring him back, just enough to get him to walk to a doctor," said the woman, "but more will have to be done to save him."

The drug certainly worked, because Nathan came around and was fully alert within a couple of minutes.

"We must get him to a doctor," said the woman. "The nearest one is thirty miles away from here."

Billy and Catrina helped to get Nathan to his feet. Amazingly Nathan could walk but he was shivering with cold, even though the air was full of Mediterranean warmth.

"Here, put this coat on your friend," said the woman as she handed Billy a long trench coat from the bishop's wardrobe. "And put this hat on him too, this will stop the little heat that he has in his frail body from escaping." She continued, "he will feel really cold because of the drugs. His body will be feeble but he will be able to walk and talk for about twenty-four hours, enough time to get him to a doctor of medicine."

Billy began to walk with his friend Nathan towards the door, followed by Catrina, when a voice boomed.

"No one is leaving this building," shouted Necho, as Jed Boot pointed his pistol once more at Nathan.

"Come on," shouted Billy, "he needs a doctor."

"Not until you have opened that book," thundered Necho.

"Billy, Billy," said a voice. "You cannot see me," said the Ghost of the Fishersgate Mariner, "and neither can anyone else. But you can hear me and no-one else can. Listen to me very carefully and follow my instructions. It is the only way that you can save Nathan from succumbing to death. Go and open the book for Necho. Once opened you must turn to page seventy-five. You must read and learn the few Latin words on the page that the book will reveal to you. Do no more than this for now. I will return soon."

Billy sat a shivering Nathan in a chair that was nearest to the lectern. Nathan said nothing but Billy whispered in his ear to stay strong, for the Ghost had spoken to him and he knew what to do.

"Ok Necho," shouted Billy, "I will open the book for you. I will open it right now."

Billy made his way towards the lectern where the book was placed.

"Keep your pistol trained on him, Jed Boot. He complied with my command too easily," said Necho. "I don't trust him."

Billy placed his hand on the front cover of the book, within the hand imprint outline, and the hasp released with a definitive click and the faint sound of multiple bells ringing.

"Stand back," shouted Necho. "I will open the book."

Necho approached the lectern and, using his index finger and thumb, attempted to lift the corner of the cover. It would not budge even though the hasp had released itself.

Billy pushed Necho's hand away and lifted the cover of the book. It opened to reveal the first page, a splendid drawing showing a mixture of inventions intertwined with each other, bright and full of wonderful colours. Billy recognised some of these items as motor vehicles, washing machines, vacuum cleaners, aeroplanes and submarines. The list was endless and the picture seemed to change as more sophisticated inventions appeared and superseded inventions that disappeared. It was a rotating moving picture show - something he had never seen before.

Necho pushed Billy out of the way as he marvelled at the moving colourful drawing displaying these progressive inventions. He attempted to turn to another page. None of the pages would move - it was as if they were stuck together. Necho realised that only Billy could turn the pages of the book so he ordered him to turn to the next page.

This was Billy's opportunity. Billy lifted a few pages and flicked through them looking for page seventy-five, just as the Ghost had instructed. He found it and opened the book on that page.

There were several sentences, once again written in the Latin language.

The first one stated, *futura ad est onerariam peregrinatione destinatio portus ipso posterus ut,* which Billy read to himself.

Necho swiped Billy around the head with the open palm of his hand exclaiming, "Open page two, not seventy-five, you are a stupid boy."

The force of the blow to Billy's head knocked him to the floor. He was momentarily dazed, but otherwise unhurt. As he recovered and stood up Necho was busily trying to change the pages once more. The pages would not budge. Necho stood back and pulled Billy towards himself before grabbing him around the back of the neck and thrusting his face onto page seventy-five of the book.

"What does this Latin mean?" he growled.

Billy could read the words and could translate their meaning but he did not understand the content. The words contained in the sentences were a series of statements.

Just then the voice of the Ghost whispered in his ear, "Billy, learn those words you will need them in a few minutes time. But you *must* get them right and do not tell Necho what they mean. These are the words that you must learn - I will remain close by," said the Ghost.

Billy read out the first line of words to Necho, "*futura ad est onerariam peregrinatione destinatio portus ipso posterus ut.*" (The cargo will travel to a destination that harbours the future.)

"What does it mean boy?" barked Necho.

"It means," said Billy, "it means… hang on a minute I will have to work this out."

"Hurry up," replied an impatient Necho.

"Let me be for a few minutes while I study the words and I will tell you soon," replied Billy.

Necho stood back and huffed and puffed like a demented wolf ready to blow down a house of straw.

Billy repeated the words over and over again out loud.

Suddenly there was a lot of noise outside the cathedral.

"What's happening?" shouted Jed Boot to one of his disciples, who was standing by the inner door.

"We are under attack," shouted the disciple.

"Deal with it," shouted Boot, "and let me know when you have defeated them."

The disciple drew his sword from its scabbard and went outside. Boot's most trusted disciple, Steve Goose, rushed over to the door and shut it firmly before fitting a large timber stay across the inside of the door frame to prevent access from the outside.

"We don't want a little battle outside to stop what we are doing Mr. Necho, do we?" called out Boot, as he made his way back into the main body of the cathedral.

"Wise man," replied Necho.

"Steve, Steve," called out Jed Boot, "stay by the door."

"Very well, Jed," replied Steve Goose.

Boot spotted Catrina who was standing next to Billy by the lectern. He made his way towards them. When he got closer he grabbed Catrina from behind and held her neck with his left hand while maintaining the pistol in his right, which was aimed straight at Billy. Catrina screamed and wriggled, but to no avail.

Necho addressed the crowd of Taranto residents.

"Just as an added precaution, if any one of you people think big things then the girl will be killed. Back away you people. Billy, you stay where you are."

The people of the city backed away to comply with Necho's orders. Murmurs and mumblings of disapproval emanated from the crowd.

"Be quiet… all of you," shouted Boot.

"Leave her alone," screamed Billy.

"Get back to what you were doing Billy," shouted Necho. "Tell me what these Latin words mean… how do I get the secrets from the book… tell me… tell me, boy."

Necho was whipping himself up into a frenzy once more. He wanted the secrets from the book. He was so close to getting them and would stop at nothing to realise his dream.

Billy continued to learn the words from the book, just as the Ghost had instructed.

Once more Billy heard a whisper in his ear. It was the Ghost of the Fishersgate Mariner.

"Billy, you must get Nathan into the hole in the ground."

"What hole?" blurted Billy out loudly.

"What did you say boy?" boomed Necho.

"Nothing… Nothing…" replied Billy.

"Have you translated those words yet, Billy," shouted Necho, "I am losing my patience with you boy."

Catrina continued to struggle in Jed Boot's arms.

"Billy," whispered the Ghost, "they cannot see me or hear me, just listen to me and follow my instructions."

"Go to the open hole in the ground, where the wooden chest was found and where the bones of an old sailor had been buried, in the Chapel of Relics. You must get Nathan into that hole so that he can sit among the smoking mist that rests at the bottom. And you must do this before the clock strikes the thirteenth hour… in five minutes."

"Why," said Billy aloud.

"What was that boy?" shouted Necho.

"Nothing, Mr. Necho," said Billy.

"You are not very good at this are you Billy?" whispered the Ghost.

Billy looked away to see how Catrina was faring in the hands of Jed Boot. She had calmed a little, but it was clear that she was aiming some Italian words of a derogative nature in Boot's direction.

The Ghost continued, "the hole in the ground is a time-portal. As the clock strikes the thirteenth chime, the panel in the stone wall will open and three ballet dancers, each dressed in a white tutu, will dance their way to the centre of the Chamber of Relics. A flute player will appear from nowhere and begin to play a tune as the dancers dance for a short while in unison. And while they dance, a golden goblet will appear as if from nowhere, into the hands of the central dancer. She will hold the goblet above her head, twirl around then lower it to sip some of the contents, before passing it to another dancer. The second dancer will carry out the same routine before passing the goblet to the third dancer, whereupon the whole process will start again. It is at this point that you, and only you, must take the goblet from one of the dancers, hold it high above your head and look for a secret parchment message fixed to the underside of the goblet. You must remove that message and put it in Nathan's coat pocket. Then you must pass the goblet to Nathan and he must take a sip of the contents. Nathan will then travel through time to the date you have set on the four cogs situated outside the chapel. You must set those cogs to October 1975. Once Nathan has drunk from the goblet you must pass it back to the same dancer from which you have taken it. You must be quick in your actions. Then you must say the magic Latin words. Say the first line from the book followed by the word *Fishersgate*. This will automatically select the correct time tunnel for Nathan. After they have performed their dance routine the dancers will take a low curtsey and as they rise to *'first position'* a huge plume of smoke and a flash of light will engulf the three of them and they will disappear. The flute player will also disappear. If you miss this opportunity you must wait until the next thirteenth hour, but that will be too late to save Nathan, for he is dying and he needs the drugs that only the future time of 1975 can provide; he must have them within twenty-four hours. You will see Nathan slowly disappear and re-appear in the hole in the ground, before disappearing for good and as he does so you must grab both the First and Second Chapters and throw them into the hole, with Nathan. You must get the Chapter books into the hole before he finally goes forward in time. We must rid these books from 1734 and send them to responsible people who can use their knowledge wisely... those people are the people of Fishersgate. The books are to be buried in Fishersgate recreational ground by Nathan."

"How can I remember to do all of that?" said Billy.

"What did you say?" said Necho.

"I am not talking to you," said Billy.

"Listen, boy, I don't know what games you are playing, but my patience is wearing thin," snapped Necho.

"Ok, ok," replied a flustered Billy. "I have read the Latin words and I now understand what we must do to release the secrets of the Second Chapter."

"And what's that," snarled Jed Boot as he held a knife close to Catrina's throat. "This better be good or she dies."

"We need to perform a burial ceremony at the thirteenth hour of the clock," said Billy.

"A burial ceremony?" snapped Necho. "What has a burial got to do with all of this?"

Necho thought for a moment. "Have you ever performed a burial before?" he barked at Billy.

"Of course I have," replied Billy, "I have buried loads of hamsters."

Jed Boot laughed that same haughty laugh followed by a long wheeze.

"You bury hamsters and perform a ceremony for them?" laughed Boot.

Billy did not reply.

Necho looked puzzled. He was not sure if Billy was telling the truth or just playing games with him. Either way, he decided that Billy needed another thump around the head. He moved towards Billy to administer the punishment but stopped when he heard several loud distinctive thuds on the door to the cathedral. Necho looked toward the door.

"Boot, let your men back into the Cathedral," said Necho.

"Oh, they can wait," replied Boot, "I've got to see this *burial ceremony.*"

Necho immediately returned his attention to Billy.

"Yes... yes, of course. Boy, prepare for a burial ceremony," said Necho.

Billy continued, "The book says that the burial must take place in the same hole where the wooden chest had previously been removed."

"Very well," said Necho, "there are plenty of dead people over there on the floor, slain by my men this morning; there are many more dead outside this cathedral, now that our forces have defeated our attackers - we shall bury one of them, take your choice boy,"

"No," said Billy, "we must bury someone alive."

Necho laughed loudly as he turned to Jed Boot, who also joined in with his own style of laughter which ended with several out of control wheezes.

"I like your style, Billy," said Necho. "You are a boy after my own heart... bury someone alive, what a superb idea."

Necho's laughter turned to hatred as he spoke these words.

"Bury your best friend... Nathan, the black boy... he is dead on his feet but still alive... just."

'Perfect', thought Billy. It simply had to be Nathan to fit in with the Ghost's plans and Necho had played right into his hands.

Billy walked over to Nathan and gave him a hug before whispering in his ear to follow his instructions without question. He continued, "Nathan, trust me... I will get you out of here so that you can get yourself well again, my friend."

"Ok," whispered Nathan.

Billy continued, "I want you to walk to the Chapel of Relics with me. I will help you. Some of the things I will ask you to do may seem strange, but the Ghost of the Fishersgate Mariner has told me what I should do to save you. There is not much time. You need special drugs to cure you and those drugs only exist in the future, so I am sending you forward in time to 1975 with the First and Second Chapters - and once you are fit and well again you must bury the books in Fishersgate recreational ground."

Billy took hold of Nathan's hand and together they slowly walked through to the Chamber of Relics where he asked his shivering unwell friend to sit by the side of the hole with his feet dangling into the ground that was soon to become his grave of 1734.

Then a nervous Billy had a thought. He was not sure he could remember all of the Latin words that the Ghost had asked him to learn.

"Mr. Necho," called Billy, "can you bring the lectern and the First and Second Chapters through to the Chapel of Relics and position them beside the grave so that I can read some of its content?"

Necho nodded his head and ordered that two of the people of Taranto city move the lectern and take the books to the place where Billy had asked.

Once the lectern was in position, Billy changed the cogs on the wall to 1975.

"What are you doing boy?" shouted Necho.

Billy needed to think quickly and he did when he replied.

"Page seventy-five of the Second Chapter, Mr. Necho."

Necho seemed to accept his response.

"And now we must wait for the thirteenth hour in a few seconds time," said Billy.

"What is this thirteenth hour?" replied Necho.

"Look at the clock, Mr. Necho," said Billy, "it's about to strike the thirteenth hour."

Just then there were several more thuds on the door to the cathedral.

"Boot, let your men in," ordered Necho. "I feel safer with them inside the cathedral."

"Ok," said Jed Boot. "Steve," shouted Boot along the length of the nave of the cathedral to his most trusted disciple, "let our men into the cathedral."

Boot turned his attention back to the proceedings.

"You can't get any better than a good funeral," he exclaimed as he moved a little closer towards the grave, while still holding his struggling captive, Catrina. "I don't want to miss *this* funeral, and neither does my dog... do you Shell?"

The dog barked in response to his master's voice.

"Once my man, Steve Goose, lets my army into the cathedral they will soon surround you all, now that they have been victorious in the battle outside," said Boot.

Steve Goose removed the timber brace and opened the door of the cathedral to the outside world with a huge smile on his face. That smile soon diminished when he saw who was standing there. It was not his comrades for they had all been slain. Steve Goose stood back in horror and he fired a shot - but it missed its target. The attackers ran towards him and bundled him to the floor before shackling him in cuffs and chains.

Who were these mysterious attackers?

Well, it was Antonio, ably assisted by Terry of course, along with their troop of Italian fighting men that now amounted to more than five hundred in number.

Necho ordered that the ceremony inside the cathedral must continue without delay. And, it seemed, he had no choice because bang-on-cue, the clock struck the thirteenth hour. The 'calling of the flute' tune began to play and the three dancers appeared just as the Ghost had said they would. The dancers performed their routine and, once the third dancer had taken a sip from the goblet, Billy took it and held it high above his head. On the underneath of the goblet was a small envelope, no bigger than the width of the base of the goblet. It was addressed to Nathan. The Ghost whispered one last instruction.

"Billy, remember, before you put Nathan into the grave tell him of these instructions and put them in the pocket of his coat."

Billy did not respond for he was focused on his childhood friend. He had tears in his eyes as he performed this final ritual in his honour. A magical ritual that would save his life.

Billy spoke some Latin words, for good effect, just as any high priest would do under these types of circumstance. He recalled the words from his burial services of the hamsters in the back garden of number 56 Duke Street, which seemed such a long time before.

"In nomine Patris, et Filii, et Spiritus Sancti, [in the name of the father, son and holy ghost,]" Billy said before taking the goblet to Nathan who was sitting by the grave.

"Take a sip of the contents of this goblet, my friend," said Billy.

Billy held the goblet to Nathan's lips and he took a small sip from the cup.

Nathan then thanked Billy for their wonderful friendship. And finally, before assisting Nathan to sit into the bottom of the misty grave Billy observed the Ghost's final instructions. He peeled the envelope from the underside of the goblet and put it into Nathan's coat pocket. "Nathan, I have put a message for the future in your pocket," said Billy, "take heed and look after yourself my friend."

Time was running out and Billy could not remember the words he was supposed to say so he returned to the

Second Chapter book, which was still open on page seventy-five.

Nathan was beginning to disappear as he sat in the bottom of his grave among the misty surroundings. The people of Taranto looked on.

"What is happening?" shouted Necho.

Nathan was in a trance-like state by this time.

Billy did not respond to Necho but focused on his friend Nathan and then to the first line of the words in the book. He read the words slowly and loudly.

"*Futura ad est onerariam peregrinatione destinatio portus ipso posterus ut.*" (The cargo will travel to a destination that harbours the future.)

'Is that it?' thought Billy as Nathan disappeared then reappeared once more.

"Billy, Billy," shouted the Ghost. Everyone in the church heard the Ghost's frantic cry. They looked around but saw no-one. The Ghost continued. "You must end with the word, *Fishersgate.* Billy, quickly, repeat the line and add the word Fishersgate," said the Ghost. "You must hurry."

Billy complied with the Ghost's request.

"*Futura ad est onerariam peregrinatione destinatio portus ipso posterus ut. FISHERSGATE.*"

Through the mist at the bottom of the grave, Nathan's mortal body began to fade into nothing.

Billy quickly closed the book of the Second Chapter, took it from the lectern, ran towards Nathan and threw it into the grave.

"No," screamed Necho, as he too ran towards the grave and lay on his belly, dangling his arms into the mist of the grave in a vain attempt to retrieve the book.

Just then Billy picked up the First Chapter and threw that in the grave too.

Necho continued to dangle his arms into the grave trying to retrieve the books.

But they were gone - and so was Nathan.

"I will kill you for this, I will strangle you with my bare hands," screamed Necho as he pulled his arms from the grave and stood to his feet. And he would have strangled Billy with his bare hands, except for the fact that Necho did not have his lower arms or hands anymore. They were in the process of being transported somewhere in time. There was no blood - just two perfectly formed, healed stumps on each of his upper arms that the very best skilled medical surgeons would have been proud of undertaking. Necho screamed and screamed and screamed as he ran past a shocked Jed Boot. But this was Boot's chance, he jumped into the grave... his whole body disappearing into the mist. Shell his trusty dog followed him but stopped short when a flash of light shone upwards out of the grave, momentarily scaring the beast. He sat beside the open grave whimpering for his lost master.

"Billy," shouted the Ghost of the Fishersgate Mariner, "quickly change the date on the cogs - any date - just spin the cogs, we must keep Jed Boot away from Nathan." Billy ran up to the cogs and randomly spun all four as quickly as he could. The cogs stopped at the year of 1930. And that is exactly where Jed Boot went, to Fishersgate 1930. It was here, a few days after his arrival, that Jed Boot changed his name to the French-sounding Jed Lavell, a mystery man said to come from the town of St. Helier, Jersey in the Channel Islands and who later became the leader of the Fishersgate dock Hufflers. Trapped in this time zone for all eternity, because he had not taken a sip of the golden goblet elixir which allowed free time travel movement through time-portals. And Necho's perfectly incised arms had gone with him to become the morbid trophy that Jed Lavell hung above his fireplace.

Jed Lavell's life ended abruptly a few years later when a contingency of Special Boat Service navy commandos crossed Fishersgate harbour under the cover of darkness in January 1944. There was thunder in the distance and dawn was about to break. Jed Lavell and his men were roasting chestnuts over an old oil drum that they had converted into a chestnut-cooker. They had regularly stolen the coal from the power station storage depot to fuel their cooking appliance. The shadows of Lavell's men stood out against the flames of the oil drum fires, casting intoxicating shadows upon the dockside decking. Out of the mist that lay upon the harbour waters, nine small boats made their way across the waterfront, each boat containing eight commandos. Their task was to surprise and take out the Hufflers - who had been supporting German spies throughout the latter part of the second world war. The commandos gently rowed their wooden rowing boats across the harbour from Fishersgate bay towards the sound of a flute that one of the Hufflers was playing. But danger was all around them and six German spies, who were waiting in the darkness for submarine transport back to Germany, opened fire. Supported by the Germans, Jed Lavell's men, the Hufflers, joined the battle, but the British special forces were too powerful for them and ninety men died that night in the ensuing skirmish. All six spies lay dead. Jed Lavell and every one of his group of fiendish Hufflers also lay dead.

Back in 1734, the grave that had transported Nathan and Jed Lavell had frozen over and had magically replenished itself with a new flagstone top. The grave had been sealed forever and the only evidence that it had ever been opened was the pile of old sailor's bones and a wooden chest that had once held the Second Chapter book. The people of Taranto would later bury the old sailor's bones in the same wooden chest in the North Taranto graveyard that was situated high on an adjoining hill overlooking the docks.

Necho, meanwhile, armless and in a state of shock had run out of the cathedral and straight into the hands of the Italian guard.

Soon, Billy was to be reunited with his brother, Terry, but he took a moment of time, a moment of reflection to think about his true friend Nathan, while held in the arms of Catrina who had run to his side and kissed him on the cheek.

Billy's thoughts of Nathan turned to tears as he looked at Catrina. He held her close in his arms, as she wiped his moist eyes with her handkerchief. They once more kissed, but this time, full on the lips. It was a long lingering kiss. For a moment in time, Billy thought he was in heaven.

Though Billy did not know this... he would never see his friend, Nathan, again.

Chapter 12

A child returns

It was proven. Patricia, who often told her random audiences of her mystical premonition during the late thirties, was right. She, you may remember, was the local fortune-teller with flame-coloured waist length hair. A bit of a nuisance some would say. Others simply thought she was a foolish misguided old woman. She had revealed her exposé during the nineteen-thirties, right up until that dastardly time in 1944 when a mark 2 German doodlebug landed flat on top of her, while she was tending to her cucumbers on her allotment at Carden Hill. But long before she died, one evening, when it was her turn to speak to the townsfolk at the local church hall, you may remember that she told them of her prediction; that a child of Fishersgate would return to Fishersgate bay.

And so it was, on an early morning in 1975, just as Patricia had predicted, on a cold but bright autumn day, Nathan, a former child of Fishersgate returned to the harbour. He arrived at Fishersgate bay in a small rowing boat. The name of that boat was indeed *Doris.* The Ghost of the Fishersgate Mariner, accompanied by the snub-nosed monkey, had rowed the boat that took Nathan home. At the shore of Fishersgate bay, the Ghost bid Nathan a fond farewell before vanishing. Nathan wore a long dark trench coat with the collar turned up and a large black hat, that hid his facial features from three sides. He had been away a long time. He had been away since 1934.

Nathan stood by the shore, looking out over Fishersgate bay. This was the day that he did indeed, survey his former playground. Soon, the drugs in his feeble body would wear-off and that shivering excruciating pain would return before death itself took hold. He was dying.

His memory was fading. He needed medical treatment for the concoction of drugs that had been administered to him in 1734, which had prolonged his life by twenty-four hours. He also required medical surgery on the gunshot wound to his hip... maybe he might survive. It was a slim chance. A fine mist hung just above the peaceful waters of Fishersgate bay. Some of the old rowing boats were laying semi-sunken in the calm water that lapped onto the shingle beach; all the boats were beyond repair, they had all been vandalised. The words on the back-rests of the once colourful boats were hardly visible but, if he concentrated his failing vision, Nathan could just make out some of the letters which once formed names like Shirley and Rose.

We know what Albert's fate was. He had choked on a brew at the Sussex Arms in 1934. But what could have happened to Tom readers of this story may have already asked? Tom had been working long hours, fixing boats in his workshop in Fishersgate just a year before, in 1974. Now he was gone - leaving his workshop to become derelict.

Glancing towards the old workshop, built into the steep grassed bank, Nathan saw that the doors were boarded over. A notice written on the doors in thick black paint and rising at an angle from left to right stated **'KEEP OUT!'**

Turning back towards the calm waters of the harbour and to the decaying rowing boats, the old quays, the Crab House and the tranquil view before him he pondered upon this image. It was a reminder of where he and his childhood friends once gathered and played nautical games many years before. He felt an air of ghostliness about the place. It was here, and only here, where he believed that his lost memories might appear before him. For the moment, a fragmented vision was all he could see in his mind. Thoughts of a lost friendship held so close to his heart. Yet something was missing. It was something he could not fully explain; something so immense but so distant - so important was his friendship with Billy. He couldn't draw this complete information from his memory, just yet. This time-travel business and his injuries had taken their toll on him. His mind was searching itself; drifting back in time; back to the summer of 1934; trying to remember what really happened; over and over again. Yet he was the same age today as when he left Fishersgate in 1934, just a boy in his teenage years. As he submerged himself within his own thoughts he did not see a Catholic nun approaching. Yes, it's an elderly Sister Alisha, his former teacher. Somehow, she knows that he has returned to Fishersgate after being away for over forty years. Somehow, she knows that the first place he will want to see is Fishersgate bay and she knows he will need a doctor to attend to his injuries. Her Mother Superior, the now late Sister Albany, had told her of this moment, for it was written in the scriptures of the convent by the Prophet Patricia, who had been a regular attendee at the convent chapel for Latin prayer.

Sister Alisha descended the steep concrete steps that took her down the steep grassed banks, towards the Fishersgate harbour shoreline; she was hurrying towards Nathan. She must tell him something. She must tell him that she needed to get him to Brighton Hospital straight away.

Suddenly, he heard footsteps. He turned around and took a long look at her. He instantly recognized her, even though she was much older with wrinkled facial features.

"Is it really you Sister Alisha?" he gently whispered in a faltering voice.

"It is," she replied. "It is nice to see you again Nathan, after all these years. I somehow knew that you would be here today. It is written in the scriptures at the convent," she continued. "Where are the other three... the scriptures do not mention them?"

The teenage Nathan fell onto his knees, holding his head in his hands as he began to cry.

"I don't know," he exclaimed. "I think they are all dead or will be very soon, but I cannot be sure."

She placed her hand on his shoulder to comfort him and said a prayer for him. It was a 'Hail Mary' prayer. Then she said the following words for all departed mortal beings from this place that is called 'Earth'.

"Eternal rest, grant unto them O' lord and let perpetual light shine upon them.

May they rest forever and ever, in peace, Amen."

Sister Alisha continued, "Come with me Nathan, I have a special taxi-cab waiting and we shall be at Brighton Hospital Accident and Emergency department within twenty-five minutes." She helped him as they ascended the steps to the high road overlooking the harbour, exiting onto the main road just opposite the old Sussex Arms pub which was, by that time, modern-day offices. The taxi cab and driver were waiting. There were three other nuns waiting beside the taxi. Sister Alisha then asked her companions to go down to Fishersgate bay and remove the First and Second Chapter books from the rowing boat named *Doris* and take them to the nunnery at the top of Locks Hill for safe keeping.

Nathan attended the hospital in Brighton where a modern-day medical assessment of his condition identified the drugs in his body that had prolonged his life. He was soon given treatment and his life was saved. The short-term life-extending medicine, that the old Italian woman had administered back in 1734, had given him just enough time to make his way to Brighton. And after a medical operation to remove the pellet that the pistol had thrust into his hip, Nathan made a full recovery. Of course, there were a few questions asked by the local police and Nathan told the whole truth of the matter about how he received that gunshot wound. But the police officer did not believe this highly unlikely story that he was a time traveller from 1934, who had been shot by pirates in 1734, some two hundred and forty years earlier, though they never cleared-up the fact that the actual bullet the doctors extracted from Nathan's hip was proven to be an eighteenth-century gunshot pellet. Later, Nathan went to live in the convent, where he spent his entire life beside a succession of Catholic nuns. He lived in a little hut in the grounds of the estate near to a stream and he worked in and around Fishersgate for many years after that, carrying out many acts of kindness in the local community at the request of the nuns, in return for free board and lodgings at the nunnery. He lived to a very old age before succumbing to one of those nice kinds of deaths in his sleep, at ten past three in the early hours of the morning, accelerated by a severe shortage of breath. Of course, though he was born in 1919, the year stated on his birth certificate, he was in fact much younger at the time of his death – because he had been away time-travelling between 1934 and 1974, when he did not age at all. Maybe that was why he stayed under the protectorate of the nuns at the nunnery for all those years for fear of being found out by the authorities. Yet, no-one would believe his real story. How could they? And no one ever questioned the Catholic nuns or anyone under their protectorate.

During his long-life Nathan's memory gradually returned and he often thought about his friend, Billy, and what had become of him and Terry, Lilly, Garrett and Wheeler. They were in a time-zone, somewhere in the universe. He never saw the Ghost of the Fishersgate Mariner again. Some say that he never saw his friends again either, but no-one knows for sure. And on some cloudless nights when he looked towards the stars in the night sky he could just imagine their smiling faces looking down towards him.

But what of the First and Second Chapter books? It was about a year after Nathan had returned to Fishersgate when sister Alisha went to see him one morning in his room. She produced the envelope that she had found in the pocket of his trench coat at the time he had arrived at Fishersgate bay. It was the envelope that Billy had put into Nathan's pocket. Nathan looked at the envelope and then he realised what he had been trying to remember when he found himself back in Fishersgate, having travelled back through time - almost a year earlier. At that moment he thought about his lost friend, Billy, and a single tear ran down his cheek.

Nathan opened the envelope to reveal a letter and instructions for the safekeeping of the two books - the First and Second Chapters. He was to go to Tom's old workshop, with the nuns, clean the place up and build a wooden casket to the design shown in the letter using all of Tom's old tools and bits of wood. Also in the envelope were the ancient deeds to Tom and Albert's workshop and the surrounding area, known as Fishersgate bay and all that the bay contained. Though the envelope was small, the deeds unfolded into a document, three feet tall by two feet wide.

Nathan's name and the name of the nunnery was magically written on the deeds. The Admiralty signed the letter - that important organisation that runs and regulates the Navy. The Admiralty also explained that Tom had been murdered at Fishersgate bay in 1974 by persons unknown. But though no one was ever prosecuted for the murder, locals believed that it was Barlott himself that had killed Tom because he found out something new about Barlott's smuggling and piracy operations. Traditional smuggling of contraband, like cigarettes and alcohol, had been replaced, on Barlott's orders, by illegal recreational drugs - and Tom wasn't going to allow such life-threatening substances on his patch... but sadly it cost him his life.

But why did the Admiralty give Nathan the deeds to Tom's old place? Was this the Ghost of the Mariner's doing? It surely was the Ghost's doing, for he had sown the seeds of this at Admiralty House when he whispered a private ghostly word into the ear of the Admiral of the Fleet, Sir Stephen Carden. And yes, Albert and Tom's old workshop now belonged to Nathan and to the nuns of St. Mary's. He cleaned up the workshop and on one of the shelves, next to the old statue of a man and a snub-nosed monkey - which once belonged to Albert the boatman - Nathan placed the old faded photograph of his father Fred, the American soldier. It was the picture he once kept by his locker at the orphanage when he was a child. He often looked at the photograph and wished that he had known his father. Sometimes he studied the detail of the statue of the sailor and monkey; for he knew exactly who they were - because he had lived the story of the Ghost of the Fishersgate Mariner.

In time, Nathan built that casket for the First and Second Chapter books and within five years he had restored all the little rowing boats to their original previously pristine condition. Later, he began hiring out the boats to the local population, mostly children aged twelve years or older, just as Albert and Tom had done. Nathan, now nearing twenty-one years old, was the first young black businessman of Fishersgate and he knew all that went on around his little empire beside Fishersgate bay. He knew of the modern-day smugglers. Smuggling is an unsavoury and despicable tax avoiding practice that continues to this day.

One night, when there was no moon in the darkened sky, at just about three o'clock in the morning, while the foxes and badgers were going about their nightly business, and while the local cats watched on, Nathan carried the finished casket containing the books from his workshop up the steps to the coastal high road. He put the books on a trolley, along with a pick-axe, fork and spade he had purchased from B&Q DIY suppliers. He pushed the trolley westwards for about half a mile before parking it at the south-east corner of Fishersgate recreational park, just beside the Albion public-house. He carefully removed several sections of grass in the park, rolling each piece up and putting them to one side for use later that night. He then began digging a hole, some three yards west and two yards north of the south-west corner fence-post of the park. He dug the hole some two yards deep. It was here, in this exact spot, that Nathan secretly, and working alone, finally buried the First and Second Chapters that were contained in the wooden casket. When he had finished back-filling the hole he carefully laid the grass over the spot and within a few minutes, with the help of a supreme external magical power that cannot be explained, the seams of the grass had jointed and there was no evidence whatsoever that anything had been buried there at all. The books remain there, in that exact location to this day, and if the contents of another part of the Ghost's letter are correct, then they will not auto-unlock until the year 2060 when the secrets of the book will once again be revealed, (so please, do not go digging up Fishersgate park… until the prescribed year.)

Chapter 13

The conclusion

Billy and his brother, Terry, were delighted to see each other once more. After an initial brotherly hug, they spoke about their separate adventures that had led both of them to the cathedral of Taranto. Lilly was delighted to see Billy too, but the reunion was tinged with sadness as Nathan was not there with them to enjoy the moment. Billy explained that Nathan had travelled forward in time to 1975 and that he had taken both the First and the Second Chapter books with him for safe keeping. The whole purpose of the children of Fishersgate being in 1734 was now redundant, for the books had gone and though Billy had opened the books to reveal some pictures of future inventions, no-one around him understood those ideas and so the secrets of the books were safe. It all seemed such a pointless exercise, the Fishersgate children travelling from 1934 to 1734 to unlock secrets from a couple of books. They had not achieved anything.

The mayor and the people of Taranto were equally disappointed that they did not have the secrets of the books in their possession, but in time they got over it.

Billy introduced Catrina to Terry and Lilly. Lilly instantly recognised that there was more than a mutual attraction between them. Catrina was to be Billy's first love - and maybe this love was to last a lifetime. But they were from two different time-zones, she from 1734 and he from 1934 - how could this possibly work? Though Catrina could not speak English and Billy could not speak Italian they understood each other by facial expressions. Of course, both had learned some words from their respective partner but it was not enough to hold fluent conversations. Billy was just happy to be with Catrina, hold her hand or hold her in his arms and she was happy too.

But Billy had another admirer. Shell the dog had followed Billy's every move since its former master, Jed Boot, had disappeared to the year 1930. Though Shell was the ugliest dog in the world, in time, Billy came to like the beast.

They were all to stay in the city hall in Taranto for the next three weeks, while they worked out exactly what they should do.

Antonio, Terry's former cell-mate in Namidia, who was a Captain in the Italian army, had been dealing with military business since his return to Taranto... but it was on this night that he visited Terry and Lilly at the City Hall. He brought with him his future bride, Teresa, who had also been captive in Namidia inside Necho's harem.

After initial greetings and the gratifying thanks they bestowed upon each other for exercising a successful escape from Namidia and the defeat of Necho's men, they sat down to dinner. Billy joined them, as did Catrina.

Servants of the city served them their food from the kitchen. Shell lay in the corner of the room waiting for titbits of food to be thrown in his direction.

After they had eaten three courses of the banquet and the frivolities of dinner conversation had ended, Antonio's manner turned to more serious matters.

Antonio was interested in Terry and Lilly's future. He had visited him that evening to offer him a job in the Italian Army as a junior officer. This was a wonderful opportunity for such a young man and would lead to lifelong security as well as a steady income. Terry did think about this offer - but not for long.

"I am not from this time," said Terry, "I should get back to 1934 where I come from, where I belong and where all of our family live."

Lilly held Terry's hand and whispered words of support. She too wanted to return to Fishersgate.

"But what of you Billy?" asked Antonio.

"I want to go back to Fishersgate 1934 too," replied Billy without hesitation.

Catrina looked at Billy - not quite understanding.

Antonio spoke in Italian to Catrina and she nodded in agreement.

"What did you say to her?" asked Billy.

"I asked her if she wanted to stay with you, wherever you went in this world - and she said yes."

Billy, who was sitting next to Catrina, kissed her on the cheek.

"Careful," beamed a smiling Terry to his brother, "I don't want you two getting lovey-dovey."

A voice from nowhere broke the conversation.

"But how do you know you can get back to Fishersgate 1934?"

It was the Ghost of the Fishersgate Mariner.

All of them, except Billy, looked around the room. Lilly was quite frightened and held Terry tight.

Antonio stood up suddenly and drew his sword. He looked around the semi-darkened room. The long, floor-length curtains were drawn, the door was shut and all was still.

"Don't worry," Billy said to them all, "it's only the Ghost!"

"What Ghost?" said Terry.

"The Ghost of the Fishersgate Mariner," said Billy. "You know, the Ghost that we followed into the dry dock in 1934. The one you don't believe in Terry."

"There's no such thing as ghosts," said Terry. "Someone is hiding behind those curtains."

Antonio moved cautiously towards the closed curtains and delicately prodded them with his sword along their entire length. Suddenly, he caught one of the curtains with the sharpness of his sword and flung the material to one side, revealing what was behind. There was nothing. He opened the second curtain. There was nothing.

Antonio turned around to face his friends sitting at the dining table in the centre of the room. As he did so the outline of the Ghost began to appear. The Ghost stood beside the far end of the dining table and all, except for Billy, were astonished.

"You can all see me and hear me," said the Ghost.

Billy, who was sitting at the far end of the table outstretched his hand, putting it straight through the torso of the Ghost.

There was a genuine 'gasp' from the other five as Billy's hand disappeared into the Ghost.

"Oh, that tickles," said the Ghost.

"You see," said Billy turning to his brother, Terry, "I did see the Ghost in Fishersgate harbour… it's him… this is the same ghost that I saw."

Terry was speechless. This was not a common trait for Terry.

All six of them sitting at the table looked towards the Ghost as he began to speak once more.

"You know, my friends, I have been listening to your conversations tonight. And so that you all can understand my words I have the power to enable Catrina to understand the English language for a few weeks."

Multiple bells rang softly and the gentle sound of a flute played for a few seconds. Catrina shook her head as if something had entered her ear.

Suddenly she spoke to Billy in perfect English and he responded. They smiled at each other and he kissed her cheek.

"Ha-hem," coughed the Ghost to attract their attention.

"Back to what I was saying… yes, yes, I know," continued the Ghost, "I shouldn't listen into private conversations but I am a ghost and there is not much else to do in this limbo land of this purgatory where I currently reside."

"No, you shouldn't listen in," said Billy.

Terry nudged Billy on the shoulder. "Don't antagonise the Ghost," said Terry.

"Oh, he's all right," responded Billy, "as ghosts go he is a bit 'camp' but he is a likeable sort of a ghost."

The Ghost laughed before continuing, "Billy, you said earlier that travelling to 1734 was a waste of time as you have not achieved anything. Well, let me tell you that you have achieved something - and something very important. You have saved all of our present-day humanity from the technical content contained in the books. You and Nathan helped to send the books forward in time where they can do no harm."

"That's all very well," said Terry, "but now all we want to do is get back to 1934 and our families."

"And you shall... perhaps," said the Ghost.

There was a buzz. The Ghost put his finger to his ear.

"What was that Boss?" he said aloud.

"Oh right, right, right," he said as he listened through his earpiece. "Yeah - got it," said the Ghost.

The Ghost dropped his hand from his ear before addressing the group.

"Well, I was not quite right there... that was the boss on the line, I should correct myself. You may get back to 1934, but that depends on what you do next."

"What should we do?" asked Lilly.

"I don't know," replied the Ghost.

There was a discussion among the group sitting at the table.

Antonio banged the table with his fist.

"Listen Mr. Ghost," he enquired, "can you get back onto your boss, *whoever he is,* and ask him what they should do to get back to 1934."

"Good idea," said the Ghost.

The Ghost pressed a button on the side of his belt and engaged in a conversation with the boss. When he had finished he relayed the entire content of his conversation to the group.

"Well, the boss suggests that you return to the ship the Star of the Sea and make sail for a time-portal, where you can travel forward in time. You cannot use the portal here in Taranto as it has been sealed. Neither can you use Wentworth's time-portal at his shop in Namidia for that was sealed for good upon his death."

"Well, where are we going to sail to?" said Billy.

"Fishersgate, England, you must find the time-portal in a part of Fishersgate known only as Brambledean," replied the Ghost.

Terry stood up.

"Mr. Ghost," said Terry, "how are we going to get onto the Star of the Sea ship? It's full of Namidians and they don't like us that much. We wouldn't get near it let alone take control of it."

"Yes, we would," said Billy, "the mayor has their leader, Necho, in custody."

"Not anymore," interjected Antonio.

"Has he escaped?" asked Lilly.

"No," said Antonio, "I had him executed this morning for ordering the killing of our people at the cathedral."

"Blimey," said Billy, "your justice system is swift."

"What are we going to do now?" said Terry.

"Well," said Antonio, "we still have Mr. Josef and Necho's wife in custody. We could use them to strike a bargain with the captain and crew of the Star of the Sea ship."

"Then that is what you shall do," said the Ghost, "and I will come with you."

Billy turned to Catrina and gently asked her if she wanted to come to England with him and, if possible, try to find a time-portal in the area called Brambledean, near to where Saint Richard is buried, and go forward to 1934. He explained that it could be dangerous but he would be at her side for all time. Catrina did not hesitate in saying yes and both left the room. They had a lot to catch up on for Catrina's newly found English, that the Ghost had bestowed upon her, allowed them to talk directly to each other for the very first time.

And that is exactly what they did. The Ghost bid his farewell for the night leaving Antonio, Teresa, Terry and Lilly to agree their plan for the following morning. The plan - the taking of the Star of the Sea ship and a trip to 1734 Fishersgate, England.

The following morning Mr. Josef and Necho's wife, Izabella, were brought from their cells to Antonio's military barracks.

"How are you keeping Mr. Josef?" asked Antonio.

"Fine, under the circumstances," said Mr. Josef.

"And you Izabella?"

"Yes, I am fine too," she replied.

"Well, I am glad to hear that you are both well," said Antonio, "for I could have made your time in my prison as bad and as cruel for you, as you did to me when I was chained in your prison in Namidia."

"I am sorry," replied Josef. "My brother Necho, Izabella's husband, runs the prisons in Namidia,"

"Well there is no need to be sorry, it's too late to be sorry," said Antonio, "anyway your brother is no more - I had him executed at dawn yesterday."

Izabella burst into tears and ran towards Antonio, fists held high, but two of the four guards stopped her and held her tightly.

"Take her away and let her go free, into the city of Taranto by the convent, where the nuns of the city live. They will take her into their care," ordered Antonio.

Two of the guards took a clearly distressed Izabella out of the room.

Mr. Josef stood motionless.

"You seem surprisingly calm on hearing the news that your brother is dead."

"Nothing surprises me anymore regarding my brother, not since I found out yesterday from your guards that he was half Scorian. It is no wonder that he had a vicious streak about him," replied Mr. Josef.

"Well, Mr. Josef, we need to arrange things between us," said Antonio.

"What sort of arrangement?" replied Mr. Josef.

"I don't want Italy to go to war with your country, Namidia, any more than you do, Mr. Josef," said Antonio. "And yet yesterday morning, I executed one of the joint leaders of Namidia... Necho himself. You are the other joint leader of Namidia and Necho's execution is enough reason for you and your country to declare war on Italy."

"Please continue," said a very interested Mr. Josef.

"Necho had to go, he was a criminal and a very nasty piece of work. So, I want you to consider endorsing his execution because he ordered the murder of innocent unarmed Italian citizens in the cathedral of Taranto - a most holy place and no-one, not even the joint leader of Namidia, is above that."

"And what will become of me?" asked Mr. Josef.

"I cannot harm you, for you personally have done nothing wrong - but there is one thing you must do for me. After that, you will be released and escorted back to Namidia with full military honours and diplomatic protection on your flagship the Star of the Sea," replied Antonio.

"And if I don't agree?" asked Mr. Josef.

"Well, let's not talk about that," replied an incisive Antonio.

"Very well..." said Mr. Josef. But Antonio cut him short. "This is what I demand," said Antonio, "I need your ship, the Star of the Sea, for about three months."

"What for?" enquired Mr. Josef.

"I feel obliged to take the children of Fishersgate back to England, but I do not have a ship of such size available to me unless you will permit me to use yours," said Antonio.

"What of the children of Fishersgate?" asked Mr. Josef. "Did they ever find the Second Chapter book?"

"Yes, they did," replied Antonio, "but before you get too excited the Second Chapter book is now lost forever - our nations will not share in its secrets for it has been sent to a place in the future where no one from this century can touch it."

"That is sad," replied Mr. Josef, "our peoples could have greatly benefitted from its content."

Antonio was not interested in Mr. Josef's sadness, for he was a practical man. Things had to be organised for the children of Fishersgate and he was going to make sure that they were done.

Antonio asked again, "Will you voluntarily let me make use of your ship?"

"Very well, Antonio," said Mr. Josef, "my men and I will take them to England."

"It will not be quite like that," Antonio responded. "All of your men, except the captain and his twelve most competent sailors, will depart the ship and wait here in Taranto while the ship sails its round-trip journey to

England. I will supply sufficient Italian sailors to man and support this ship under your captain's command during its voyage. Once we have delivered the children of Fishersgate to their destination, in order that they can find a time-portal, the ship will return here to Taranto and you, your ship and men will be free to leave."

"Very well," said Mr. Josef, "I agree."

The following morning two small rowing boats left the docks of Taranto making their way towards the finest ship of the Namidian navy, the Star of the Sea. Captain Pickering was informed of his new command and his imminent journey to England. The rest of that day saw the transfer of men between the ship and shore and by the following morning the Star of the Sea had set sail for England.

On board was Antonio, Terry, Lilly, Billy and Catrina. Teresa had stayed at home tending to Antonio's mother. Mr. Josef stayed in Italy with his crew of sailing men awaiting the return of the Star of the Sea while enjoying the fruits of Italian culture.

The Ghost of the Fishersgate Mariner sailed with them too, but through most of the journey kept himself to himself, just as friendly ghosts often do - occasionally popping up to tell the most wonderful ghostly stories to Billy and Catrina. One of those stories came through on his earpiece one morning from the boss, who told him that the wrath of the Admiralty had avenged his death and that every Barlott up until the present Barlott had been hung by the neck until dead and all were now in a place called hell, along with Necho. A travesty of justice one might say, all hung for one single murder - but they were all murderers anyway. The problem was, sighed the Ghost - there were plenty more offsprings of Barlott and all were ready and willing to take command of the smuggling and piracy operations at Fishersgate.

One week into the journey Billy asked where Garrett and Wheeler were located and found they were still imprisoned below decks. He ordered that they be brought on deck immediately.

Garrett and Wheeler were escorted onto the main deck still clad in their chains.

"It's time to keel-haul both of you," shouted Billy. "Guards, prepare for the punishment."

Garrett and Wheeler stood silently in a dazed shock awaiting their fate.

"But I thought we were now friends?" shouted Wheeler.

Billy walked the deck for a few minutes, head bowed in pretend, deep thought. Suddenly he stopped and turned towards the condemned men.

"Only joking," screamed a delighted Billy, "Guards, release them for they really are my friends. We have been through quite a few adventures together." Both stunned by this experience Garrett and Wheeler fell to their knees echoing howls of laughter and delight. They promised to Billy, there and then, that they would change and never bully anyone else again.

"There is one thing I need to ask you both," said a smiling Billy.

"What's that Billy?" asked Garrett.

"How did you two get here - back in time from 1934 to 1734?"

"Well," replied Garrett, "in 1934, after we left Fishersgate bay and began to row our boat eastwards to the harbour basin - we suddenly changed our minds and decided to turn about and row westwards towards the lock-gates. We saw you, in the distance. We saw you row your boat into the dry docks and saw the lock-gates close behind you..."

Wheeler continued, "We couldn't get through the gates so we moored the boat at the bottom of a vertical steel ladder bolted to the outside of the quayside and climbed onto the top of the dock before breaking into the building that extends over the area. It must have taken us an hour or more but once inside, we made our way to the edge of the quay when," Wheeler stopped and turned to Garrett, "do you want to tell him this part of our story Garrett?"

Garrett continued. "It was dark and, silly me, I tripped and fell into the water in the dock. Wheeler jumped in to help me and, suddenly, the waters in the dock began to empty. The water must have dropped by five yards before stopping. Almost immediately the lowered waters revealed a large hole in the wall of the quay so we scrambled into it. Then, just as suddenly, the waters lowered completely so we were trapped. Then we saw a light at the far end of a tunnel - so we followed it."

"Did you follow the sound of a flute," asked Billy.

"Yes, we did," replied Wheeler, "and soon we were lifted into the air and travelling at great speed on a gust of wind."

"And you came across a shop in a cave where you sipped the content of a special traveller's elixir?" said Billy.

"That's right," said Garrett, "a strange shopkeeper named Wentworth said we were his first customers that day. But we didn't hang about when he demanded money - which we did not have. So, we ran - but straight into the arms of the Namidian guards. Unfortunately, we were arrested, chained and taken aboard the Star of the Sea ship which was anchored in the Namidian harbour."

"I think I probably know the rest of your story," said Billy. "I guess that after we had passed through the bottom of the dry dock – and into the tunnel – the dry dock filled up with water again, shortly before the two of you arrived. You then went through a different tunnel – a tunnel in the wall of the dry dock – and somehow got to the shopkeeper's place before we did, because I remember him saying that we were his second customers that day. Anyway, whatever happened on the day I am really glad it did – because things have worked out well for us all and, of course, we are friends now."

Garrett and Wheeler agreed.

The six-week journey to Fishersgate, England on the Star of the Sea was uneventful and they had the advantage of good weather en-route.

Billy turned fifteen years old on the journey to England and the sailors made him a cake in the galley. It was a little strong of rum but tasted wonderful. The party went well, shanty songs were sung by the crew and everyone had a good time. That night Billy and Catrina looked up into the cloudless skies to see the moon and the twinkling stars of the constellation of Lyra. It was during this voyage that Billy and Catrina formed a close bond, and they both decided that once they came of age they would spend the rest of their lives together - wherever that life might lead them, be it 1734 or 1934.

It was on December 20^{th,} 1734, on the high-tide, that Austin and Jack, the semi-frozen boys in the crow's nest of the Star of the Sea, shouted, "Land ahoy!"

Captain Pickering immediately set his telescope towards the land in the distance. Antonio stood beside him on the poop-deck and glanced in the general direction of a mass of land.

"We have arrived. Fishersgate harbour is 500 yards over there, beyond the peninsular of Finger Island," shouted Pickering. He continued. "Lay the anchor, we shall dis-embark our guests here. Prepare to release two rowing boats into the water."

The rowing boats were lowered into the water by the sailors and held firm against the side of the ship by an intricate arrangement of ropes and pulleys. Two rope ladders were flung over the side of the ship - one for each of the rowing boats below.

Antonio stood at the head of the rope ladder and bid farewell to each of his friends in turn. Billy went down the ladder first, Catrina followed and lastly, Lilly. Terry stood in front of Antonio and the two embraced before looking closely at each other in mutual admiration.

"Terry, are you sure I cannot get you to change your mind? Stay with me and join my Italian army," said Antonio.

"I am sure," replied Terry. "My destiny is with my brother, Billy, my family and with my future bride, Lilly. When I get back home to England 1934 I will marry Lilly and we will make each other happy for the rest of our lives. But I will never forget you, Antonio, or the people of Taranto."

"Well my friend," said Antonio, "I wish you Godspeed to your destination and a happy and long life with Lilly and the rest of your family."

Terry climbed down the ladder into the rowing boat, took the oars and cast-off towards the harbour of Fishersgate. They waved goodbye to those looking down from the Star of the Sea and the sailors chanted the words 'Hip…Hip, Hooray.'

They made their way across the calm waters of the English Channel. Garrett and Wheeler followed in a rowing boat behind.

"Hello," said a voice quite suddenly and abruptly. "It's me! I thought I would come along with you," said the Ghost of the Fishersgate Mariner as he appeared before them at the bow of the rowing boat.

"Have you come along to show us where the time-portal is in Brambledean?" asked Billy.

"Oh no," said the Ghost, "you will find the time-portal without my help."

The ghost then looked intently at Lilly, "My dear girl, I have to tell you something." said the ghost.

"Yes, what is it?" replied a surprised Lilly.

"I understand that you trained to become a ballerina when you were younger?" he said.

"Yes, I did," replied Lilly, "but I broke my ankles in an accident and though the bones repaired themselves, I was never again able to perform on stage to the exacting skills necessary for me to become a professional dancer."

"Yes, yes I know all that my dear and that is why I had a word about you with the Boss."

"The Boss?" said Terry, "who is he?"

The ghost did not reply to Terry but continued to look at Lilly

"And the Boss has agreed to fix the problem," said the Ghost. In a few moments, you will feel a tingle in your feet - the Boss will be fixing your bones and once fixed, it will be as if you had never broken your ankles at all. When you get home promise me that you will go back to your ballet training and become a big star."

"Oh, I will," replied an excited Lilly as she felt a systematic tingle start in each of her big toes, rise through her feet, past her ankles and up to her knees. Lilly wiggled her toes before replying to the ghost. "My feet feel so different already – much different from a moment ago. Thank you, Mr. Ghost, and say thank you to the Boss - if I could give you a big hug then I would.

"Oh, I really wish you could give me a hug," replied the ghost, "I haven't been able to have a hug with anyone for a very long time - how I miss those human moments."

All the while, Terry was watching. "Lilly," he asked, "do your feet really feel different?"

"They do," replied an elated Lilly.

"That's fantastic," said Terry as he kissed Lilly. "I cannot wait to see you in your tutu."

Lilly smiled before responding, "Terry, you will not be seeing me dressed like that until I have had some ballet practice under the guidance of my old dance teacher Mrs. Goatcher."

"Right then," said the ghost. "It is now time to leave you all."

"Where are you going?" asked Billy.

"The boss is calling me in... my work is done," said the Ghost.

"Calling you in... where?" replied Billy.

The Ghost did not reply to Billy's question. The Ghost unexpectedly turned towards the bow of the boat and appeared to be looking for something. The little rowing boat was now mid-way between the Star of the Sea ship and the shoreline of Finger Island.

"Terry, be a good boy and stop here for a moment," said the Ghost.

Terry pulled back the two oars on either side of him and rested them lengthways along the boat.

"What's up?" enquired Terry.

Just then a flute began to play and multiple bells gently rang - as they had always done, shortly before something magical was about to happen.

A huge cloud dropped slowly from the otherwise clear wintery sky, onto the calm sea waters, about ten-yards from the rowing boat. The cloud parted, revealing a sunny place full of happy people, some going about their business, some relaxing, others playing cricket. The sea water suddenly froze between the boat and the cloud. The Ghost of the Fishersgate Mariner got out of the boat onto the ice-covered path. He glided a few yards on the ice before he turned and looked back towards the little rowing boat.

"Farewell to you all - I am leaving this purgatory of a place called Earth for somewhere known as paradise."

Suddenly, the snub-nosed monkey appeared beside him.

"And where do you think *you* are going?" demanded the Ghost as he looked down at the laughing beast who was still wearing its diamond-encrusted collar. The monkey looked up at the Ghost and pointed towards the open cloud.

The Ghost shrugged his shoulders and, with a sigh of dismay, he accepted the fact that he was stuck with this monkey for all eternity. Taking the monkey's hand and holding it firmly, the Ghost and his primate partner turned towards the open cloud and walked those last few yards into their final resting places in paradise. Once among the people of paradise, both the Ghost and the monkey disappeared into the crowd. At the front of the crowd was father and son, Albert and Tom, the two jolly boatmen, laughing and joking with each other beside a small clinker rowing boat. Mother superior of the convent, Sister Albany, stood watching them. Molly Martin, Nathan's mother, was also there in paradise with her chickens. She was holding hands with her lover, Fred, the American soldier. Billy felt a momentary sadness that Nathan was not with them to see his mother and father together. Patricia, the mystic came walking by, cucumbers firmly in hand, just as Wentworth the soothsayer stood upon a marble table and began singing out loudly, *"Good old Sussex by the sea. Good old Sussex by the sea..."*

And it was then, at that very moment, that Billy spotted Grandad at the front of the crowd of people in the cloud, in paradise. He was sitting beside a beautiful woman. He had his arm around her shoulder. It was Granny - Billy recognised the relatively young Granny Burton from photographs that he had seen on the sideboard at home at number 56 Duke Street. Beside their feet, on the floor, scampered several hamsters. It was Henry the first, Henry the second, George, Fred, Bill and all the other hamsters that had once lived at the Burton house and had been buried in the back garden. They were all there doing the same wicked things that hamsters often do... and doing it in paradise of all places. Watching over the hamsters with a smile on his face was the grandfather of Whiskers the cat, also called Whiskers, and his lifelong feline mate, Whiskerina.

"Grandad, Grandad," shouted Billy.

Grandad had seen Billy.

In his excitement, Billy got out of the boat, onto the frozen pathway and began to run towards the open cloud into paradise. Grandad's, facial expressions changed from happiness to a look of horror as he stood up from his chair and began to profusely wave his arms about.

"No Billy," shouted Grandad, "it is not your time… go back and live your life on Earth. If you cross that line into paradise you will have to stay here for all eternity. Go back and live your life to the full, treat every single day as a new adventure. Life on Earth is so very worth living - never forget that and be honest in everything you do and be happy with those around you… stay with those people on Earth who you love more than anything."

Billy suddenly stopped… he turned around to look at Catrina who was beckoning him back to the rowing boat.

"Come back Billy," shouted an astonished Terry, "your life is here with us."

"Yes, come back Billy," screamed Catrina, "I want you to stay with me for the rest of our lives."

Billy soon decided his own fate. He slowly turned and walked back to the boat and into the arms of Catrina as Grandad shouted, "Well done boy and goodbye, Billy… goodbye, Terry… goodbye to you all… go and live your lives and find your way in life, find your own paths of destiny. And when your time on Earth is done and when you have lived honest lives, been true to yourselves and to others, don't worry, we will see you again - but only when it is your time. And when we see you again we can have a party together, just you, me, Granny and the rest of our late departed ancestors. That's about a thousand of us in the extended Burton family. What a party that will be."

Grandad Burton kissed Granny Burton and they stood waving as the cloud slowly closed. It then rose to the heavens above. Suddenly it was gone.

"What do we do now?" said Billy.

"Well, brother," said Terry, "I guess that we four in this boat and our friends Garrett and Wheeler, who are following in the boat behind, had better row the rest of the way to Fishersgate harbour, go and find that place known as Brambledean, and try to find the time-portal so that we can go home to 1934, where we belong. What do you think of my plan, Billy?"

"It sounds good to me," said Billy. "Catrina is not from the 1934 time-zone and I want her to come home with us. That is Catrina, if you want to come home to 1934 with me?"

"You know I do," replied Catrina.

"I hope we can get you through the time-portal," said Lilly.

"We will try our very best," replied Terry, as he picked up the boat's oars - preparing to row the small vessel towards the entrance to the harbour at the far end of Finger Island and into Fishersgate bay.

"Let's go home then," replied an excited Billy as he squeezed Catrina's hand before wrapping his arms around her and holding her close. After their short embrace, Catrina looked deeply into Billy's eyes and exclaimed, "Oh, Billy Burton, my Billy Burton - I want to stay with you forever."

The End.

Acknowledgements

Thank you to the following people who assisted in proof-reading the draft text and making honest critical storyline comments which greatly assisted in the production of this book.

Mrs.D.Mitchell   Mr.G.Vardy

Mrs.J.Lessels   Mrs.S.Vardy

Mrs.S.Reeve   Mr.M.Mitchell

Also to:

Shoreham Port Authority, and the workers and residents of the harbour – past and present, for setting a real-life scene that helped to establish the making of this fictional story.

And finally, to every single one of those teenage children of Fishersgate, Hove, Portslade, Southwick, Shoreham and the surrounding areas, who frequented the harbour during 1965-1974, all of whom played a small part in helping to create this story.

These pages are intentionally blank

Printed in Great Britain
by Amazon

23261680R00205